Growing Together

Meant to be Together, Volume 4

Richard Alan

Published by Village Drummer Fiction, 2019.

Growing Together

Copyright © 2018 by Richard Alan and Village Drummer Fiction

Cover design by AuthorPackages

https://www.authorpackages.com[1]

www.villagedrummerfiction.com[2]

ISBN: 978-1-970070-06-4

This book is available at most online retailers.

---

1. http://www.authorpackages.com/

2. http://www.villagedrummerfiction.com/

Also by Richard Alan

Meant to be Together
Finding a Soul Mate
The Couples
Finding Each Other
Growing Together

Watch for more at https://villagedrummerfiction.com.

This series of books would be impossible without the love and encouragement of my partner, wife, publisher, and soul mate, Carolynn.

Many thanks to my editor, Lisa Dawn Martinez, who understands my style, improves my novel's flow, and whose critiques improve my characters.

Also thanks to Craig Latham and Mike Van Strien, both men I met while serving with the 101st Airborne Division in Vietnam, who made the effort to stay in touch and have remained friends during the last forty-three years.

Chapter One ~ Megan Cohen

MEGAN COHEN HAD ARRIVED at a place in her late twenties where she didn't like what she'd become. With her three-year-old master's degree in chemistry she'd been working diligently as the only female engineer in, what she had once thought, was a wonderful company whose owner cared about his employees.

She had advanced quickly to become a manager in the company, and with a manager's level of remuneration, Megan had purchased a large, fully furnished condo. Her residential perch was situated on the twentieth floor of a building in the City of Angels, which provided her and her frequent guests a view of glorious sunsets over the Pacific Ocean while they dined.

But Megan had been spectacularly unsuccessful in relationships with men, such that when she went on dates she was well-practiced at neutralizing any feelings that may arise, in order to avoid the pain of yet another failed relationship. However, with a lovely wardrobe and a small luxury car, Megan reveled in the single life.

Sadly, what she'd believed to be a fulfilling life was soon to head over a cliff. All because of one brief kiss—and from a man who meant nothing to her.

It had started when Todd Portman had been hired by her company to advise them on composite structures. He was plain looking, slim, and not much taller than her petite, nicely endowed five-foot frame. His wife and two young children lived in San Diego, so he stayed in LA during the week and drove home weekends. He was an excellent team member on their project and they all enjoyed working with him.

During one of their lunch meetings, Megan had mentioned to her group that she was buying a condo. Todd had asked where it was, as he was thinking of buying something in LA because most of his work was there.

The following Wednesday, she was heading over to her future home to pick out rugs, wall coverings, and furnishings. "I'll be done around seven," she'd told him. "So if you want to see my place in its undecorated state, you can meet me there."

Afterwards they went to dinner at a well-appointed seafood restaurant and sat next to each other in a large U-shaped, leather-covered booth.

"Look over there," he'd said, directing her attention to a tall, thin woman who had porcelain skin, flaming-orange hair, and gaudy purple earrings that flashed as her head moved. Her balding date had a terrible comb-over and a Hawaiian shirt that was mostly unbuttoned to reveal his spray-on-tanned chest and large gold chain suspending an equally large silver peace sign.

"Leftovers from the seventies," she'd whispered. "Do you think she looks in the mirror when she gets dressed?"

"A writer in Chicago named Mike Royko called California the world's largest outdoor asylum," Todd said. "If some of our fellow diners are any indication, I'd say he was right."

As they'd pressed against each other to exchange their whispered observations, Megan's body began reminding her that she hadn't had a sexual dalliance in over two-years.

The more they'd pressed against each other, the funnier Todd's pitiful attempts at humor became. He'd placed a brief kiss on her lips, watching her expression to see if she'd object. When she didn't, he'd kissed her longer. As they sipped a fine after-dinner port, Megan had made sure she was firmly pressed against him and that her hand was massaging the top of his thigh.

As they drove to her apartment that night, she'd rationalized what she was about to do by telling herself his wife was far away and had had him for years. Megan hadn't had anyone for years, so why shouldn't she enjoy him for a brief sexual escapade.

They'd entered her apartment and she'd guided him straight to her bedroom, where she'd gotten him out of his clothes as quickly as she could.

He'd moaned and gasped at her touch.

Megan had stripped down, too—a difficult maneuver as Todd's hands were all over her.

She'd consumed this man's scent and sensations. He'd manipulated her body in so many ways it felt like he had more than two hands. And those hands and lips played her body like a musical instrument.

***

When she'd seen him at work the next day, they'd acted as if nothing had happened. She liked this. Two consenting adults taking care of their sex drive with no commitment. Without any effort or planning her one-time dalliance soon become a weekly event. His wife had him on weekends and Megan had his body once a week, for an hour, on Wednesday evenings.

That had seemed like a fair deal to her.

There'd been no emotion and certainly no sense of them becoming a couple. Todd was satisfying a basic need. It was simple. She'd satisfied him and he'd satisfied her in return.

It became like an artist creating an ice-sculpture, removing tiny chips from a fairly nebulous piece of ice to reveal a hidden shape. Megan hadn't realized it initially, but each dalliance with Todd was chipping away tiny pieces of her character, revealing a mean-spirited woman who thought nothing of destroying a marriage in order to satisfy herself.

Chapter Two ~ Megan's Story

MEGAN WAS RAISED BY two loving parents who did their best to convey an excellent set of values to her and her identical twin sister. But the older she became, the more she realized how far away from those values she'd moved. So much so she hadn't even spoken to any of them in the last three-years.

She had long ago determined that her problems began at age-sixteen, when her boyfriend, David Kaplan, broke up with her after many years of dating. They had met at camp when they were twelve-years-old. David and his twin, Ethan, and her and her sister, Sheryl. They were the four musketeers. Ethan and Sheryl had long since married and were still blissfully happy.

After the breakup happened, Megan had attempted to impugn David's integrity by raging to her parents that he had cursed and sworn at her while telling her their relationship was over. Of course, none of it was true, but better to lie and save face she had thought.

However, unbeknownst to Megan, David's younger brother and his Uncle Meyer overheard the entire shouting match and witnessed the fact that the only foul-mouth during the breakup had belonged to her.

It had seemed an inevitable progression that soon after, Megan and her parents began having loud and angry arguments. Her adolescent mind was furious they hadn't taken her side as the injured party, even though she had been caught in a lie about what transpired.

After the big breakup she tried to soothe her wounded pride by dating a guy named Teddy. They went to movies and dances together and occasionally doubled with Sheryl and Ethan. But that proved to be too much for Megan, with Ethan being David's identical twin brother, it seemed that the closer Sheryl and Ethan became, the more jealous she was. In true teenage form, she expressed her displeasure with her sister's happiness with, and eventual marriage to, Ethan by continually finding reasons to argue with her.

As soon as Megan found herself in a relationship, she was on the lookout for signs of trouble. The moment she saw even the hint of a warning sign, she ended it. Although, she did experience momentary pain one time when one boy actually cried.

As her body filled out during her high school years, it became obvious she could use it to get dates practically anytime she wanted. And from the glow on her sister's face, she knew exactly when she and Ethan had started doing it. It was during the summer after high school graduation.

Megan was determined to keep up with her twin, and when she met a good-looking junior named Terrance during her freshman year of college, she decided that he would be her first. After a few weeks of dating she let him do the deed and the dismal experience was over quickly. He'd took care of his needs, and mumbled, "I gotta go home and feed my dog." Then he ran off in the direction of his dorm.

She soon came to find out he didn't have one. A dog, that is.

The difference this time was the pain of another failed relationship was mirrored in the pain between her legs. To top it off, a few days later she learned Terrance's fraternity brothers had given him the vile nickname of Cosmo the Cherry Stomper.

So, gradually she learned how useful it was to make herself emotionally numb to the efforts of men, even those who chose to lavish their attention on her. She tried to make sure she was always the taker in her relationships—if you could call them that—and not the giver, figuring it was the best way to avoid the pain of any real entanglement.

Her sexual dalliance with Todd, however, was different. It was even causing her after-work exercise routine to suffer. After working up a good sweat, she normally luxuriated in the hot tub to remove the lactic acid that accumulated in her sore muscles. But shortly after she had begun using Todd to satisfy her, she had joined three other women—all wearing wedding rings—in the soothing warmth of the bubbling water.

One of them suddenly put her hands to her face and began sobbing hysterically as her friends rallied around and pulled her into their arms.

"I'm only thirty-four," the woman had wailed. "And my body still looks pretty good for someone who's given that bastard three children. Why would he feel the need to screw some bimbo?"

The other women tried to console her. Then they stared directly at Megan as if she too should have some sage advice. After all, women were supposed to have an instant bond with each other, especially in times of need.

So, she made the effort and jumped in. "That's terrible," she said in a way that she hoped sounded commiserating and would prevent them from seeing the flash of guilt she felt. But when no nods were forthcoming, she was sure they knew her dirty little secret.

She never used the hot tub again.

The incident upset her, but only because, for a just a moment, she thought she'd been exposed as the harlot she was. Not that it would have necessarily stopped her from continuing her affair with Todd.

A number of months went by after that when Todd's wife flew to the east coast for a weeklong trip to see her parents. So, the two of them flew to the Caribbean for a long weekend, where they actually got to know each other. She discovered they had nothing in common and Todd was a terrible conversationalist.

"Now that I'm done with school I don't read anymore," he told her during the flight. "My weekends consist of drinking beer with my buddies and betting on pro-sports."

Really? And this was whom she was choosing to spend her time with?

When they reached the resort, it quickly became apparent that he'd only invited her so he'd have a partner at the couples-only nude beaches. Not that she minded. Her body was in great shape due to all her time at the gym, but it would have been nice if he had told her before they arrived.

The sun-drenched beach was covered in white crystalline sand. They stripped down and began soaking up the rays on a couple of lounge chairs. Megan loved the warm tropical air coming off the water, but noted the strange new sensation of having her curly hairs down below swaying in the gentle sea-breeze.

Another couple, who'd been swimming in the ocean, came over and introduced themselves. The droplets of ocean water still on their nude bodies glistened like tiny diamonds in the bright sunlight. The man was medium height and quite muscular. The woman had a nice tan, was a bit taller than Megan, and came well endowed.

As gracefully as possible, she stood up and shook hands with the man and his wife. Todd did the same.

"We're having a robe party in our room tonight with a few other couples," the man said. "Would you like to join us?"

From the way his eyes were appraising Megan's body, she didn't have to ask what a robe party was. She knew they wouldn't be wearing them for long.

They both agreed, Todd with a bit more enthusiasm, but hey, she didn't mind the thought of doing someone else at that point. What the hell, she figured she was a tramp anyway.

At about eight, they wrapped their robes around themselves and headed over to their new friends' room.

"Ah! Everyone, our last couple has arrived," announced the woman from the beach, aptly named Kitty, who led them into the enrobed crowd.

Rather quickly after the announcement of the final two players arriving all robes were discarded, littering the floor, revealing lots of lovely naked bodies.

Kitty's husband Greg wasted no time, and before Megan had a chance to react, he was in her face, kissing her and caressing her. Soon she fell into step with all the other promiscuous couples, feeling as if she was not alone for the first time in years. There were others like her. Maybe she wasn't damaged goods after all.

Meanwhile it seemed as if Todd had died and gone to heaven. Kitty was sucking on Todd's lips and another woman was stroking his business.

After she got used to the idea, she took the initiative. When in Rome, right?

She was just beginning to think this was going to be kind of fun, when suddenly—and without warning—her long-dormant conscience sprang to life.

"I'm sorry," she said, taking a step back, "but I can't do this." She turned to Todd, who had clearly forgotten her existence. "Todd, I'm leaving."

The stunned look on Greg's face was enough to propel her to the floor in frantic search of her robe and then to the door to make her escape. Megan heard him call after her, but all she could manage was another pitiful apology on her way down the hall.

Back in her room, she indulged herself in a good cry for a little while, thoroughly ashamed of what she'd let her life become. What had happened to the little girl who only needed a good book or a light breeze and a small sailboat to find happiness for hours at a time? What had happened to the woman who had a wonderful relationship with her parents, but then quit talking to them when they had the audacity to suggest she date a nice man they knew?

Megan gathered her belongings and headed to the airport. She had plenty of time to think on her long wait for the next plane.

Then again on the even-longer flight home. She had nothing to think about *except* what a sad state of affairs her life had become.

She'd constantly rationalized her bad behavior, so this descent into an emotional hell was entirely of her own making. Her greatest goal in life had always been to have a family and raise her own children. Where had *that* dream gone? Had she become so shallow that she thought a well-paid career would bring her a lifetime of happiness? Who would want her now that she had become such an awful person? She was already in her late twenties—her mommy- clock was no longer just ticking, but was thundering in her ears. A nice morsel of added resentment to her already bitter soul.

***

Todd entered her office the following Monday.

Without hesitation she made her orders clear. "You are not to speak to me unless it's business related."

Seemingly unsurprised, he turned without saying a word and left.

Fine, she thought. No confrontation was good. She buried herself in her work for the next-two-weeks and determined that she would avoid any type of social interaction. This worked quite well until the two police detectives showed up at her door.

Chapter Three ~ Dana Jacobs

DANA JACOBS HAD HEARD the story many times. Her parents were raised in poverty, living in Ghana, and were always hungry during their childhood. When they came to the United States, they couldn't believe the amount of food available every day of the year. They swore to each other that their children would never see a day of hunger.

Her father had found a job as a helper on a garbage truck and had quickly moved up to supervisor while her mother was earning a degree in accounting. One day he'd asked her to help him finance a garbage truck. They'd invested their hard-earned money as a down payment for their first truck. He drove it around and picked up wastepaper and occasionally scrap-metal, while her mother ran the office. That first truck was the beginning of a firm that would take care of them and their future children, not to mention the next few generations of their family.

At the time that they were about to take delivery of their second truck, her mother delivered their first child, a daughter, who they named Dana.

The lesson to never waste food and to clean their plate every time was one that had been drilled into Dana her entire life.

Unfortunately for her, she was a sedentary child. She'd also learned that when she felt sad or upset, she could eat her way into a good mood. In a house with an endless assortment of her mother's delectable pastries, cookies, and cakes, a quick snack was always at hand.

While her parents must have realized she was much heavier than the other neighborhood children were, they also reminded her that they remembered how painful hunger was. They simply couldn't refuse her request for food.

They actually seemed more worried about the health of Dana's brother, who was three-years-younger and always skinny due to his ball mentality—as in baseball, football, basketball, soccer ball and any other sport that entailed the use of a ball.

At seven-years-of-age he'd heard that his favorite soccer star ran a few miles every morning. His parents seemed shocked when, at that tender age, he began a daily habit of getting out of bed first thing in the morning to run.

Dana never connected her brother's exercise habit and his general fitness. She'd always just chalked it up to his being a boy.

***

Twelve-year-old Dana had just alighted from the school bus on a Monday morning, the last week of school, when she saw her friend Freddie. He was one of the few kids at school that was kind to Dana. Perhaps it was because on some level he understood her pain— Freddie had genetic problems with his right hip and knee that caused him to spend many years on crutches as his doctors did their best to repair his joints. Having just had surgery on his right hip, he was on crutches again and he moved slowly with small steps.

"Hi, Freddie," Dana said as she slowed down to walk next to him.

"Hey, Dana!" Freddie said as his face brightened. "I've got some great news. I've been accepted at the university summer program for middle school students who are gifted in math. All summer I'll be learning math, and most likely be surrounded with math geeks like me. I can hardly wait."

"Sounds perfect for you, Freddie." She held a door open for him and watched him inch his way through.

"What are you doing this summer?" Freddie said as he stopped in front of his locker.

Dana glanced right and left, up and down the hallway. She opened her mouth to tell Freddie about the camp she would be attending, but nothing came out. Her eyes filled with tears as she tried to speak again but was overwhelmed with shame. She shrugged her shoulders, gave Freddie a brief smile, and ran to the nearest girls washroom where she hurriedly entered a stall and locked the door. Putting her hands over her face, she tried to stifle her sobs.

She'd been chubby all her life, and huge since fourth-grade. Her female friends didn't seem to care before, but now that they had discovered boys they didn't seem to want her around. The only boy who talked to her was Freddie.

And he's the biggest slob in the school. Maybe that's why we go together.

Dana tried to have a neat appearance, but with fat coming out in all directions, she felt she looked awful no matter what she wore. Her body was beginning to develop and she had nice-sized breasts coming in, but they barely showed because her belly stuck out so far.

Dana wiped at the tears on her face and hung her head. *I hate my life.*

A bell rang, indicating classes were about to start, so she checked her appearance in the mirror, briefly considered running a comb through her hair, shrugged her shoulders, shook her head, and didn't bother trying to improve her appearance. What would be the point?

***

It would be another summer of hunger, sore muscles, and general anger at having been sent to, what her parents referred to as health camp, but Dana called the fat farm. The only bright spot in an ocean of humiliations at camp was that there would be at least two or three other campers who would be more obese than she was.

The seemingly endless humiliation would begin the moment she arrived. Her luggage would be searched for any contraband like candy, chips, or snack cakes. Then the worst moment of camp occurred—the dreaded scale. She would have to step on a scale which had a digital readout in numbers that were twelve-inches- high, which everyone around her could read. Dana would find out how much she had gained since last summer. Their weight was made public because the staff thought a display of the campers' poundage would inspire them to follow the program.

The first morning, the walks would begin. By the second morning, the pain in her ankles would start, along with aches in her calf muscles. Boring classes on nutrition would follow. The afternoon, which followed a lunch of salad and bottled water, would begin with canoeing and end with exhausting laps in the swimming pool. By the end of the third day her knees and thighs would be sore and by the end of the week her hips would ache as well.

As they started their first walk, she looked around at her fellow campers—just a bunch of fat losers like herself.

"Hey, kid," a similarly sized girl said.

"I'm Corrine."

"I'm Dana. Welcome to the fat farm."

"I'd tell you that I'm glad to be here, but we both know that would be a lie. I'm twelve and from Denton, Texas near Dallas."

"I'm twelve too, and from Mercer Island, Washington. It's near Seattle."

"This is my first time. You?"

"My third summer. I really hate this place."

"I was hoping to meet a guy, but the only ones here have all the sex appeal of trampled marshmallows."

Dana laughed. "That's probably what they think of us."

"I had a boyfriend for most of last year, but the jerk tossed me aside for a skinnier model right before the spring dance," Corrine said.

"I have one guy who talks to me, but he's just a friend. The rest of the guys won't even look at me. I go out of my way to be nice, but it doesn't get me anywhere. I've never been invited to a dance."

"I know what you mean about trying to be nice. All this weight seems to imply that we're just losers and nobody wants to be around us."

A rather rotund boy walked ahead of them.

Corrine nodded in his direction and quietly said to Dana, "I tried to talk to him, but he let me know he was going to lose a lot of weight this summer and find a normal-looking girl."

"What a jerk. But then I'm thinking most boys are jerks."

They walked in silence for a while then Corrine asked, "Are your boobs coming out?"

"Yeah. Why?"

"Mine just started and they itch a lot."

"Mine too. I guess that's normal."

"Something funny about them."

"It feels good when you pull on them?"

"Yeah. Crazy that."

Corrine continued speaking, but in a quiet voice. "I have a brother two-years-older than me. He and his buddy were talking about their things and didn't know I could hear them. Guys play with them almost every night."

"What?"

"They call it spanking the monkey." Dana laughed hysterically.

"You been in a canoe?" Dana asked.

"Sure. Lots-a- times."

"Let's make sure we're partners. Last year my partner leaned out nearly every time she tried to paddle. I spent more time in the water than in the canoe."

Corrine laughed. "Okay, friend. Canoe partners it is."

***

"I know we've been hiking up and down trails for the last-two-hours but I feel like ninety-percent of this hike has been uphill," Dana said through her rapid breathing as they topped another ridge and saw the trail continued upward.

"Let's stop here for a break," one of the counselors said.

"My legs are killing me," Corrine groaned. "They feel as if they're loaded with lead."

"You guys are putting in a great effort," the counselor said. "You guys are winners."

Dana shook her head—she was tired of the counselors' endless positive talk.

"Let's be honest for a minute, can we?" she said. "If we were winners, we wouldn't even be at this camp. If I was a winner then I would get invitations to school dances instead of hearing fat jokes behind my back. The only guy who talks to me is the biggest slob at my school."

"I'm trying to be positive," the counselor said.

"This is my third-year here," Dana continued angrily, "and the only things I'm positive about are that I'm furious at my parents for sending me here and that I'll put the weight I lost here right back on when I get home."

Dana glared at the counselor in silence for a moment. "I'll bet you've never been fat a day in your life. You don't have a clue what it's like to be big and ugly."

Corrine put a hand on Dana's arm. "Enough, Dana," she said quietly as she nodded to the other campers.

Dana looked at the other campers, many of whom were crying. She felt bad for making them cry, but everything she had said was true. She couldn't take that back.

***

At dinner one of the last nights of camp, Corrine turned to Dana. "I sure would give anything to have a plate loaded with pasta and meat sauce instead of a mound of brown rice with brussels sprouts on top."

"If nothing else," Dana said, "this place makes me appreciate my mom's cooking."

After a moment of silence, she added, "I'm awfully angry with my folks for sending me here. I know they're doing what they think is best for me, but except for a handful of new friends, I hate this place."

Corrine nodded in agreement. "I can't wait to get home and sneak out to the bakery for churros."

"Churros?" Dana asked.

"They're a Mexican dessert thing. It's like a long string of fried dough with brown sugar on it."

"I can't wait for fried anything," Dana said causing her friend's laughter.

At the end of four-weeks of depressing and physically exhausting camp life, Dana said good-bye to her new friends, and any desire to exercise.

Chapter Four ~ Carrie and Freddie

IT WAS A BRIGHT June day in Seattle, Washington, when twelve-year-old Carrie Levin walked into the university classroom to begin her advanced mathematics class. She held a pink notebook in her hand and wore her favorite pink sandals on her feet. She'd decided they coordinated nicely with her brightly colored pink-and-yellow paisley top. Her sand-colored jeans matched her straw-colored straight hair, which hung down to just above her shoulders. Carrie thought she looked quite stylish for a girl going into the seventh-grade.

She chose a seat in the front row, near the center of the room. The other six students sat together, close to the middle, but a few rows back from the front. They looked a couple of years older, but she knew they were all middle school students like her, gifted in mathematics.

Carrie was nervous and excited at the same time. She had imagined a class where she would be surrounded by math geeks like herself. Sadly, her teachers in public school didn't have a clue what to do with her. During the previous school year she had completed most of freshman high school algebra plus some basic concepts of geometry. This was mostly self-taught, but ably assisted by her techie parents, Michael and Anna Levin.

For now, until her parents moved out to Washington from Idaho, she was staying on Mercer Island with Jonah and Holly Kaplan, friends of her parents, who had known her since birth.

Carrie hoped she would be surrounded by other students who also knew how difficult it was to be different. Her classmates at home in Idaho didn't think much of her math ability, and couldn't understand why she wanted to spend so much time studying. She had acquaintances but no close friends, as none of them shared her love of math. When her public-school classroom had a math lesson, Carrie was sent to the back of the classroom where she studied the material she had brought from home. It was obvious to Carrie that her teachers resented her brilliance and were embarrassed that they had no idea what to do with such an exceptional child.

"Hey, we got a midget this year," one of the older students proclaimed looking at Carrie.

"I heard freaky Freddie will be here this year," another one said.

Great, Carrie thought to herself, *a class full of buffoons.*

The instructor walked in precisely at nine o'clock and began taking roll. The door to the classroom opened one more time. A boy about Carrie's age hobbled in.

"It's freaky Freddie," she heard one of the older students say, none too discreetly.

Freddie was on crutches. His right leg dragged a little behind him as he maneuvered across the classroom. He was average height for a seventh grader, but with big shoulders and thick muscular arms. A man, presumably his father, walked behind him carrying a notebook and pencils.

His father was a large, rugged-looking man whose tall, muscular frame filled the doorway as he entered the room. Carrie decided if he had been a truck, he would be one of those huge diesel powered, off-road, four-door pickups with a lift-kit and huge off- road tires.

Freddie smiled weakly at Carrie and sat down next to her.

"Hi, freaky, glad to see you," one of the older students said sarcastically.

Freddie turned to the speaker and said in a quiet, high-pitched voice, "Hey, Neil." Then Freddie waved to his departing dad, and the instructor, Mr. Coop, began telling them what they could expect from the class.

"We're going to do evaluations after our first break today. Right now, I'd like each of you to write a few paragraphs on what you believe your knowledge level of mathematics is and tell me why you're here and what you'd like to get out of the class."

They busied themselves writing their papers and after they finished, Mr. Coop announced there would be a ten-minute break.

Freddie leaned toward Carrie. "I'm Freddie Lipinski. I'm a seventh-grader."

She offered him a smile. "Hi. I'm Carrie Levin and I'll be in the seventh too."

"I need some water," he whispered.

"Me too."

As Carrie stood, Freddie struggled to get his crutches off the floor and was in obvious pain trying to stand.

"You okay?" she asked.

"I had surgery a couple-of-weeks-ago and it still hurts."

He had taken a few steps from his own desk when one of his crutches caught on the edge of another one. Freddie tumbled to the floor with a great splat, as his crutches went flying.

"Nice move, Freddie," Neil called out, laughing at him. Carrie immediately tried to help him up.

Freddie's face turned red and he yelled at her. "I don't need any help!"

Carrie was taken aback by the ferocity of Freddie's voice. She took a step back and watched as he used one of his crutches to slowly, and rather painfully, stand up again. He had a most frustrated and uncomfortable expression on his face. The moment he was upright, his glasses slipped off his face.

"Oh, no," he exclaimed.

He tried to catch them but they were headed for the floor—that is, until Carrie's lightening reflexes pulled them out of the air just before they could hit the ground.

She grinned and handed him the glasses.

"Thanks," said a relieved Freddie. "If they broke..."

He didn't need to finish. Carrie had the feeling he'd be lost without them.

They went into the hallway and found a water fountain.

"I'm sorry I yelled at you. There are lots of things I have trouble doing because of my right hip and knee. I like to be able to do the things I can manage by myself."

"How long have you been on crutches?" Carrie asked.

"Since my surgery. It was supposed to repair my hip but it doesn't look like it did any good. I've needed a cane to get around since I was little."

Carrie changed the subject, hoping to cheer him up. "I'm from Meridian, Idaho."

"You've come a long way for a class. I live in Hunts Point, Washington."

"I'm living on Mercer Island until my parents move out here next month. I'm staying at the home of some of my parents' friends. Mrs. Kaplan teaches languages here. She's driving me to class every day."

"My dad works here sometimes. He's working in the aerodynamics lab now," Freddie said.

"We're the only seventh-graders," Carrie said as they walked back into the classroom. "I think we should hang out."

Freddie looked at her, seeming pleasantly surprised. "S'all right with me, I guess." He shrugged and spoke a little grudgingly, as if it were hard to admit he would enjoy spending time with her too.

"And that means if you drop your books or something—" Carrie saw his face and quickly amended what she was going to say, "not that that's going to happen, of course, but if it did, um, I'd help you. You, know, because that's what friends are for."

She waited for Freddie's reaction but none was forthcoming.

Had she been too bold?

"Yeah, but I couldn't help you if you dropped your books," he said finally. "I'd probably fall down trying."

"At least if you fell on them, no one could steal them."

Freddie stared at her for a second as if trying to decide if she were serious. She stretched a smile across her face and then he laughed. "Okay, friend, I guess you got a deal."

The instructor passed out evaluation exams as class began again.

"You're not being graded on these. I need to determine what level of mathematical knowledge each of you possesses. Do your best. There's a number at the top of each exam. Each one is different. I want you to tell me why the number is significant."

When Freddie got his exam he smiled, looked at Carrie, and pointed to the number at the top of his paper. "One seven two nine—taxicab number!"

"Um...not," Neil said in a voice that dripped with sarcasm. "There are rational numbers, whole numbers, complex numbers, and irrational numbers. No taxicab numbers."

Freddie turned red again. Carrie spun around in her seat.

"On the contrary, dude, taxicab numbers were discovered by the French mathematician Frénicle de Bessy and are defined as the smallest number that can be expressed as a sum of two positive algebraic cubes in n distinct ways. In the case of the number one seven two nine, n equals two."

In the stunned silence, Neil scowled at Carrie, who turned back to the instructor, who suddenly seemed to have a new perspective on one of his youngest students.

"Sorry, Mr. Coop," Carrie said, "but I read about them in that book—the one about the Indian mathematician Ramanujan."

Mr. Coop nodded and looked at Neil and then the rest of the class. "Ms. Levin is correct. And seeing as she's shared with us why Freddie's number is significant, perhaps Freddie can tell us why the number on Carrie's exam is significant."

Carrie held up her exam so Freddie could see the number sixty.

Freddie thought about it.

"What's wrong, Freddie? The number too boring for you?" Carrie couldn't believe that Neil still had the nerve to be teasing Freddie. The guy was nothing more than a big bully.

Freddie smiled at Carrie and turned to Neil. "Au contraire, Neil. Sixty is the smallest number divisible by each of the first six positive integers, and the smallest number with twelve factors—one, two, three, four, five, six, ten, twelve, fifteen, twenty, thirty and sixty."

"I think," Mr. Coop stated while glaring at Neil, "that should be the end of making fun of our erudite seventh-graders. Everyone start working on your exams, please."

Carrie and Freddie exchanged a brief smile and began working on their exams.

***

At noon, Holly Kaplan stopped by the classroom to pick up Carrie. "It's nice you have someone your own age in the classroom," Holly told them.

"Yes," Freddie agreed. "We've decided to be friends for the duration of the class."

As they were leaving the university campus, Holly asked Carrie how her first day went.

"It was incredible," Carrie said. "We had a math test, an exam the instructor called it, which took nearly two-hours! It was so great. Just one math problem after another. There were so many problems I didn't even get to finish all of them. Holly, I was made for this stuff."

Holly smiled at Carrie. "I'm very happy you're made for that stuff. I've been asked to teach a beginning Italian language course from one to two o'clock each day. I was thinking we could have lunch together after your class and then you could come and study math for an hour while I teach. Would that be okay? Your math class comes first, so if you think that will be a problem, I won't take the job."

"Can I sign up for your course? I remember speaking to you in Italian all the years you lived near us."

"Well, I didn't really think...I suppose, if nothing else, you can audit the class. You can attend all the lectures. I can give you the same homework my students get and you can take the same exams as they do. It'll be a lot of work, Carrie, and your math class has to come first."

Carrie rolled her eyes. "Holly, in my world, math always comes first."

Holly laughed. "And boys?" she asked, referring to Freddie. "Oh, Freddie's okay, I guess. He's just, well, a little..."

"Is he a nice person, Carrie?"

Carrie didn't have to think about it. "Yes."

"Then that's all that matters."

Carrie explained what she knew of Freddie's disability and how he seemed to be in constant pain.

"It must be awful to have to deal with pain every day of his life," Holly told her.

Carrie thought for a moment. "We're friends, so maybe I can think of some way to help him."

"That would be very considerate of you, Carrie."

That evening, Carrie called her mom to tell her about the class. "We had a two-hour exam. We had word problems and math sentences to solve. I even have some homework. Some of the older kids act like clowns, but there is one other person my age in the class. His name is Freddie. We decided to be friends as long as the class lasts. He looks like kind of a mess but is good at math."

"Is he a nice person?" her mom asked.

"Hey, that's what Holly asked me. You guys must be reading from the same script. Don't worry, Mom, he's nice."

***

The following day, Freddie brought two bottles of water and two small plastic containers with strawberries for them to share—and he even arrived in class with his hair combed and his shirt tucked in.

"Hello, Carrie."

"Hello to you too, Freddie."

"These are strawberries from Watsonville, California, near the Monterey Bay Aquarium. Apparently the weather along the coast down there is ideal for growing juicy strawberries."

At breaktime, Carrie bit into one of them and her mouth was immediately filled with sweet strawberry flavor.

"Good thing you brought a pile of napkins for us," Carrie exclaimed as she wiped strawberry juice from her chin.

As he walked past them, Neil spoke in a mocking voice. "Did you bring something to share with your girlfriend, Freddie?"

Before Freddie could reply, Neil's girlfriend nudged him. "Hey, bozo, he's only a seventh-grader. I'm your girlfriend. What did you bring me today? He's being nicer to her than you are to me."

Freddie and Carrie shared a smile as they finished the strawberries.

At the end of class that day, Freddie was still making a few notes and Carrie was standing next to his desk waiting for him. The classroom was empty by that time except for the two of them and Neil, who saw an opportunity to put Freddie in his place. He walked over to the still-seated Freddie.

Neil grabbed Freddie by the front of his shirt and bent forward. "Look, you little freak, you and your shit girlfriend—"

Those were the only words Neil got out of his foul mouth. Freddie put both of his hands on the back of Neil's head. Using his powerful arms and shoulders, he slammed Neil's face onto his desk and held it there. It landed with the sound of a bowling ball dropping on a wood floor.

"If you ever talk that way about Carrie again," Freddie sternly and quietly told him, "I'll shove your head so far up your ass, you'll have to open your mouth to take a crap."

A now-terrified Neil looked at Carrie, who had grabbed one of Freddie's crutches and was ready to wield it like Babe Ruth at the plate. He briefly tried to pull away, but with Freddie's iron grip on his head and the threat of being used for batting practice by Carrie, he apparently decided that discretion was indeed the better part of valor and he should stay where he was, if for no other reason than to be near his head.

Carrie slowly lowered the crutch and put her hand on Freddie's arm. He let go of Neil.

Holly entered the room just as Neil straightened up. "Is there a problem here?"

"No, Mrs. Kaplan," Freddie stated. "I was just advising my friend Neil, it would be nice if he talked to Carrie and me in a more pleasant manner."

Neil tried to smile at Freddie as he started walking out of the room. "Sorry, Freddie. It ain't going to be a problem."

***

They discovered they didn't live far from each other and Freddie's dad agreed to drop him off at the Kaplan's home on Saturday morning so he and Carrie could study together.

Freddie arrived and Holly introduced him to Jonah.

"My brother is going to drop his sailboat off at our dock this afternoon," Jonah said. "Would you two like to go for a sailing lesson?"

Carrie was excited, but Freddie seemed more reticent. "I don't think so. I can't swim and I can't imagine maneuvering around a sailboat with my crutches."

"Crutches or not, you can learn to sail," Jonah said. "Besides, there's a pool in back of our house. Why don't I start teaching you to swim?"

"My right hip and knee aren't formed properly. I've had a limp since I started walking. Since my surgery, my hip hurts a lot."

"We can easily work around that," Jonah said in an enthusiastic voice. "We'll practice in the shallow end and I'll have you swimming in no time. Even Carrie needs help with her swimming. Isn't that right, Carrie?"

Carrie stared blankly, until she realized Jonah was trying to encourage Freddie by stating that she needed help as well.

"Right."

"I don't have a swimming suit to wear," Freddie said. "We'll run to the store to get one."

"It's a sunny day, so can we take the old Auburn and sit in the rumble seat?" Carrie asked.

"Of course," Jonah replied.

Carrie opened the rumble seat on the old car and assisted Freddie as he climbed in.

"This is so cool, they should have these on modern cars," Freddie said after they headed out and the cool wind was blowing on his face and in his hair.

They drove over to a department store and bought a suit. He seemed nervous about the swimming, but he and Carrie had so much fun riding in the rumble seat of the old Auburn, that he nearly forgot about his fear of water when they got back.

They changed into their suits and headed out to the pool. It was a bright, warm day with a blue sky overhead and a gentle breeze coming off the lake at the back of their yard. Before they got in the water, Jonah had them practice the crawl stroke and side breathing. Jonah climbed into the pool first. Freddie seemed to be getting scared again, so Jonah put a flotation device around his hips and told him he would walk next to him and keep his hand on Freddie's stomach so he wouldn't sink.

"Hey," Freddie exclaimed upon entering the pool, "the water is supporting part of my weight. My leg and hip don't hurt so much."

"Just keep your legs straight and pull with your arms like we practiced."

Jonah and Freddie started going up and back across the shallow end of the pool. After the fourth-lap, Jonah was next to him but was no longer supporting him. Two-laps later and Freddie realized that the flotation device had come loose when he ran into it on his next length of the pool.

"I don't need that thing, Mr. Kaplan," he said proudly as he continued doing laps.

Jonah stopped him after watching his progress for a few more laps. "You're doing great. Come over to the side of the pool and let's work on developing your kick."

Freddie was so excited, he didn't even seem to notice what a smooth swimmer Carrie was. Jonah gave her some advice to improve her kick and began showing Freddie how to do the flutter kick.

"If your right leg and hip hurt, try not to kick so hard on that side, and don't worry about going fast."

Freddie practiced for a quite a while, pushing against the side of the pool. Next, Jonah showed him how to use the kick board. He continued to motor up and back in the shallow end of the pool, pushing the kick board ahead of him.

"Freddie, you're doing great!" Carrie said when he stopped to rest.

"Thanks, Carrie," a very proud and out of breath Freddie told her. "I really think I can do this!"

"Freddie, when you're ready again, let's swim the length of the pool," Jonah told him. "You can swim next to the side of the pool so if you get scared you can grab the side. I'll swim next to you just in case."

Freddie said he was worried about swimming over the deep end of the pool, but with Carrie and Jonah encouraging him, he decided to try.

As he swam along, Carrie walked next to him on the pool's edge cheering him on. As soon as he touched the far end of the pool she yelled, "Way to go Freddie!"

"Wow," he exclaimed. "I made it!"

"I think that's enough for today," Jonah said, "but come back next Saturday and we'll keep practicing."

"Thanks, Mr. Kaplan," Freddie stated. "I really had fun!"

Carrie looked at the poolside clock and was astonished to see two hours had gone by.

"Dry off and put some clothes on you guys," Holly called to them. "Lunch will be ready in fifteen-minutes."

As Freddie pulled himself out of the pool, Jonah looked at his broad shoulders and well-muscled arms. "Freddie, are you working out with weights?"

"My dad bought us a weight machine two-summers-ago and I do upper body workouts every-other-day."

"I need to remember that. I'll bet you could learn the butterfly stroke with an upper body like you have."

After a lunch of *Tako Sunomono* and *pasta fagioli*, Carrie commented to Holly. "Japanese salad and Italian pasta. It really feels like home, Holly."

"Thank you, Carrie. Between your mom and my mom, I've learned an amazing amount of international cooking."

"I don't think I've had a salad like this," Freddie said. "It's really great."

"It has *Tako*—that's octopus, Freddie—cucumber, and sweetened rice vinegar in it," Holly told him.

"I've loved *Tako nigri sushi* since I was little," Freddie told them. "My father has taken me out to eat sushi many times. I sure can't wait to tell him I'm learning to swim. Thanks, Mr. Kaplan."

"My pleasure, Freddie."

"I sent a video of you swimming to your dad's phone, Freddie," Holly told them. "I invited him to go sailing with us. He'll be here about three."

Chapter Five ~ Freddie and Carrie Study

MR. COOP HAD DECIDED they needed to begin learning Euclidian geometric proofs. The idea of a proof was new to them and they worked together to understand the concept.

"First we're given some information and then we're given something to prove," Carrie said as she opened her class notebook in the Kaplan's library.

"Then we have to use the given information to construct a step-by-step logic chain to reach the conclusion," Freddie added.

"Let's review the definitions and axioms we learned this week," she said.

Holly walked by the library and looked pleased to listen to Carrie and Freddie. "What a delight it will be when I have my own children studying in our home, too," she said. Then she looked down and spoke to her seventh-month swollen belly. "You'll be living in a real *Bet Midrash*!"

"What's that?" Freddie asked.

"A house of study," Holly explained as she left the two students alone to do their homework.

After an hour of review, Freddie and Carrie were standing in front of a whiteboard. They had written a problem on it and were straining to write down logic statements and reasons for the statements.

"I know what's next," Carrie blurted out. She began writing her statement on the whiteboard.

"Yes," Freddie called out as he started writing. "And this is the next statement."

"Done!" Carrie yelled as she high-fived Freddie.

He put his arms around her and yelled, "We did it!"

Suddenly they each seemed to feel embarrassed they were in an embrace. They let their arms drop.

"I think we should try another problem," Freddie said. "Yeah, but let's sit down for this one," Carrie agreed.

***

Ryan Rifkin's wife, Lucinda, stopped by to visit Holly. They sat on the patio enjoying the bright sunshine of that warm June day. Lucinda, too, was pregnant, five-months-along.

"How's the pregnancy going?" Holly asked.

"I'm okay. Some mornings I feel like I have cotton in my head, but Ryan is still going nuts. If he sees me lift anything heavier than a washcloth he gets upset. It's almost a relief that Jonah and he are both working in Austin during the week. Also, I'm glad I'm taking classes. It gives me something else to think about other than worry about what kind of a mother I will be."

"I know what you mean on both counts," Holly agreed. "I think if it were up to Jonah, I'd be restricted to bedrest until this baby arrives. I'm teaching a couple of classes at the university this summer, so that helps."

"We should review our class schedules and see if we can share some of the driving."

"That's a great idea."

"You know, Holly, I remember when I first told Ryan I was pregnant. I was frightened to death, and he put his arms around me and held me so tight against him I could hardly breathe. That's when it hit me—we were pregnant and he would be my partner through this whole pregnancy. He's a real together kind of partner. We do almost everything in our lives as a team. That really works well for us."

"Well, there are a number of things Jonah and I don't do as a team," Holly said. "Jonah has a love of high-end audio and antique cars. He detected something called oscillations in one of his amplifiers last week. I listened but couldn't hear them. He was on the phone to one of his audiophile buddies in Livermore, California nearly all of last Saturday morning. They sounded like two doctors consulting about a sick patient—I just don't understand—but I can, however, enjoy his enjoyment of those things."

Lucinda smiled and nodded her head.

"Also, Jonah loves driving, which I certainly don't. He's willing to spend hours doing it. Last year we drove out to the Sand Hill Crane Festival in Othello, Washington. Four-hours there, three- hours birding, and then four-hours home—all in one day. He wasn't even tired when we got home. Since I'm a scenery junky it works out well for both of us."

"I know what you mean, Holly. Sometimes teamwork is not about doing things exactly the same, but more about complimenting each other's strengths and balancing each other's weaknesses. I can remember being such a frightened girl when I met Ryan. But he always knew when I was worrying and he would put his arms around me and explain how we would work things out. That felt so reassuring. The weekend we met, when Ryan and some of his university friends had a study weekend at my parents' home, we fell asleep on the living room floor and he called me his partner for the first time that night."

"That must have felt so nice," Holly said.

"It did. I held him so tight after he said that. Then there was a neighborhood get-together in Meridian a week later with tons of people who were new to me. Ryan was laughing and joking with your brother, Drew, and his friend, Andy. I was standing all alone and Ryan stopped what he was doing and came over to me. He called me his special lady and stayed beside me the rest of the night."

"Speaking of enjoyment, Jonah's mom is coming over for dinner tonight. I like Michelle so much. Everyone should have such a kind mother-in-law. Ethan and Sheryl will be here as well. Sheryl is going to announce her pregnancy. I only found out because she called me when she was having terrible morning sickness. Can you and Ryan come over? I'm going to order sushi trays rather than cook. I'm at the point in this pregnancy where almost any food smell makes me feel ill...except, oddly enough, sushi."

Lucinda looked worried. "But my doctor told me sushi isn't safe in pregnancy."

"Yeah, I have heard that too, but my doctor told me his wife is Japanese and she ate sushi with all her pregnancies. You just have to be safe and eat fish with low mercury levels. Then it is okay in moderation. So I have ordered some with salmon and shrimp rather than tuna so we can have some too."

"Well then, in that case, sushi sounds wonderful. Of course we'll come. Can I bring over miso soup and a fruit tray for dessert?"

"Great, if you're up to it."

"No problem," Lucinda told her.

Holly became serious. "Did you check the threat level today?" "Ryan did. He calls first thing every day."

"Who could have imagined the two of us would end up marrying math guys involved in classified military work such that we'd be wearing concealed pistols all the time," Holly said.

"I know. Sometimes my head starts spinning when I think about the danger we could be in."

"Jonah and I are going travel up Puget Sound to Victoria, British Columbia in two-weeks. Are you guys coming with us? We're going to borrow Jonah's cousin's antique trawler. Ari and his wife Leah just finished restoring it last spring. It should be a great time, and the Butchart Gardens in Victoria are to die for. If we have time we'll also stop to see the San Juan Islands, plus Jonah is anxious to overnight in the harbor John Wayne loved. It's up near Port Angeles."

"You know, Ryan helped Jonah and Ari rebuild one of the engines on that boat. He can't wait to go for a cruise on it, so we'll be there. I understand it took them three-years to get it restored. Leah's and Ari's dads spent almost all of last winter up here working on it. Apparently they restored an old Chris Craft Connie when they were in college back in the sixties. I've never been on a cruise before, but let me tell you, I can't wait to see the Butchart gardens. Their website is so informative and I've read through it so many times, I won't need a map when we get there."

"Cruising is close to heaven in my opinion," Holly said as she shifted in her chair to get more comfortable. "We won't be on a big ship, but it's stable and I enjoy coming home, so to speak, rather than staying in a hotel room. Also we should see whales and seals around the San Juan Islands. Carrie is excited because of the bird life we'll see."

Holly and Lucinda glanced toward the lake at a forty-two-foot Hinckley Daysailor sailboat being maneuvered into their dock.

"Ethan and Sheryl are here," Holly announced. "Ethan and Jonah are taking Carrie and Freddie out for a sailing lesson. They've borrowed the boat from Ethan's Uncle Meyer."

"Are you doing *Havdala* tonight?" Lucinda asked.

"Yes, but I need to replenish my spice box." Holly loved the Jewish ritual that marked the symbolic end of *Shabbat* and holidays and ushered in the new week.

"Don't worry, I'll bring mine over."

"That would be great—oh, my Lord!" Holly exclaimed. "I don't think sailing agrees with poor Sheryl. We better get out there."

They ran out and Ethan was standing behind Sheryl with his arms around her waist while she vomited into the lake.

Sheryl stood and said something to Ethan and then they walked up to the patio where Holly and Lucinda were.

"This kid is going to owe me big time for putting me through all this!" Sheryl declared.

Chapter Six ~ Megan leaves LA

THERE WAS A LOUD demanding knock at Megan's door. She opened it a crack to find a detective flashing his badge. "Are you Megan Cohen?"

"I am."

"We need to talk. Can we come in?"

"What's this about?"

"We need to ask about Todd Portman."

Megan shut the door, slipped the security chain off, and invited them in. "I work with him," she said. "I think he took the week off to be with his family in San Diego."

"Word is you've been having an affair with him."

"How is that any of your business?" She put her feet together to keep her knees from shaking.

"Todd Portman is in the hospital, ma'am. He's been cut up pretty badly. His wife and children are missing. When we went to his home we found some photos in an envelope addressed to Mrs. Portman. These are copies."

The detective handed her a large manila envelope that contained photos of Todd and Megan as they walked on the nude beach and kissed. There was even one photo of him caressing her breast. She was disgusted and appalled at the implications. "Where did these come from?"

"Can't say for sure yet, but someone probably paid a private detective to take these and send them to his wife."

"You don't think I had anything to do with his injuries, do you? I stopped seeing him as soon as I returned from that trip."

"As far as things stand right now, no, we don't. We're trying to find Mrs. Portman. Has she tried to contact you?"

"No, and I wouldn't know her if I saw her."

"Ms. Cohen, to be honest there was a threat against you along with these photos, and due to the brutal nature of the attack on Mr. Portman, we think it might be a good idea if you left town for a few weeks until we locate the perpetrator—as long as you let us know where you're going. Is there someone you could stay with?"

"I have a sister in Seattle."

"Let me have your cell number and I'll call you when we have the perp in custody."

"How soon should I leave?"

"There's a black-and-white outside to take you to the airport right now."

"I'll call my sister while I pack a bag."

Megan was distraught. What choice did she have? She hadn't spoken to her sister in so long and now she had to up and visit her under shady circumstances. As she threw some things into her suitcase, she also called her boss and told him she needed some time off. Oddly enough, he didn't ask why but simply said he'd look forward to her return.

***

Carrie and Freddie looked out at the pier from the library and saw the sailboat.

"Do you think we'll be sailing on that?" Freddie asked.

"What a nifty sailboat. I hope that's the one. Let's put our stuff away and go check it out."

They were just about to head downstairs to the patio when they heard the doorbell ring. The two of them followed Jonah to the front door.

Marvin Lipinski greeted them and introduced his six-year-old daughter, Olivia, who had a pretty smile, bright eyes, and shoulder-length brown hair.

"I think that's the boat, Dad," Freddie enthusiastically said while he pointed out the large window.

"That's a nice one," Mr. Lipinski said. "I hear you're turning into a dolphin."

"Dad, wait until you see their big pool. I swam a whole length today."

"And," Carrie said proudly, "he swam over the deep end without any help."

"That's a fine accomplishment, Freddie," his dad told him.

Jonah led them out to the patio and they greeted everyone just as Sheryl's cell phone rang. She stepped off to the side to answer it. When she returned from the call, she announced that she still felt nauseous and not at all up to sailing. When she also announced that her sister was coming for a visit, Ethan decided to stay with her.

Changing the subject, Jonah turned to Marvin. "I have a child-sized life preserver on the boat if Olivia would like to come with us."

"Oh please, Dad," Olivia implored her father. "Please, Dad? Can I go?"

Olivia turned to Jonah. "I'm little but I'm getting to be a big girl and my dad sometimes calls me his big helper."

"If we go out on that boat," Mr. Lipinski said, "you have to do exactly as you are told, without any argument."

"Dad, I'm not that little!"

Jonah looked at Marvin, who winked his okay.

"I think we certainly can use a big helper today," Jonah said as he took Olivia's hand. "Come on, sailors, it's off to the boat we go."

Marvin helped Olivia with her life jacket. Then, using both hands, she brushed her hair back from her face. "Dad, do I look like a sailor?"

"You certainly do," he replied.

It was a partly cloudy day with soft, gentle breezes. As they were about to get underway, Freddie asked, "Will you use the engine to get away from the dock?"

"Let me tell you, I had an excellent teacher—my cousin Leah. She showed me how to get under way just using wind power. I'm going to teach you the same thing."

Jonah turned to Carrie and instructed her as he untied the last line holding the sailboat to the dock. "Okay, Carrie, start pulling in the jib as Freddie pulls in the main sail."

The sailboat began gently and silently gliding away from the dock. They had traveled all of twenty feet when Carrie exclaimed, "This is great!"

"Great nothing," an enthusiastic Freddie yelled. "This is fantastic."

"This is so cool! It's like we're just gliding on the water," Olivia added.

Jonah had Marvin take the helm as he began teaching the children how to perform various boat and sail handling skills. They all seemed to readily absorb the nomenclature of the boat as Jonah described the points of sail and demonstrated how the sails had to be set for each.

After forty-minutes on the water, the wind momentarily died. The sails drooped and the boat slowed to a standstill, but maintained a slight rocking motion. Jonah looked at the surface of the water and saw an area of dark ripples moving across the top, indicating a puff of wind was coming toward them.

Olivia was seated on the windward side of the boat and Jonah called out, "Olivia, I need some help. When I tell you to, please blow on the sail."

An instant before the puff hit the boat he told her, "Now, Olivia!"

She stood up, took a deep breath, and blew toward the sail. Within a second, the puff hit the sails, and as they filled, the boat began to move again. Olivia's eyes opened wide and were filled with wonder at her accomplishment.

"Thank you, Olivia," Jonah shouted to her.

"Wow! I did it. Dad, did you see what I did? Did I really do that?"

"Thank you so much, Olivia," Jonah said. "It's a good thing you decided to go sailing with us."

Olivia turned to Carrie. "See? I told you I was little but I could do things like a big girl."

"I'm sure glad you're helping us sail today," Carrie said, smiling at her.

"Marvin, I want to demonstrate how to fly the spinnaker for Carrie and Freddie. Set a course for downwind, please."

"Olivia, I'm going to turn the boat, but then I'm going to need you to steer the boat for me."

"Okay, Dad. I'll be right there."

She ran across the teak deck to her father. He had her sit on his lap and hold onto the big wheel.

"This wheel is bigger than I am, Dad," she told him.

"Okay now, I want you to line up the front edge of the jib, that's the sail in front, with that white house on the shore. I want you to sail right at it."

"Okay, Dad, but those people will be mad if I hit their house."
"You are correct, so we'll turn before we get there."

The large powder-blue spinnaker was maneuvered into position and filled with wind.

"That's beautiful, Dad. It makes the boat look even prettier."
"Good job, guys," Olivia yelled to Carrie and Freddie, who were still near the bow looking up at the spinnaker. "That spin- whatever thing looks great!"

"Thanks for keeping us on course, Olivia," Freddie yelled back. "You're welcome!"

Marvin looked in heaven watching Freddie maneuver around the boat—he seemed so wrapped up in sailing he didn't pay much attention to his lack of mobility. After three-hours on the water they tied up at the dock once more.

"Thank you, Mr. Kaplan," Freddie said. "Anytime you need crew for this boat let me know and I'll be there."

"You're welcome, Freddie. I love to teach beginning sailors." "Count me in when you need crew as well," Carrie stated.

"Thanks so much, Jonah. I think sailing is going to be one of my favorite things to do."

"I'm glad to hear that, Carrie."

"Anytime you need someone to steer the boat or blow on the sail," Olivia said. "I'll be glad to help you, too."

"Sounds great, Olivia."

"How did it go?" Holly asked when they walked into the house.

"Fabulous," Carrie stated.

"Fantastic," Freddie agreed.

"I was a big help, Mrs. Kaplan," Olivia said. "I steered the boat and blew on the sail to get us going."

"You are certainly a big helper, young lady."

"How about I give you guys swimming and sailing lessons again next Saturday?" Jonah asked them.

"Yes," they yelled in unison.

"You should plan on coming over to the house during the week to practice swimming when Holly has time to keep an eye on you," Jonah told them.

"I'm sure I can find time for that," Holly said.

She turned to Marvin. "Why don't you three stay for dinner? We have lots of family coming over."

"I don't want to intrude on a family get-together."

"Please, we have more than enough."

He smiled and nodded. "All right. Thank you, we'd love to." Jonah sat on the patio with Marvin and Ethan. Holly had Carrie, Olivia, and Freddie take each of them a large glass of iced tea.

After Ryan had joined them, Jonah turned to Marvin. "What specifically is wrong with Freddie's hip and knee?"

"The bones stopped growing too soon, so the joints aren't fully formed."

"If I could get access to Freddie's medical records I might know someone who could help him," Jonah said looking to Ryan, who raised his eyebrows.

"That would be kind of you. I'll set that up."

Then the four men began chattering away about boats and boating.

"There's just something magical about being on the water," Marvin stated. "I've felt that way since I was a child."

"Sheryl and I have loved sailing since the first moment we tried it when we were at camp," Ethan said. "We've spent many peaceful hours in our little twenty-two-foot sailboat."

***

Just before the sushi trays arrived, Jonah's mother, Michelle, arrived from the airport with Megan—Sheryl's identical twin. Lucinda noted that Megan would have indeed looked identical to Sheryl, but for her more flamboyant dress and predilection for makeup. She had Sheryl's petite body, but wore tight dark-colored slacks and a top that did its best to reveal as much of her chest as possible. She also wore sling-back high heels that matched the color of her top.

As she was introduced to everyone, Lucinda observed another difference between Sheryl and Megan. Sheryl's expression radiated happiness, while Megan's expression consisted of an obviously forced smile.

She mentioned that to Holly when they were alone in the kitchen.

"She hasn't spoken to her family in years. It's a long story," Holly began, "but the short version goes like this. You've heard Ethan and Sheryl have been together since they met at camp when they were around twelve. Well, what you may not have heard is that Ethan's twin brother David was there too. He and Megan became a couple until sometime in high school. Megan was angry as hell when David broke up with her, and she became a very bitter person. It seemed like the happier Sheryl became, the angrier Megan became. She was engaged a couple of years ago, but it didn't last."

"I can see how that might be hard, but shouldn't she be over it by now?" Lucinda said as they set the table.

Holly shrugged. Then as everyone sat down for dinner, Marvin stood and pulled out a chair for Megan.

"I can manage my own chair, thank you," she snapped.

Lucinda exchanged a quick glance with Holly as if to say what a sad lady Megan was.

Freddie watched his dad and then pulled out a chair for Carrie. "Thanks, Freddie," Carrie said, flushing with the attention.

The adults all smiled, but when the husbands had helped their wives into their seats, Olivia remained standing.

"What's up, Olivia?" Ryan asked. "What about my chair?"

He smiled and then pulled out her chair. "I'm sorry, Olivia." She sat quickly, thanked him, and put her napkin in her lap.

The adults laughed and the tension from Megan's comment was lifted.

Much of the dinner conversation dealt with pregnancies and relationships until Carrie reminded everyone that she and Freddie had completed their first week of class at the university.

"We even studied together today," Carrie said.

"Plus we had a swimming lesson *and* a sailing lesson," Freddie added.

"What did you think of the sailing, Freddie?" Ryan asked.

"I really wasn't sure what to expect, but when the wind grabbed the sails and we started moving, I was amazed the gentle wind could move us right along."

"And you, Carrie?" Sheryl asked.

"I thought it was great. I also really liked being at the helm while Freddie tended the jib. The two of us were really in control of that big sailboat—just the wind and us. I felt like a real sailor, controlling the boat like that."

"I liked the quiet as we moved across the water," Freddie added. "We just had the crashing of the water against the side of the boat, the occasional whoosh of the wind in the sails, and the squawking of the birds flying over the lake."

Carrie paused, looking pensive for a moment then announced to the group, "Math, swimming, and sailing...now that's a great Saturday."

"You said it, Carrie," Freddie said in an enthusiastic voice.

Jonah grinned. "Carrie, please tell everyone what you said as you took over the helm."

Carrie sat up straight and positioned herself as if standing at the helm. "Ahoy there, you swab jockeys, wrap the clew around the captain's barnacles, and batten down the boson's mate."

"When she said that," Marvin said as everyone laughed, "Freddie and Olivia started laughing so hard, I was afraid they were going to fall overboard."

Megan wore an almost-smile, her face appearing as if she was fondly recalling a memory.

Olivia leaned in and whispered to Lucinda. "I laughed, but I really don't know why it's so funny."

Lucinda whispered back, "It's really just nonsense words that sound like sailor talk. It's kind of a running joke with this bunch. I can teach that to you sometime."

As dinner ended everyone moved to the patio. When the conversation returned to relationships and pregnancies, Megan excused herself and wandered down to the lake's edge.

Lucinda whispered to Holly. "She's got her ass closed so tight I think she may have had it vacuum sealed."

Holly's eyes filled with tears as she covered her mouth with her hand to avoid laughing out loud. She leaned toward Lucinda. "I'm actually surprised she's visiting for as long as she is. She barely gets along with anyone in her family. Something must be going on."

***

As far north as they were, it was still light out until nine-thirty in the evening. Megan slipped out of her heels and walked across the lawn. The damp grass felt comfortably cool on her bare feet.

She saw Marvin standing nearby as she arrived at the water's edge.

"I find it tough to hear stories about other people's happy relationships," Marvin said to her as he shrugged.

Megan could relate to that. She smiled and nodded, but did not speak, allowing Marvin to continue.

"I did have one wonderful relationship, but my wife died a year after Olivia was born. Losing her was so painful. I never want to go through that again." He shook his head as if he was remembering the experience. Then he turned back to her. "Would you like to go for a walk along the shore?"

Megan wasn't sure how to respond so she just stared at him. "Don't worry," Marvin said. "I'm not much on small talk so I won't be invading your space. I spend all my emotional energy being a dad, and a mom, for my kids."

Megan didn't think much of Marvin but she started walking next to him. They walked in silence for a while.

"No doubt you've heard, at least according to my family, that I'm a bitter person."

"Whatever I've heard from others doesn't matter much to me, Megan. I tend to make my own decisions when I meet people."

"My sister, Sheryl, is always smiling and happy. People expect that I should be the same—like because we look the same, we should be the same. That's not me."

Marvin was quiet for a bit. "If it will make you feel better, you can curse at me, call me names, even say bad things about my mother, and I won't care because I don't know you."

Megan smiled for a moment and then burst out laughing. She thought that if the other members of her family had been watching, they would have been in shock to see her relating to someone like this.

Marvin smiled too, and they continued walking in silence for a quite a while longer.

He looked to the horizon. "The sun is getting low in the sky," he said. "We should head back."

Megan nodded and they turned and began retracing their steps. "So, what do you do, Marvin?"

"I work on airplanes. You?"

"Organic chemistry—research."

"Sounds challenging."

Megan shrugged and there was little further conversation as they continued back.

They returned to the house and Marvin told Freddie and Olivia to get their things together and they would head home. Then he turned to Megan. "I'm taking Freddie, Olivia, and Carrie to the Space Needle and the Seattle Aquarium tomorrow. Interested?"

As far as Megan was concerned anything would be better than listening to more discussions about pregnancies and how happy everyone was. "I haven't been to the Space Needle in years," she said. "Why not?"

"Good. I'll pick you up at ten."

Megan noticed a number of family members looking at each other with surprised expressions, likely shocked that someone could get her to agree to do something outside her comfort zone, let alone in such a short time. It likely seemed all the more remarkable being someone as quiet and reserved, as Marvin appeared to be.

Lucinda lit the candle for *Havdalah* then blew out the match. She leaned toward Sheryl and spoke quietly, but Megan could hear every word. "According to Freddie, Marvin never goes on dates."

Sheryl, being more aware of how good Megan's hearing was, whispered her response quieter. Still, Megan could imagine what her sister would say to that. She envisioned her telling Lucinda that Megan likely hadn't gone out with anyone in years and that she was far too wrapped up in her career for such things.

Chapter Seven ~ The Arrival of Nancy Grace

FEW MONTHS BEFORE the trip to the gardens, Drew and his bride, Beverly, had just setup their first home in a small three-bedroom house in Meridian, Idaho. They had both grown up in that vibrant town just west of Boise and thought it the perfect place to settle down.

On one particular day, Drew had already left for work and Beverly was just getting her things together to go to her job helping her friend Shelly setup the office for a senior citizens' activities center. Her doorbell rang and she opened it to find a young lady, seeming near her own age.

"Hi. I'm Drew's sister, Nancy Grace," the young woman said. Then before waiting for Beverly to respond she continued. "Helga was our mom. We were taken away from her when I was two. Drew somehow ended up in Seattle and I bounced around between foster homes in Oakland. I have my birth certificate with our mom's name on it so you can see I'm not lying. Also, a social worker in Seattle that Drew knows can vouch for me. I have her number so you can call her."

A shocked Beverly let the young woman in and then called Drew to tell him the news. She spoke to him for a few moments before putting the phone on speaker. "All right, Drew, you're on speaker now."

"Hey, Sister," he yelled into the phone.

"Hey, Brother."

"Thanks for finding me."

"Mrs. Hollings, from the State Child Welfare Agency, told me where you were living."

"I remember her. Can't wait to see you in person. I'll be home from work around five."

"See ya then."

After saying good-bye to Drew, Beverly turned to Nancy. "I have to visit a senior center this morning. Would you like to come with me?"

"Sure. I'll do that with you. I enjoy talking to seniors."

Beverly drove them over to the senior center. They walked into the cafeteria where an elderly woman was upset and shouting.

"I was a famous actress, and no one is treating me with respect," she yelled.

"Mrs. Corbett, you need to eat," an attendant angrily told her. "I won't." She pushed the plate of food away.

The attendant looked at Beverly and Nancy, shrugging. "What the hell am I supposed to do?"

Nancy quietly walked over and sat down next to Mrs. Corbett. "They're not nice to me. I'm a famous actress and I refuse to eat until I'm treated with respect," she told Nancy.

"That's awful. You hold my hand and tell me about it. They shouldn't treat a famous actress like that. That's not fair at all."

Nancy deftly calmed the elderly woman, and while they talked, she gradually started feeding her in between discussions of how badly she was being treated. By then end of her meal, Nancy had the woman smiling and calm enough to quietly watch television with some of the other seniors.

One of the center's administrators came up to her. "Who are you?"

Nancy hesitated and looked to Beverly.

"She's my sister-in-law." Beverly smiled. "This is Nancy."

The administrator broke into a smile too. "Honey, if you ever want a job helping seniors, I'd hire you in a flash."

"Thank you, but I'm just visiting."

***

Drew arrived home, and in his excitement, took the stairs to their apartment two at a time. He flung open the door and was greeted by Beverly.

"Drew, this is your sister Nancy," Beverly said. Nancy looked at Drew and offered her hand.

Drew ignored the hand and threw his massive arms around her. "Sisters get hugs," he said. "I am so glad we finally get to meet—again. I always wondered, you know..."

Me too," Nancy said. "I heard that you lived in a nice town, so I thought I'd drive out to meet you."

"I'm really glad you did. How long will you be in town?"

Nancy shrugged. "I've been thinking about moving and I've heard good things about Boise."

"We love it here," Drew said.

"We don't have much room," Beverly said, "but you can sleep on the couch until you find your own place."

"Thank you. That's very nice of you." Nancy looked relieved. That evening, during dinner at Drew and Beverly's apartment, Nancy mentioned the poor state of her old car.

"You've come to the right place," Beverly told her. "Your brother has a degree in automotive engineering and has been working on, and restoring, cars since his high school years. If it has wheels and an engine, Drew can fix it."

"That's quite a talent, Brother."

"My adoptive dad taught me an awful lot of what I know. He's been my dad since I was six, though, so as far as I'm concerned, he's my real dad."

"Oliver is even rebuilding an old nineteen-thirties airplane with a neighbor right now," Beverly said as the threesome cleaned up the dishes from dinner. "And by the way, we run every morning."

"I'd like to do that with you. I was on the cross-country team in high school," Nancy told them.

"Nancy, did you find out anything about our birth-mom? I don't remember and no one ever told me anything about her."

"I can tell you the little bit that I have found out about her." Drew agreed and Nancy told him what she knew.

"Well, our mother, Helga, was raised by a single mom, in a rough neighborhood near Oakland, California. Her father had abandoned their family many years before. It seems it was her goal to get pregnant and have a baby by the time she was sixteen in order to get the government to pay for her to have her own apartment and everything."

"That would be me," Drew said.

"Right," Nancy said. "And when you were four and I was two, it seems Helga was expecting a friend one night and when she heard knocking on her door, she answered it without thinking. Instead of seeing her friend she found herself standing in the doorway with a crack pipe in her hand, face to face with a policeman who had been canvassing the neighborhood looking for witnesses to a crime."

Drew shook his head quietly as Beverly reached out for his hand.

Nancy shrugged. "So she was hauled off to jail, and Drew and I were placed with child protective services."

"She didn't even try to get you back?" Beverly asked.

"They said that at her trial she told the judge she needed her children back, but when he told her she wouldn't be allowed to have us back until she attended drug rehab, she screamed something about keeping the damn kids for all she cared. So that's what the judge did. And here we are."

Chapter Eight ~ Megan and the Children

MARVIN, WITH FREDDIE AND Olivia, picked up Megan and Carrie the following morning. "I received a call from a boat dealer early this morning," he said. "A certain boat I'd previously inquired about has just come in on trade. If you don't mind, I'd like to head over there and we can all go for a brief ride on the it."

They agreed and Marvin proceeded to drive them over to the dealer, on the northwest side of Union Bay.

Sitting at the dock next to the dealer was a sleek-looking forty-six-foot boat with a fully enclosed cabin and a flybridge. The cabin had a nice u-shaped dinette with a three-person couch opposite. The helm had a number of electronic displays in front of the pilot's chair and there was a forward-facing bench seat opposite the helm. The aft cockpit had a nice sitting area, and below deck and forward were a kitchen, head with shower, and two cabins with queen-size berths. The workmanship on the boat was exemplary, with beautifully finished teak flooring and satin finished teak trim.

After a tour of the boat's interior and engine space, the dealer's agent fired up the engines. "The boat may be used, but there are only a few hundred hours on each of the Cummins diesels. They're rated at six hundred horsepower each."

Indeed, the boat looked like new. Marvin took over at the helm while Megan and Olivia sat on the bench seat.

"Great view," Megan said as they gently cruised into Lake Union.

"Let's head out through the locks and onto Puget Sound to see what this boat is like at speed," the agent said.

"I've never been on a boat when it goes through locks," Carrie said.

"Me neither," Freddie added.

"Freddie, what does that mean, locks?" Olivia asked from the bench seat.

"The boat drives into this special chamber. We are then isolated from the body of water that we used to enter the chamber. A big valve is opened. It is used to hydrodynamically diminish the level of water in the chamber until we're equal to the level of Puget Sound."

"Thank you, big Brother."

Olivia turned around to face forward, and then glanced up at Megan while shrugging her shoulders, as if to say she still didn't understand.

Megan smiled. "It's a kind of water elevator for the boat, Olivia."

"Thanks, Miss Cohen. My big brother is very nice, but," she leaned closer to whisper to Megan, "sometimes he tells me more than I want to know."

"Big brothers'll do that sometimes."

As they gently cruised along the canal leading to the locks, Megan kept watching Marvin. His smile seemed to be broadening with every mile that slipped under the boat's keel. She'd always liked being on the water, too, but this was different from the small power boats she had experienced. It was smooth and quiet. Being inside the cabin was nice and warm on that cloudy, cool morning.

She turned and looked at the kids who were pointing at, and discussing, the various boats and ships they passed. Freddie had brought a book of math puzzles because, he said, he had thought riding in the boat might become boring, but the book sat unused on the dinette as they chattered with each other and viewed the many sights.

"Do you have a boat now?" the agent asked.

"We have a twenty-eight-foot Boston Whaler Outrage," Marvin said. "It's a stable and seaworthy boat for the kids and me to cruise around Lake Washington, and occasionally head out onto the Sound."

They tied up in the locks. As the boat began its drop to the level of the Sound, Freddie and Carrie, wearing bright orange life vests, were assigned to watch the two boats which were tied up to their boat. Olivia stayed inside the cabin.

Megan was pleased to hear the calm voice Marvin used as he gave Carrie and Freddie precise directions on what was expected of them. They readily complied. Marvin nodded to her and she kept an eye on them.

Once the locks opened, the smaller boats were allowed to leave first. As their boat cruised out onto the Sound, Marvin opened the throttles on the powerful twin Cummins diesels and they were soon cruising a comfortable twenty knots.

Again Megan was surprised how smooth and quiet the ride was. As they were traveling north on Puget Sound, they passed shorelines edged by sandy beaches, many of which had gray driftwood logs strewn about them. Long rows of tall evergreens met at the beach's edge and provided a colorful green contrast to the dark water of the Sound and the tan beaches. Their beauty was emphasized as the sun began to peak out from the diminishing cloud cover, illuminating the water and stately forests. Looking to the west, she saw the snow-capped Olympic Mountains.

"I'd forgotten how beautiful the Sound is," she told Marvin. "Not to mention how relaxing and peaceful it is to gently cruise along like this."

"I used to dream about having one of these to take my family on. I can finally afford one and I'm afraid I'll need someone to help me with it. Freddie would enjoy it, but as you can see from our experience at the locks, it really takes two adults to safely handle one of these. Piloting is a full-time job and I'd have to have someone to watch the kids and do other things while we were cruising. I may have to wait until Freddie is older."

"That may be true," Megan said, "but if you kept it on Lake Washington for a couple of years, you could still enjoy it on the lake and head out onto the sound when you had assistance."

She was quiet for a while, then she glanced around the boat and Megan noticed that the children were riveted to the windows. "The children certainly think it's a lovely way to travel," she said.

"You guys, look over there!" Carrie suddenly yelled.

They all looked in the direction she was pointing just in time so see a large dark-feathered bird glide down to the water. It reached below the surface with its talons, pulled a fish out, and flew away with the fish suspended below.

"That was a golden eagle. I've never seen one before," Carrie stated.

"Looks like salmon sushi at the nest tonight," Freddie declared. "That poor fish." Olivia shook her head.

"You like sushi," Freddie reminded her. "Yeah," said Olivia, "but sushi's already dead."

Ten-minutes later the tall, shiny black fins and water spouts of a pod of Orca whales came into view. The three children were glued to the windows as they watched the whales.

Olivia moved from the dinette and sat next to Megan on the bench seat. She yawned a few times and soon fell asleep with her head on Megan's lap.

Megan surprised herself by patting the little girl's back as she slept. "She's precious, Marvin," she said.

They continued cruising on the Sound for an hour and then returned to the dealer.

Marvin told the dealer he would call him after he thought about the purchase for a few days.

Megan carried a sleeping Olivia off the boat. "I can carry her," Marvin offered.

"I'm fine," said Megan.

Actually she was more than fine. All her life she'd loved children. The thought of being childless terrified her. Holding that precious child in her arms, and interacting with her, would truly be the highlight of that lovely day.

As they got back into his car to drive to the aquarium Marvin turned to Megan. "This is when I really miss having a partner. I need another voice to see if this is a reasonable purchase."

"I'm not your partner, but what questions would you ask if your partner was here today?"

"I'd point out that I know I can afford this and would ask if we would use it enough to justify the expense."

"Let's see. You could serenely cruise down to Gig Harbor to see their colorful art show in July. You could explore all the gorgeous areas of southern Puget Sound. You could head down to Olympia and yell at your legislators. You could go to the Glass Museum in Tacoma. You could weekend in the San Juan Islands, and you could explore Hood Canal, not to mention heading up to Vancouver, BC. Those activities would occupy a few years at a minimum. You could also go fishing, bird and whale watching, and crabbing."

"Crabbing?" Freddie asked. "We could go out and catch our own crab?"

"That would be neat," Carrie stated. "Imagine pulling a big crab out of the water, dropping it in hot water, and then eating the crab you just caught!"

"See that?" Megan said jovially. "The kids think it's a great idea."

"I'm sure they do," Marvin said. "They don't have to pay to maintain it. These things can get expensive to operate if you're not careful."

"So you setup a budget for the year and when the budget runs out, that's the end of boating until the following year."

"What if something breaks?" Marvin asked.

"The repair money comes out of the yearly boat budget. It's easy. I'll setup a spreadsheet for you, if you like, and show you how to populate it for something like this boat."

"That's where a partner comes in. I would need someone to keep me on the budget."

"I've never been a successful partner," Megan ruefully stated. "Therefore I don't know how a partner would keep you on the budget. But, Marvin," she added buoyantly, "that was really a lovely boat. You could spend every weekend for years meandering around Puget Sound. That would be so nice for Freddie and Olivia."

"Meandering? That's a lovely way of describing how we could explore the Sound," Marvin stated. "Meandering. I like that."

They arrived at the Seattle Aquarium. The kids walked ahead of them with Carrie holding Olivia's hand. They couldn't wait to see the new baby sea otter.

The two adults were quietly observing Carrie, Olivia, and Freddie's excitement at viewing the little baby. Carrie continued to hold Olivia's hand while she pointed out things in the furry mammal's seawater enclosure. Olivia was positively entranced by their antics.

"Tell me about your wife," Megan asked.

"Elisabeth was perfect for me. She understood my love of working on airplanes and she was a great mother for Freddie and Olivia. We were together for a little over six-years. Just after Olivia was born, she developed a rare liver infection that killed her within a year of being diagnosed. I've been Freddie and Olivia's dad and mom ever since then. I think I'm doing okay on the dad part, but I worry about the mom part."

"Olivia seems to be a happy child. Freddie seems to be a sweet child as well. The way he and Carrie get along, I'd say he's developing into a fine young man."

"Thank you for saying that but I think it's mostly Carrie. She seems to know just what to say to him. A mom would be able to tell him how he should be treating her in return."

Megan looked back at Carrie, who was laughing at something Freddie had said. "From the expression on Carrie's face when she's around Freddie, I'd say he certainly knows how to treat her. Also, watch how easily Carrie relates to Olivia. Carrie's a real people person."

They began exploring other parts of the aquarium.

"They decided to become friends after they met in class and they alternate bringing snacks to share. Freddie asked me how to iron a shirt last week. He was so insistent that I took his shirts over to the cleaners to get them pressed. He's carefully brushing his hair every day and tries to look as nice as possible for her. I've tried to get him to improve his appearance for years but Carrie did it in a few days. She has this kind and patient way of talking to him. He'd walk through a wall for her if she asked him to."

"Wow," Megan said. "Sounds like Ethan and Sheryl. How did he hurt his hip?"

"It was a birth defect. It affected his right knee as well. He had some surgery a few weeks ago and it did little more than cause him a huge amount of pain."

They looked in on a tank that had many types of starfish. "I heard you had a young romance," Marvin said.

"We changed over the years and suddenly our personalities didn't fit any longer."

"I'm not sure what you mean by fit."

"The things I wanted out of life were no longer the things he wanted out of life. We started arguing all the time. David wasn't interested in going to the concerts or plays that I loved. He wanted to perform in concerts or act in plays rather than watch them. I saw how my sister and Ethan got along, and it hurt when I realized I couldn't manage the same type of relationship. I was young, so I blamed David, of course."

She shrugged. "In hindsight, we had simply grown apart. I see how happy he is with his wife, Linda. His happiness angered me at first, but gradually I realized I wanted a different kind of partner. I like to do things on my own and need time to work on life issues by myself before I can make a decision. David and Linda work out problems immediately. I can't make quick decisions. I need time to think through problems. When I'm pressured, I get angry and I want to put off the discussion until I calm down. That quality killed my engagement as well. I had found someone I thought was like David, and it turned out he was, so that relationship failed for the same reasons. I thought I could find another David and prove I could have a successful relationship with him."

"When Elisabeth died, I wanted my life to end," Marvin admitted. "Having the responsibility of the kids kept me going."

Their conversation got sidetracked by the children, who were mesmerized by the wide variety of bird and sea creatures at the aquarium. They couldn't seem to get enough of the marine life on display.

Soon, they drove over to the Space Needle and had lunch at the top, in a restaurant that slowly rotated while they ate. During lunch, Freddie and Carrie asked Megan questions about the chemistry of sea water. It was obvious they enjoyed talking to her. She provided explanations with just enough information that their young minds could grasp the concepts she taught them. While she talked to the older kids, she kept making little drawings with Olivia, who was laughing and giggling at the silly drawings she was creating with Megan. Marvin spent most of the lunch staring out at Puget Sound.

"Thinking about the boat?" Megan asked.

"As you said, it would be a lovely way to travel. As much as Freddie loves science and the natural world, it would be good for him.

Olivia has been curious about nature since she was tiny. They're such good children. They deserve everything I can provide for them."

***

Late the following Wednesday afternoon, Marvin called Megan to see if she wanted to attend a movie with Freddie, Carrie, and him.

She had been in a bad mood all day while she beat herself up over the path her life had taken. She had told Sheryl and Ethan it was best to leave her alone when she was in such a depressed state. Megan was also wondering if Todd had survived his wounds and when she might hear from the LA police.

"I'm sorry, Marvin," she told him, "but I'm in a foul mood—rather depressed—and I know I wouldn't be good company for anyone."

"Please help me with this," Marvin calmly stated. "If you are in a foul mood, I certainly don't want to have you around me, but the kids had so much fun with you last Sunday, they're looking forward to seeing you again. They just spent the last-twenty-minutes choosing a movie they think you'll like. How shall I explain to them you're too upset to spend time with them?"

Megan became defensive. "You don't know anything about me. Well you can tell those kids...you can say I...well...you can..." Megan became quiet as she mentally reviewed Marvin's words letting her know Carrie and Freddie looked forward to seeing her again. Forcing herself to calm down, she sighed. "You can tell them you're picking me up in thirty-minutes and we're going out to dinner after the movie—my treat."

Half-an-hour-later, as she got in Marvin's car, he told her Olivia was playing at a friend's house but they would pick her up after dinner. Freddie and Carrie instantly bombarded her with questions about chemistry.

"We need to know about molecules and stuff," Freddie told her. "Like how do the molecules stick together and how do they know what to—what's that word, Dad?"

"The word you're looking for is bond."

"Yes! How do they know what to bond to?"

"And how do they decide when to bond to something?" Carrie added.

"Oh yeah," Freddie said, "and how come some are heavy and some are light?"

Megan smiled at them. "I guess we'll have to have a discussion about electrons, protons and neutrons, plus Avogadro's number, not to mention moles."

They were wide eyed in excitement as Megan began explaining atomic structure. Marvin seemed pleased to sit and listen to their enthusiasm.

Megan opened her purse and pulled out a copy of the Periodic Chart of the Elements. She described some of its features. "You can study this for months and not learn all it can tell you about chemistry."

"Dad, did you know about this stuff?"

"Not me, Freddie. I'm just a guy who works on airplanes."

"That periodic chart is really neat," Carrie stated. "I'm going to ask Dad to buy me one when he and Mom get up here next week."

Marvin pulled his car into the parking lot at the theatre. The kids were disappointed they were going to end the discussion about chemistry, so Megan promised them they would continue at dinner. Her foul mood had completely evaporated. It had been pushed out of her mind by Freddie and Carrie's bubbly enthusiasm as she taught them about chemistry.

As Marvin was about to exit the car, Megan put a hand on his shoulder, leaned toward him, and kissed his cheek.

"Thanks for inviting me," she said, realizing her time with them had indeed improved her mood.

Marvin smiled at her. "You're certainly welcome."

Megan enjoyed the movie, but she especially enjoyed Carrie and Freddie choosing a sci-fi flick because they thought she would like to see something science based. Then after the movie, they went to a wonderful deli and the science-filled discussions continued at dinner.

Afterwards, Marvin dropped Megan off at Sheryl and Ethan's home. "You're a beautiful lady when you let the sunshine through," he told her.

"Thank you for saying that, Marvin." She smiled when she said that but didn't believe it was true.

She looked at Freddie and Carrie. "You guys certainly made it a sunshine-filled evening."

She said good-bye and when she entered Sheryl and Ethan's home, they looked pleased to see her wearing an ear-to-ear smile.

"How was your evening with Marvin and the kids?" her sister asked.

"It was so much fun. I really had a nice time with them. Carrie and Freddie asked me all kinds of questions about chemistry." Megan laughed. "They're so funny. They kept calling Avogadro's number Avocado's number. I thought I would die laughing at them."

She giggled again and continued. "We had dinner at a Jewish-style deli. I ordered matzo ball soup. It came with two big matzo balls, so I carved them up to explain shared atomic orbitals and covalent bonding. Then Carrie said, 'If I order a plate of spaghetti, will it help me understand string theory?' We all cracked up."

Ethan was a music major and Sheryl was a sociology major, and both were clueless when it came to covalent bonding or string theory. Megan was sure they had no idea what Avogadro's number was, let alone why that was funny, but she could tell they were overjoyed their always-angry and somber sister had returned to their home laughing and smiling.

As Megan lay in bed that night, reviewing the evening, her pillow began absorbing her tears. "Why can't I manage to have my own children to teach and love?" she quietly implored the dark room.

***

The following Saturday, there was a gathering on the patio of Jonah and Holly's home.

"Carrie, come over to the pool please," Freddie asked just after he arrived. "I want to tell you about Reynolds number and viscous versus turbulent flow."

"Freddie," Megan asked, "where did you learn about Reynolds number and types of flow?"

"My dad taught me," he said proudly.

"Watch this, Carrie." Freddie moved his hand through the pool water at varying speeds. "In fluid mechanics, the Reynolds number is a dimensionless scalar. It gives a measure of the ratio of viscous forces to inertial forces, which quantifies the importance of these two for given flow conditions."

Megan thought it was odd for someone who repaired airplanes to have knowledge of Reynolds number and types of flow.

"I think they talk like that so I won't understand them," Olivia complained.

"Why don't you sit between Miss Cohen and me?" Lucinda suggested. "We'll talk about things Freddie and Carrie don't like to talk about."

"That should be easy," Olivia told them. "What do you like?" Lucinda asked her.

"I love flowers and trees. My dad bought me some flower seeds and some tree seeds. He had me put dirt and fertilizer in some containers. When the flowers were about six-inches, I planted them around the yard. I have the most beautiful flowers in our backyard. The trees have to stay in containers for a couple more years."

Lucinda, the botanist in training, perked up. "Why don't you and I walk over to my house and I'll introduce you to the flowers in my backyard."

"Can Miss Cohen come with us?" Olivia asked with tons of enthusiasm in her voice.

"Of course she can."

Olivia jumped off her chair. She grabbed Megan's hand and then Lucinda's and they proceeded toward the path leading to Ryan and Lucinda's back yard.

Olivia looked back at Holly. "You can come with us, if you like."

"Thank you, Olivia, but I'm going to keep an eye on the swimmers."

After the garden tour, Olivia put on her bathing suit and joined her brother and Carrie in the pool. They immediately stopped their swimming practice and began playing games with Olivia.

"What brand of boat were you on last week?" Ryan asked Megan.

"I think it was called an Eastbay forty-six."

"Carrie told me it was made by Grand Banks," Holly said. "The boat cruised serenely and quietly across the Sound. It was amazing to look at the workmanship. Even the screw heads lined up. It had a lovely kitchen, big cabins, and a roomy living area. I can imagine a million fun adventures Marvin and his family could experience on a boat like that."

"Moshe and Samantha bought a Grand Banks last summer," Jonah told them. "They are going to use it to cruise up to Alaska next spring. I don't know much about the GB boats, but the value of the boat you were on was most likely in the upper six-figure range when it was new."

"It's hard to imagine how a man who repairs airplanes for a living can afford a boat like that. He seems so bright. I'm surprised he doesn't do something more intellectual."

"What? Who told you he repairs airplanes?" Holly asked. "That's what Marvin told me. He said he works on airplanes."

"Megan," Jonah said, grinning at her, "he is one of the top aerodynamicists in the Northwest. He consults for companies from all over the world. He also teaches advanced aerodynamics at the university. He's an incredibly quiet, and certainly very modest, guy. He has one PhD in aeronautical engineering and another in the chemistry of composite structures."

"Really?" Megan was shocked. Jonah laughed and nodded his head.

Megan quietly stared at the kids in the pool for a few minutes. She loved the melodious sound of the children's laughter as they played.

"Come on in the pool, Miss Cohen," Olivia called out. "I can tell you need to get wet!"

"I can't take it anymore," Megan announced. "Ladies and gentlemen, with your permission, I'm going to put on my suit and get wet."

She went and changed into her bikini, which didn't leave much to the imagination. Hesitating for a moment as she regarded her image in the mirror, she then headed out the door with a large white terrycloth robe wrapped around her. As she neared the pool, she slipped out of the robe and felt every eye looking at her.

She decided to use humor to alleviate the awkwardness of the moment. "I call this my bum suit," she said as she turned to the adults. "Not because you can see my bum, which you can, but because I wore it on a cruise last summer and it attracted every bum on the ship."

The adults broke into laughter.

As soon as Megan was in the water, Olivia came over to her. The older two went back to their swimming practice, with occasional guidance from Jonah, who also began teaching them open-water-rescue techniques. It was obvious Olivia loved having her around. They started playing little games, and then Megan gradually started teaching her techniques so she would become more confident in the water. Within a few minutes she had Olivia floating motionless on her back with only her little face sticking out of the water.

"Look at me, Mrs. Rifkin and Mrs. Kaplan. I'm doing the jellyfish float!"

"Good work, Olivia," Holly called to her.

"You certainly look like a great big jellyfish from over here," Lucinda shouted to her.

Megan started showing her how to kick her feet and "push the barge" as Megan referred to the game of pushing a kickboard ahead of her. Under Megan's watchful eye and enthusiastic encouragement, Olivia and the kickboard were zipping up and back across the shallow end of the pool like a baby duck chasing its mother.

"Come on, everyone, lunch is ready," Holly called out.

Olivia climbed out of the pool with Megan right behind her. Then Olivia began running. She tripped, skinned her elbow and one knee on the rough pool apron, and started to cry.

Megan immediately picked her up and held her. "I'll get a first-aid kit," Holly called out.

Megan wrapped Olivia in a big towel and carried her into the house to the pool-level bathroom. Olivia had large tears running down her face and was trembling.

"I'm going to put some antiseptic spray on your arm and knee," Holly told her after Megan had cleaned off the scraped areas.

"Will it hurt?" Olivia asked.

"No, it will just feel cool and make the pain go away." Within a minute, Olivia's tears had nearly stopped. "Shall we get dressed?" Megan asked her.

Olivia nodded her agreement as she sniffed away a tear. Megan carefully helped her out of her suit so it wouldn't touch the areas that had been scrapped. She took a large fluffy towel and gently dried her off.

"I'm going to put my clothes on. You get dressed and then we need to brush your hair. I have something special for you."

With a brush and hair dryer, Megan gave Olivia a quick hairstyle. Olivia looked in heaven as she watched the new style appear.

"Now, you have to wear my ribbon in your hair, because it is a special ribbon."

"Why is it a special ribbon?"

"When you wear it, you look prettier and you feel better."

Olivia looked at herself in a full-length mirror. She put her hands up to feel her new hairstyle. "This is great. Thank you so much." She hugged Megan. "The ribbon is working. I do feel better. Will you teach me how to take care of my hair like this?"

"I'd love to."

They returned to the patio to have lunch, and Olivia was walking particularly straight with her head held high.

"Olivia," Lucinda exclaimed. "Your hairstyle is perfect."

"Very grown up, Olivia," Holly added.

"They like it," Olivia whispered to Megan.

"Thank you so much."

"You are certainly welcome, little lady."

"Will you sit next to me, please, Miss Cohen?"

They sat together, and Olivia spent most of the lunch talking to Sheryl, Megan, Lucinda, and Holly about school, boys, and the flowers she saw in Lucinda's yard.

"My favorite was the Iris Latifolia which is from the Spanish Pyrenees. It has lovely blue petals on its flowers and yellow stripes in the middle of the petals."

Lucinda smiled. Olivia could be another Freddie, but in botany instead of math. "What about the Iris Wattii?" she asked Olivia.

"It was beautiful to look at and really different. I think I like plants that are different, but also the real colorful ones."

The four of them talked plants for the rest of the meal, until Holly spoke. "You know, in a couple of years I might need a babysitter."

"As will I," Lucinda added.

"Would you like to do that?" Megan asked Olivia.

"Yes. I would even know how to take care of them if they scraped their knee like I did today."

Marvin arrived. Megan was proud when Olivia told him about their day.

"Miss Cohen started teaching me to swim today, and I can do the jellyfish float and kick like a motorboat."

Sheryl looked pleased as Megan interacted with Olivia, and Marvin smiled every time he looked at the two of them doing something together.

He told his daughter she should try to rest for a while as she had been up late reading the night before.

"But, Da-a-ad, I want to go sailing with the big kids."

"Do you still have the Comedy Craft?" Megan asked her sister.

Sheryl nodded. "We thought of selling it, but it has too many fond memories. I can call Ethan and have him bring it over here."

"Olivia, with your father's permission, you can come over and sit on the couch with me for a while and I'll read you a story. Then after you rest, you and I will go sailing on our own sailboat...just the two of us."

"Wow. Just us?"

"Just us, little lady. We don't need the big kids for sailing."

Marvin nodded his approval and they moved to a couch that was located under the shaded section of the patio. Within four pages, Olivia had put her head on Megan's lap and had fallen asleep.

"I can move her," Marvin offered.

"Don't you dare!" Megan told him, pretending anger.

"There is a paperback book next to my purse. Would you please bring it out here for me?"

When he returned, Megan patted the cushion next to her, indicating where he should sit.

She was in heaven with Olivia sleeping on her lap. She looked out at the pretty summer scene on the lake. There wasn't a cloud in the sky. All manner of boats were out plying their way across the lake's dark blue surface.

She looked down at Olivia. *You are the one who really brings sunshine to my day, little girl.*

Marvin gazed at Megan. He, too, looked happy that she and Olivia were becoming so close and creating so much happiness for each other. But his expression said more, too. Was he thinking that his children needed a mother in their life?

Megan also wondered if the only reason she was being nice to Marvin was to enable her to spend more time with Olivia.

"I've learned that I'm talking to a man with two PhDs," she said. "Why didn't you tell me?"

"I've found that many people don't like to talk to an über-geek."

"That wouldn't have bothered me."

"I realize that now. I'm sorry if I've offended you."

"You didn't. You're a good man, Marvin Lipinski."

"I try," he said cheerily.

Sheryl had called Ethan and asked him to bring the Comedy Craft over to the Kaplan's dock, and although he was in the middle of staining a new oak door they had purchased, he agreed to have it down there in twenty-minutes.

An-hour-and-a-half later, Olivia awoke and stretched. "Are we going sailing now?"

"Yes, we are," Megan said, putting her book down. "See that sailboat over there? That's the one we'll use to take us out on the lake."

"How about taking some snacks along?" Holly suggested. Olivia smiled. "That would be great, Mrs. Kaplan."

Holly handed Megan a cooler with bottled water and sliced fruit inside.

"I can help carry that," Olivia exclaimed as she held one end of the cooler's handle while Megan held the other end.

As they arrived at the boat, Olivia stared at the boat's name. "Comedy Craft? Why is the boat named that?"

"Because a long time ago, some good friends sailed on this boat and told each other funny stories." For Megan it really did feel like a lifetime ago. She held back a deep sigh.

"I think we should do that." Olivia climbed into the twenty-two-foot Ensign sailboat with Megan's assistance. "This boat is just perfect for us girls! Don't you think so, Miss. Cohen?"

"I couldn't agree more, Olivia." Megan fitted Olivia into a life preserver. "But now I need to teach you about some things first."

Megan began showing Olivia how to use a winch and a cam cleat. "The cam cleat will hold a line until you pull back and up on the line. Try it now with this practice line."

Olivia tried it a few times and then they moved to a winch. "Now, a winch makes you stronger. We'll wrap a length of line around it and when you pull the line tight, I won't be able to pull you."

Olivia was delighted as she saw she could hold Megan tight with the winch's help.

"Okay, now loosen a bit and tighten again."

Olivia seemed amazed she could easily let out a little line, allowing Megan to move, and then retighten and prevent her from moving again. "I can do this. I really can."

Megan raised the main sail, while Olivia carefully coiled the line for her. The wind that day was coming from slightly behind them. Megan untied the boat and moved to the tiller. "Okay, Olivia. Pull the line that is farthest from you out of its cam cleat and run it three times around the winch."

She did as she was told.

"Pull the line in," Megan said.

Olivia's eyes opened wide as she saw she was unfurling the jib. Then they cruised away from the dock and out onto Lake Washington.

"Remember the sea otters at the aquarium?" Olivia asked. Megan nodded.

"I think we're sailing across the water's surface like the sea otters, when they rolled onto their backs and went across the pool. We're kind of like a baby otter riding on top of its mother while she swims."

"That's how sailing feels for me as well." Megan smiled at Olivia.

"Coming about," Megan yelled as she pointed the boat so it would cross the wind. "Loosen the line you're holding, grab the line on the far side from the first one and run it around the winch then start pulling it in."

Olivia looked enthralled as the boat changed course and she pulled the jib over to the other side. "Am I turning into a real sailor?" she asked.

"You're becoming an absolute Limey!"

Olivia looked perplexed, so Megan explained. "A long time ago, British sailors were called Limeys because they ate limes to prevent vitamin C deficiency, which could make them sick."

"Limey—that's a funny name." "We're coming about again, Olivia."

Megan watched with pride as Olivia immediately loosened the line on the port side of the boat and pulled in the line on the starboard side to bring the jib over on the new tack.

After a few more tacks, she turned to Olivia. "I'm getting tired of steering. You need to steer for a while. Put the line you're holding in the cam cleat and we'll change places."

Olivia grinned and took hold of the tiller as she was taught about the main sheet which controls the main sail.

Then Megan showed her how to determine the wind's direction by listening. "When you have an equal amount of wind noise in each of your ears you are looking in the direction the wind is coming from."

Olivia rotated her head a few times. "I can hear the wind just like you said!"

Megan demonstrated luffing by having Olivia bring their direction close to the wind so she could see and hear the jib begin to flutter.

"That noise is called luffing," she said. "Just turn back a little bit, away from the wind, and you'll be fine."

"Wow. I really can do this."

Megan proudly watched Olivia's growing excitement as she reveled in her nautical accomplishments. She opened the cooler and they shared the snacks that were inside.

"What do we do if a big storm comes over us?"

"That's a good question, Olivia. First we would take in or furl the jib. If it got worse we would reduce the amount of main sail."

Olivia carefully contemplated Megan's reply. "Oh, that's what you do."

She was quiet for a while when she looked up at the top of the main sail. A hawk was circling far above them in the cloudless sky. After pointing out the hawk, Olivia moved so she could lean against

Megan. She turned and looked up at her. "If I forget to tell you, I had a wonderful time today."

"Thank you, Olivia. I'm having a wonderful time as well."

"I bet this is what it's like to have a mom," she commented.

"Nearly all my friends are forever telling me about the stuff they do with their moms."

Olivia looked up at Megan and sighed. "I dream about having a mother in my life all the time. Sometimes I pretend I'm shopping with her, or that we go to the movies, or she comes and sees one of my performances in school. I know it's not true, but lately I've been dreaming that you are my mom. Is that okay?"

"I'm not your mom, Olivia, but thank you for thinking that I might be a good enough person to be your mom."

Megan loved the sparkling expression on her sailing companion's face. She felt so fulfilled when she did things with Olivia. She realized she was experiencing the joy and sense of accomplishment a mother must feel when she's doing things with her children.

They decided to sail back to the Kaplan's home. They saw the much larger *Young Love* up ahead of them.

"Pull in the jib, Olivia."

The boat started to heel more than it had the entire day. "Is this safe?" Olivia asked.

"Not only is it safe but it's also fast."

"Are we going to catch the boat with the big kids on it?" "Catch them? I think we should pass them and get back to the dock first. What do you think?"

"Tell me what to do and I'll help," Olivia said in a most excited voice.

Megan sat at the tiller while Olivia was holding the jib sheet. The Comedy Craft began responding to Megan's skilled hand, heeling over until its lee rail was nearly in the water.

As they caught up to the larger sailboat, Freddie must have noticed they were about to be passed. "Mr. Kaplan!" Freddie said in an excited voice. "Quick, let's do something so they can't pass us."

Jonah looked over at the Comedy Craft and laughed. "Sorry, Freddie, that sailboat has a real racing sailor at the helm."

"Is that true?" Olivia asked. "Are you a sailboat racer?"

"Yes, it's true. I raced sailboats in high school and college."

Olivia eyes sparkled in delight as she screamed at the other boat. "Ha, you guys! My mom's a real sailboat racer!"

Olivia instantly realized she had referred to Megan as her mother and she put both hands over her mouth, hesitated a moment while looking at Megan, then dropped her hands. "Oops, I'm sorry. I shouldn't have called you Mom."

Megan put her arm around Olivia and pulled her against her side. "That's okay, sweetness." She felt tears forming in her eyes.

"What's wrong?" Olivia asked.

"Doing things with you makes me very happy, Olivia. Happier than I deserve."

"I think you deserve to be lots of happy," Olivia said as she put her little arm around Megan's waist.

The *Young Love* started to slow as the Comedy Craft drew abeam.

"Hey, that's not fair! You guys are stealing our wind," Carrie complained.

"You guys are bigger, but we're faster!" Olivia triumphantly yelled.

They arrived at the Kaplan's dock two boat lengths ahead of the *Young Love*.

"We win!" Olivia yelled.

"We did indeed. Now we have to furl the jib and we'll take down the main."

After everything was secured, they started walking up to the house.

Carrie walked over to join them. "Next time I want to sail with the fast girls."

Jonah and Freddie joined them, too. "I didn't know that little boat could move like that," Jonah said. "I think you should take the kids out for next week's sailing lesson. I've taught them all I know."

"I received a call this morning that let me know I'll be here for two-more-weeks. I would be happy to run the sailing lesson next weekend, but the following week we have the trip and I go back to LA the following Monday."

Carrie and Freddie looked disappointed, but Olivia's expression was downright sad. "I didn't know you were leaving."

"I'm just here for a few weeks. My home is in California and I have a job there."

Olivia quit walking and looked at Megan with a saddened expression. "I thought we had a good time."

"We are having a wonderful time."

"Then you should stay up here so you can visit us."

"It's not so simple, Olivia. I have a home and a job in LA." "You could get a job up here."

"I'm sorry, Olivia, but I have to go back to my job, or I'll lose it. But I'll still be here for two-more-weeks."

***

On the following sunny and warm Friday afternoon, Megan and Lucinda were visiting Holly. Freddie and Carrie were in the pool practicing their swimming, so the ladies sat on the patio to keep an eye on them.

Freddie's swimming was improving on a daily basis. The choppy movements that were evident during his first time in the pool were being replaced with smooth purposeful motions. He still didn't have much of a kick, but he found he could use his powerful arms to swim four lengths of the pool before stopping.

Carrie was already a strong swimmer, but Jonah challenged her by setting goals for her as well. She didn't have powerful arms and shoulders like Freddie did, but she had a textbook overhand stroke. Jonah had her start with a rate of three kicks per arm stroke at first but soon had her start practicing with four kicks per stroke. A couple of laps at that rate and the muscles in her legs would get sore, but Carrie didn't complain. She said she thought her legs were getting stronger.

Freddie and Carrie finished their swimming by practicing some of the open-water rescue techniques that Jonah had taught them, and then they swam four laps together.

"Carrie's going to need a new swimsuit," Lucinda mentioned to Holly. "She's almost falling out of the top of that one."

"I think she's going to be big like her birth-mom," Holly told her.

Then Lucinda turned to Megan. "Why don't you join us for dinner tonight? Holly and Jonah, plus Ethan and Sheryl, are coming over and you can invite Marvin if you like."

"Thanks, Lucinda. I'm not sure about inviting Marvin, though. I don't want him to think I want to get involved in a relationship. Marvin is kind, a great father, and I certainly enjoy spending time with his children, but a successful relationship may be out of the question for me. I don't want Marvin thinking our friendship will go anywhere."

"I used to think the same way, Megan. I thought I was nothing but a throw-away girlfriend who got dumped as soon as someone better came along...until I met Ryan," Lucinda told her.

"The moment we began to talk to each other, I was drawn to him—actually, drawn isn't a strong enough word. When we're together, our personalities fit like a key in a lock. It frightened me at first. Then one day I realized I was more worried about taking care of Ryan than taking care of myself. At that moment I knew we were made for each other—*Bashert.* From the first moment we were together, Ryan has gone out of his way to take good care of me."

"When Jonah and I first met, I was a twelve-year-old who had no use for boys," Holly told Megan. "But when we were sitting next to each other and our shoulders were touching, that warm touch was magic. Plus I loved talking to him. I immediately started feeling close to him. Not love at first sight, but more like a sense of closeness. Six-months-later, I put my arms around him for the first time. He had just given me one of the most thoughtful presents I had ever received. I can still get excited thinking about the warm feeling which came over me while we held each other. Through the years, he has treated me in a way that constantly demonstrated what it means to be loved by a partner."

Megan shrugged. "That's what I thought my relationship with David Kaplan was...until we grew apart."

"Megan, that relationship was a long time ago. How do you feel when you're with Marvin?" Holly asked.

"I do my best to feel numb whenever I'm out with someone.

That way I can avoid getting hurt again."

"Sometimes you have to take a chance in order to find someone," Lucinda offered.

Megan thought spending time with Marvin was pleasant enough. He was so calm and low key. She decided to take Holly's and Lucinda's advice and call him. He arrived shortly before dinner, bringing Olivia with him.

Megan was helping Lucinda prepare dinner at the time.

As soon as Freddie saw his dad arrive he ran up to him excitedly. "Did you get the tickets, Dad?"

Marvin grinned and removed a small envelope from his shirt pocket. "Fifth row behind the first-base dugout."

"Wow! Those are fantastic seats," Freddie yelled.

"I have five tickets," Marvin said, looking at Carrie. Carrie quickly looked at Holly, who nodded yes.

Then Marvin and the children looked at Megan.

She shook her head. "I'm sorry, guys, but baseball's not my thing. You'll have to count me out on this one."

"But we get fun stuff to eat and we can cheer for the Mariners and Dad lets us pick out a t-shirt sometimes," Olivia encouraged.

"It's a great game. Purely scientific." Freddie grinned. "One of the players stands at the base of a diamond shape which has been inscribed on a grassy field. The pitcher propels a spherical object toward him and the player begins converting adenosine triphosphate into adenosine diphosphate by giving up one phosphate molecule, therefore releasing energy."

Yeah," Carrie agreed with a smile. "Using the energy released by the conversion from ATP to ADP, the player strikes the spherical object using a large semi-rigid piece of cellulose, sending the sphere out of the park. Then we all use our own ATP to ADP conversion to stand up and cheer. How can a chemist not be fascinated by that?"

Megan looked at the three of them and started laughing. It suddenly didn't matter that she loathed watching baseball. She wanted to spend more time with Olivia, Carrie, and Freddie.

"Okay, you've convinced me. I certainly wouldn't want to miss a display of ATP being converted to ADP, not to mention having fun stuff to eat. I guess I'll have to join you guys."

"You can sit next to me and I'll tell you what's going on," Olivia volunteered.

"I'll look forward to that, Olivia."

Megan looked up at Marvin. "So you don't know anything about chemistry, Dr. Lipinski? Did you set them up to convince me to go to the game?"

"Me? Would I do that?"

Megan thought that if she were going to get serious with someone, it would certainly be a joy to have a man as kind as Marvin to go out with. Not to mention someone who had so much patience for his children. She considered the life she'd led and felt that maybe she didn't really deserve to have anyone like that.

"Time to light the *Shabbat* candles," Lucinda announced. Each of the women in attendance gathered around and lit a candle. She turned to Megan. "Would you do us the honor of chanting the blessing?"

Megan stepped forward, covered her eyes, and sang the blessing in dulcet tones. Everyone started shaking hands or hugging while they wished each other "Good *Shabbos.*"

***

The following day, they arrived at noon for the baseball game. They walked over to the sushi stand and started ordering sushi rolls.

"We're eating sushi at a baseball game?" Megan asked.

Freddie replied with pride in his voice, "You're at Safeco Field! We have one of the top ten rated baseball parks in the nation when it comes to food. Besides, it's really great sushi."

Marvin said, "I'll get you a hot dog if you would rather have that."

"You have to be kidding. I love sushi!" An usher helped them find their seats.

"Do you really enjoy baseball?" Megan asked Carrie.

"I don't like to watch it so much on TV, but it's different when we come to the park to watch. It's fun how excited Freddie gets. That kind of makes me feel happy as well. It's kind of like when I was watching your face on that nice power boat. It seemed like your smile kept getting bigger as Mr. Lipinski's smile got bigger. I think that's called getting joy from someone else's joy."

"Carrie Levin, you are a most observant and perceptive young lady."

"Thank you. I think Freddie and I are friends because we can enjoy what the other person likes. We go around the neighborhood sometimes looking for birds. I like that more than Freddie does. He gets into it, though, and likes watching me have fun."

"We're trying to memorize some bird calls," Freddie told her. "I wouldn't have done that, but it gives Carrie and me something else we can do together."

"And Freddie's teaching me Morse code. Dah dit dah dit space dit dah dit space dit stands for CRE, the abbreviation we use for my name."

Megan marveled at the two of them. They appeared to have their relationship worked out better than any relationship she had ever had in her entire life.

As the kids enjoyed their sushi, she looked at Marvin. "They know how to make each other happy...and they're just kids."

"Maybe they're setting a good example for you and me," Marvin said.

"With what we've each been through, we don't have a chance."

"I don't mean with each other. Just that there might be someone out there we can get along with, although I don't know where I'd find the time."

"Thank you for saying that, but we've both been alone for a long time." She engaged in a long sigh. "I'm certain we must have lots of habits we've developed over the years which could get in the way of our happiness."

"That may be the case, yet here you are at a baseball game, eating sushi, surrounded by people you just recently got to know, and you're having a good time."

"You're right," she said, laughing. "Thank you for pointing that out."

Marvin's phone rang.

He answered, listened for a bit, and then put his hand over the phone. "Jazz Alley has two tickets for dinner and the Big Bad Voodoo Daddy concert tonight. Do you want to go?"

Megan thought quickly. *Why not?* She nodded.

Megan heard Carrie say to Freddie, "That's like they would be going on a date."

"That would be cool. I never saw my dad go out with anyone."

"I can call Mrs. Kaplan," Carrie offered, "and ask if you and Olivia can come over to their house for dinner."

"That would be fun. Maybe we could watch a movie in Dr. Kaplan's media room."

"He has a new B.B. King DVD that we can watch," Carrie said.

"Wow! B.B. King is the greatest. I can't wait to hear that." "Olivia, would you like to come with us and watch a music video?" Carrie asked.

Olivia looked at Megan, who told her, "I think you would have fun doing that."

"Yes," she replied. "I'd like to do that."

Olivia leaned toward Megan and quietly told her, "I'll be on my best behavior so they won't think I'm a little kid."

"That would be most thoughtful of you, Olivia"

***

Marvin and Megan had a pleasant evening at Jazz Alley. The driving swing music, brilliant musicianship, and on-stage commentary enlivened everyone's spirit, even Megan's.

In between numbers, Marvin turned to her. "I'm going to sign papers for the boat tomorrow. I'd appreciate if you'd come with me. I'm going to be so excited that I might sign anything they put in front of me."

"Marvin, I'd be happy to help you with that."

Marvin was quiet for a moment. "Are we starting a relationship?"

"I doubt it. We can be friends, but that's it. I don't love you and you don't love me. Even if things improve to the point that we moved in together, it would be little more than two adults playing house, and that wouldn't be fair to the kids."

"I agree with you. There is something I would like to discuss, but it's a bit delicate."

"Go ahead. I'm listening."

"I was wondering if we could...*do* something before we pick up the kids tonight. It has been six-years since I've, you know, done any-thing...and we are at least friends."

Megan was frightened as she considered the cost of her last sexu-al dalliance. But Marvin wasn't married, so this might be okay.

Is that why he asked her to dinner? Was the time he let her spend with Olivia a setup for getting her in bed?

She must have been wearing her feelings on her face, as he turned to her and said, "I'm sorry if I've suggested something which has of-fended you."

She smiled. "We're adults, so as friends we can decide to do some things to help each other. It would be fine, Marvin."

They had sex in a perfunctory manner. Their hands manipulated each other's body without enthusiasm and only enough to excite their partner sufficiently to bring them to a state where they could use each other to relieve their sexual tension. There was no love in-volved—they each had trained their minds to ignore any emotion. Sadly, it was little more than masturbation using someone else's body...with one tiny but significant exception.

When Megan did it with Todd, they were simply using each oth-er for sex. With Marvin, a small part of her mind enjoyed doing it with him because she knew she was giving her body to a kind and gentle man, who had let her become part of his family, if only for a brief time. She was giving more than she was getting, which somehow seemed so right.

***

The following day, Marvin had just signed the last paper to acquire ownership of the boat.

"Are you driving it home today?" Megan asked.

"Not today. They have a little work to do on it. I'll pick it up later in the week. Thank you so much for coming with me. Let me buy you lunch."

They drove over to Ballard Park, had lunch at the Lockspot Café, and wandered around the lovely gardens. They followed the pathways across the locks and observed the season's first salmon going up the fish ladder.

After Megan remarked about the large, fast moving silver and red sided salmon,

Marvin told her, "If you think this is amazing, you need to come out here the first weekend in October and attend the Issaquah Salmon festival. The stream over there gets so full of salmon you can hardly see the stream bottom."

"That would be special," she replied as she brought up her calendar on her phone. "I'll mark my calendar to make sure I come back for that."

"I can't begin to thank you enough for taking Olivia sailing. She's been talking up an absolute blue fog, telling and retelling everything she did on that sailboat. She can't wait to go sailing with you again."

"I've been around kids numerous times in my life, but Olivia and I seem to have a special relationship. It's a relationship I can feel more than describe. I don't know why that's happening to us, but I certainly enjoy it."

The hum of the boats going in and out of the locks combined with the *whoosh* of a gentle breeze working its way through the tree tops. Many birds added their voices to the sounds around them as well. They found a bench to sit on where they could watch the boat traffic at the locks and enjoy the sun-filled blue sky.

"Marvin, I love spending time with the children and I'm leaving the following week."

"Would you like to do something special this coming week?"

"I have an idea. With your permission, I think I'd like to spend lots of time with Freddie and Olivia each evening when you've come home from work this week. We have the trip on Friday. I'm hoping you'll let me spend more time with them."

"I'll give you a key to the house so you can be there in the afternoon when Holly brings Freddie home from class and an hour or so later when Olivia comes home from day camp."

"If you allow me to do that, I can have dinner ready for you guys each night."

"That would be lovely. Let's get you a key."

When Freddie arrived from school on Monday, he enthusiastically discussed the activity that took place in his class.

"So, Freddie," Megan said. "I heard from the neighborhood grapevine that you said something quite vile to one of your classmates."

"I did because Neil called Carrie my...well...poop girlfriend."

"And what kind of respect are you showing Carrie when you talk like that in front of her?"

"I apologized to Carrie, but I got pretty angry with Neil."

"Let's talk about what happened and see if we can think of a better way to handle a situation like that."

Freddie was quiet, so she continued. "If you want to earn Neil's respect, apologize to him even though your behavior was less than desirable and Neil caused the situation."

"What? Why should I be the one to apologize?"

"Because you're more mature than he is."

"Yes, ma'am," Freddie said reluctantly.

***

As Marvin and Freddie entered the doctor's office at the medical center for a new procedure to alleviate some of Freddie's constant pain, they were surprised to see Jonah and Ryan leaving.

They exchanged greetings.

"What are you doing here?" Marvin asked.

"We needed to talk to Doctor Epstein about some stuff we work with," Ryan told them.

"Hey, he's my doctor, too."

Freddie and his dad entered the office and Dr. Epstein explained. "The procedure is completely new and not tested on human beings yet. It's based on a mathematical basis for gene expression that's been developed in the last few years. We know it works on some primates and we're optimistic it will help you, but there is a chance it will not work or may cause other problems. It could be a number of months before we know if the treatment is working. It's not magic, Freddie."

Freddie looked at the doctor and said sternly, "No, it's not magic. It's better than magic. It's math—so let's get busy."

***

Megan felt fulfilled each afternoon and evening she spent with Marvin's family. Each day, Freddie arrived first, bursting with excitement to explain to her what he had learned in summer school and what his day was like. Then, upon Olivia's arrival from camp, the three of them drove over to the Kaplans' home to practice swimming with Carrie.

Olivia helped Megan prepare dinner in the evenings and Megan always found numerous activities to share with her, as well as helping Freddie with his homework.

As Megan had been running each morning with Sheryl, she had lost seven pounds since she'd arrived. After the first few days, her level of anger had diminished and she seemed to be having a nice visit with her sister and Ethan. This hadn't happened in a long time. After Olivia and Freddie went to bed, Megan and Marvin sat outside on his patio and talked for a while, after which she drove home to Ethan and Sheryl's house.

This particular evening, her sister was sitting in the living room when Megan arrived. "How's it going?" Sheryl asked.

"Being with the kids is the most natural thing I have ever done," Megan told her. "From the moment I arrive to the moment I leave it's nothing but occupying my time doing things with, and for, the children. I'm frightened I'll wake up and find this is a dream. You can't imagine the relationship I have with Olivia and Freddie. When Holly drops him off after school, he doesn't stop talking until he's told me every little detail of what's occurred at school. I've started doing some cooking things with Olivia and she sets the table for me every night. I've assigned some after dinner cleanup to Freddie. They respect me and help me as if they're my own children. Marvin is kind to me as well. I mentioned to Marvin that Olivia could use a step-stool. An hour later he returned from his workshop with the right sized stool for her. He told me he'd stain it and put a finishing coat on it so it would be ready tomorrow."

"That sounds great."

"Yes. It's gorgeous, too. He made it out of some old mahogany boards. Olivia showed me some shelves and the dining room table he made from the same material. They're all so pretty. I just assumed he'd bought them. I started looking around the house and everything from pens to quilt racks were handmade by Marvin. When I asked about his woodworking he told me, 'It's just a little hobby of mine.' Sheryl, you have to see some of the beautiful woodworking he's done. Freddie said he even has trophies for the dining room table and other things he has built. None of the trophies are displayed. I had to ask about them before Marvin would show them to me. We talked for three hours tonight. And, you know, he's not pushing me, which is so nice. He rarely suggests anything about a future, only occasionally mentions things we can do together. That's just what I need. I hate to say the words, but he really seems to understand me."

"Megan, is he like David?"

"Not even a little bit."

"Sister, I am so happy for you."

"Let's not kid ourselves. Marvin is nice, but only friend-nice and I intend to keep it that way and so does he. He even told me he doesn't date and his entire life consists of raising his children. Next Monday I go back to my life and job in LA. That will be the real reality check for me."

***

The following day Megan took Olivia and Freddie shopping for school clothes. It was difficult to tell who was more excited, Olivia or Megan. Fortunately Freddie brought a book to read while his sister tried on different outfits. Megan bought her quite a few dresses, skirts, slacks, and tops that could be combined into many different lovely outfits. She bought shorts and jeans for Freddie plus a number of t-shirts and polos.

When they arrived at an athletic shoe store, Freddie stopped Megan, turning serious. "Don't waste your money buying me running shoes. I can barely walk fast."

"A good cross trainer will give you good support whatever you are doing. Well-made shoes that fit properly are never a waste of money."

Freddie tried on a pair of excellent quality cross trainers the sales consultant recommended after he watched Freddie walk across the floor. They had air cushioning in their soles.

"These feel great," he told her. "I'd run like the wind with these—if I could run, that is."

As soon as Marvin arrived home, Freddie and Carrie insisted he look over all their purchases.

"Dad," Olivia said, "come see what I got! I can combine these separates into lots of different outfits. Miss Cohen is going to teach me how."

Freddie demonstrated the air cushioning and stabilizing padded construction of his new cross trainers. "Carrie says they sound like boogey boots."

"They don't get that excited when I take them clothes shopping," Marvin teased Megan.

"It was nothing but fun," she told him. "Nothing but fun."

"Thanks for taking them. I'd like to pay you back for what you spent on the kids."

"Don't even think about it. I feel so fulfilled when I'm with those two. I should probably be paying you for letting me spend so much time with them."

***

On Thursday night, Olivia and Megan began preparing minestrone soup to take on the next day's trip.

Megan instructed her on what to do. "First, I need you to seed and tear up the tomatoes I peeled today. Squish the tomatoes over the bowl to get the seeds out and then tear them up with your fingers. I'll get the broth going and cut up the vegetables."

Marvin came into the kitchen and asked if there was anything he could do to help.

"Thank you for offering, but we're fine," Megan told him. "I'm squishing and tearing tomatoes over here, Dad."

"I see that, Olivia. I hope you washed your hands before you started doing that."

"Dad," she said in an exasperated voice. "Of course I did."

Olivia turned to Megan. "Don't worry. He always talks like that."

Megan couldn't help but laugh.

"This is going to be a great meal to eat on the boat Saturday night," he told them. "I think they're all going to appreciate that you're doing most of the cooking for this trip."

"With Holly and Lucinda being so far along in their pregnancies it seemed like the considerate thing to do."

After all the ingredients had been added, Megan put the soup on a low flame to simmer. She started reading aloud Dr. Seuss's *To Think I Saw it on Mulberry Street*.

"I love Dr. Seuss's books," Olivia told her.

An hour later, Marvin helped them store the soup in containers and took them out to the refrigerator in the boat.

"I'll run the small generator for a while to make sure the batteries are up. The fridge will be running fine all night after I do that," he told Megan.

Chapter Nine ~ The Trip to Butchart Gardens

THE THREE-DAY WEEKEND arrived when the Kaplans, Rifkins, Lipinskis, plus Megan and Carrie were all going to cruise up to Vancouver, BC.

Carrie's parents, Anna and Michael Levin, came over to the Kaplans' home to see them off. They would have loved to accompany the boaters but were busy setting up their new home. Their son David Linn, who was a month older than Carrie, was not with them as he was on his way back from camp but hadn't arrived yet.

Ari's sixty-two-foot restored antique boat sat at the dock, resplendent in its new paint and recently polished-bright woodwork. Marvin, Olivia, and Freddie were expected momentarily, and Megan saw them first. "Here they come!" she said smiling hugely. "I don't see his Whaler," Ryan said.

"Is that them in the GB forty-six?" Jonah asked.

"It is," Megan told them proudly. "I went with him when he signed the papers for it."

"That's why you didn't want us to load your things in our boat," Holly said.

Megan nodded. "We loaded some food in our boat last night but it still has lots of empty storage space. We expect everyone to join us for dinner tonight and tomorrow night. We're serving homemade beet borscht and brisket sandwiches tonight, and have minestrone soup with clam linguine prepared for Saturday night."

"Sounds like you're going to have a floating feast this weekend," Anna declared.

As they approached the dock, Freddie waved and yelled at the top of his lungs, "My dad bought the boat, Carrie!"

Anna looked at Michael. "It seems our daughter has found a beau," she said.

Michael winked at her in response.

Carrie's supplies for the trip had already been placed on the restored boat, but she decided to ride with the Lipinskis and Megan on that day's cruise up to Victoria.

Ryan and Jonah quickly tied Marvin's boat to the dock. He smiled broadly as they both congratulated him on his purchase. As Megan crossed the transom, she saw the name of the boat had been changed to *My Meanderer*.

"Excellent name for your boat," Megan said.

"Thanks for the suggestion." Marvin was still beaming widely.

He went below with her. "I've put Freddie's and my things in the master cabin, so you and Olivia can share the guest cabin."

"That will not do." Megan looked at Marvin. "Unless you think it will be bad for the children, please move Freddie's things to the guest cabin so you and I can share the master."

Marvin raised an eyebrow. "We can talk to the kids, but I doubt they'll mind. They'll be excited that you're spending the entire day with them. But are you sure?"

"I've thought about it all week. There is no polite way of saying this, but I enjoyed having you the other night. For some reason that I can't quite fathom, it was, let's just say, rewarding, to be with you. It wasn't exactly love that I experienced, but it was more than just sex and I can't for the life of me tell you why."

Marvin put his arms around her.

She wondered if he felt sorry for her. After the way she had been relating to his children, he likely saw her as a caring lady living a lonely life.

She embraced him. "Thank you for putting up with me these last few weeks."

"Gentle lady, it's been easier than I imagined it would be, adding you into our little group. The smile you put on the kids' faces has made it more than worthwhile."

"This has been like something out of a dream for me, but I go back to the real world Monday. Besides, you don't need someone in your life who has managed to become a continual failure at relationships."

"And you deserve to have a man who can take care of you and not spend all his time worrying about, and parenting, his kids."

"Marvin Lipinski, the time I've spent with your children may possibly be the happiest time in my life."

"Will you come back and see us?"

Megan looked to her feet. "I'm sorry, Marvin, but I don't know for sure."

They went back up and everyone had a delicious going-away breakfast of Belgian waffles with fruit toppings, scrambled eggs, and chorizo sausage that was served on the patio and prepared by Michelle Kaplan.

After that, Carrie said good-bye to her parents and six-month-old twin siblings.

***

During the low-speed twenty-minute cruise to the locks, Megan sat with Carrie and Freddie at the dinette in the living area, while Olivia sat on the bench seat near her dad.

She used the opportunity to talk to them about boy-girl relationships.

"You know, when I was your age I had a boyfriend and thought I was in love with him. But instead, I was in love with being in love. I was so blind I didn't see we had very little in common. Also, as young as you are, you need to know that sometimes we grow at different rates. I'm referring to growth as a maturing person. Those will be the times that test your relationship. Sometimes people change as they grow. That's why it's important to always talk to each other."

The kids nodded and exchanged a look with each other as if confirming to her, as well as each other, they understood.

Then, after they went through the locks, Megan sat on the bench seat near Marvin. They passed through and were on the Sound. Marvin positioned his boat behind the *Young Love II* and set the throttles to maintain a leisurely nine knots to match speed with Jonah and Ryan.

He checked the charts and called to Freddie and Carrie. "Do you two want to take the helm for a while?"

"Yes," Freddie yelled.

"For sure I do!" Carrie added.

They shared the pilot's chair as Marvin explained which instruments they should watch and told them they needed to stay three boat lengths behind the *Young Love II*.

"You can adjust the throttles in tiny increments to maintain that distance." He gestured to the control panel. "Watch each engine's RPM on these gauges. Both engines should be running at the same revolutions."

Carrie and Freddie immediately began discussing how they would take turns at the wheel.

"How about we switch every ten-minutes?" Carrie suggested. "Ten-minutes is perfect. You go first."

Olivia took their place at the dinette with Megan, while Marvin sat on the bench seat to keep an eye on the helm as he gradually started teaching them how to read where they were on the nautical chart and how to view the same information on one of the boat's electronic displays.

Sitting at the dinette, Megan opened a cloth bag and removed a large-format hard-cover book entitled, *Plants of the Northwest*.

"Lucinda gave me this book last night and said we could borrow it during the trip. She thought you might like to look through it with me and plan what plants you would like to put in the ground for next spring."

"Wow," Olivia declared as she turned the pages of the book. "This is neat."

Megan opened the bag again and removed some sheets of construction paper, plus a box of crayons. "I thought you might like to draw some pictures of the plants you like, and maybe you could draw what a garden with those plants will look like."

"I don't draw so well," Olivia said. "I'll help you."

"Okay! Hey, I bet we could give a drawing to Lucinda, I mean Mrs. Rifkin, to thank her for letting us use her book."

"That would be most considerate of you, Olivia. I'm certain she would love to have one of your drawings."

Marvin looked over at Megan and Olivia. He looked pleased to see Olivia's expression positively sparkling as Megan talked to her. He smiled as they talked and laughed while discussing plants.

"Let's draw this one," Olivia said pointing to a primrose. "Mrs. Rifkin said this was her favorite flower. How should we start?"

"Let's find a nice shade of green that matches the stem of the flower first. Then we'll use a darker green to draw the leaves." Olivia started working on the drawing with Megan's assistance.

She was never going to be an artist, Megan observed, but she was having fun. She concentrated once she started doing something, and her excellent work ethic was apparent in the pool as she was learning swimming skills, as well when they were sailing together. *This little cookie is going to make something of her abilities by sheer force of will.* Megan smiled at the thought. Then she outlined the petals of the flower and had Olivia fill them in.

"How about a little blue in the sky and then we'll print the Latin name of the flower at the top of the page. Then we can write your name on the lower right corner."

"Nice," Olivia stated as she held up the completed drawing. "Look you guys," she called out.

They all turned to take a look at her drawing. "Nice, Olivia," Marvin agreed.

Freddie looked at his little sister's drawing and then grinned at Carrie. "I hope she didn't waste too many phosphate molecules doing that."

Carrie clearly knew better than to laugh.

When Freddie looked back at Olivia and Megan. Megan was no longer smiling and was now looking at him, most displeased. When he saw that look Megan could tell he immediately knew he had committed a huge error.

"I'm just joking, Olivia. You have a very nice drawing," Freddie quickly said.

"You guys think you're so smart," Olivia yelled, "but you wouldn't know a ladybug from a potato bug."

"Olivia," Megan chastised her while trying not to laugh. "Just because Freddie said something that wasn't nice doesn't mean you should reply in kind."

She still had an angry look on her face, but apologized anyway. "Okay. I'm sorry I said that."

After a couple of hours of taking turns at the wheel and watching the instruments, their radio crackled to life. "Ahoy, *My Meanderer*. This is Jonah in the *Young Love Two*."

Carrie looked at Marvin. "Pick up the mic, and push the side button when you talk, then release it to listen."

"Ahoy, *Young Love Two*. This is Captain Carrie. Captain Freddie is at the helm."

"Captain Carrie," Jonah said with laughter breaking up his voice, "there is a small cove up ahead where we can raft up and have lunch together. Will you ask Captains Marvin and Megan if that is acceptable?"

"Captains Marvin and Megan have informed me that a lunch raft is acceptable, sir. Captains Freddie and Olivia have informed me they are hungry."

"Follow us into the cove and pull up on our port side." "Follow you into the cove and pull up on your port side. Aye,

Aye, Captain Jonah!" Carrie saluted.

Freddie grinned at her. "He can't see you saluting, Carrie."

"Oh yeah," Carrie giggled. "I forgot."

"I'll take over the helm," Marvin told them. "You Captains put two bumpers on the starboard side of our boat."

"What should I do?" Olivia asked.

"I think we need some video," Megan suggested as she pulled a small video camera out of the cloth bag. "Let's put on jackets. Then you and I will climb up to the flybridge and shoot some video. Will you please get our jackets from below deck, Olivia?"

"I'll get them," Olivia stated. "Oh yeah, this is going to be great! Drive careful, Dad. We're going to be making a video movie of you parking the boat."

"I'll certainly keep that in mind, Olivia."

"You're spending a lot of time with her," Marvin said as Olivia ran down to the closet in her cabin to get a jacket.

"That little girl makes my heart glow. I've never been happier in my life than when I'm with your children. Never!"

"Every moment you spend with the kids takes pressure off me and certainly brightens their day. All this last week, I didn't have to worry about the kids because I knew you were with them. When I arrived home they weren't fighting for my attention like they usually do. Best of all, I feel their sense of happiness when you're doing things with them. It's almost like you're their mom."

"Thanks for saying that, but I'm not anyone's mom."

***

Holly and Lucinda were bringing dishes out and placing them on the large dining table in the big open cockpit at the rear of their boat, as Megan and Olivia climbed the stairs to the flybridge.

Marvin carefully placed his boat alongside the already anchored *Young Love II*, and Jonah and Ryan quickly tied the two boats together.

"You guys, I'm up here making a video movie," Olivia called out.

They looked up at the adorable six-year-old and waved to her.

Megan was on her knees at her side giving her tips on how to use the video camera. Olivia said something to Megan and they both laughed. "After lunch we'll get out a laptop and edit the video," Megan told Olivia as they sat down to lunch. "If you keep taking video, we'll have a whole movie of our trip."

"Wow, you and I sure can do a lot of stuff together!"

"Yes, we certainly can." Megan put her arm around Olivia and gave her a brief hug.

"We have a choice of New England clam chowder or Manhattan clam chowder," Lucinda announced. "There are oyster crackers and rosemary-olive bread for those who want them."

"There's olive oil and crushed garlic on the table for the bread, as well as butter," Holly added.

"I'm the video taker on this trip," Olivia told Jonah.

"That's just what we needed," Jonah told her. "If we do anything wrong you'll have a video record of our mistakes."

"I just knew you would like that," Olivia cheerfully told him. "Wow, this is great," Olivia said after trying the New England chowder. "No, wait a minute." She turned to Megan. "What's that word we learned this week?"

"Scrumptious."

"This is scrumptious!"

"Good vocabulary, Olivia," Holly told her.

"Thank you, Mrs. Kaplan. We played a vocabulary game every day this week, so my vocabulary is increasing and expanding. And Mrs. Rifkin, I drew a picture of a primrose flower for you."

"Thank you, Olivia. I can't wait to see it. In fact, if you think it would be okay, I'd like to put your drawing in the nursery so when our new baby wakes up she'll see your pretty picture."

"That's okay with me. Is that okay, Mom? Oops, I mean, Miss Cohen."

"That would be lovely, Olivia."

Ryan turned to Freddie then. "Since you had the special treatment, how are your hip and knee feeling?"

Freddie thought about it. "Well, until this last week I would have told you it made little difference, but my hip and knee don't seem so sore when I do stuff now. I can actually take a few steps without my cane, and it doesn't hurt like it used to."

"Yes!" Jonah screamed punching his fist into the air. Everyone looked at him.

He shrugged it off. "Hey, I'm happy for Freddie. That's all."

Jonah and Ryan couldn't seem to get the proud grins off their faces for the rest of the meal.

***

After lunch they cruised another five hours and stopped at the harbor in Oak Bay for the night. Everyone came over to Marvin's boat for dinner. Megan and he served cold beet borscht with sour cream and warm brisket sandwiches. They put out three kinds of mustard.

The first was stone ground to a fine texture, the second coarse ground with horseradish and a third flavored with Tabasco sauce.

"Let's light *Shabbat* candles," Megan said.

"Carrie, would you do us the honor of chanting the blessing, please? And then I'd appreciate if Freddie recited the blessing over the wine, and Olivia the blessing over the *challah*."

They each chanted the blessings to a most appreciative audience.

"Miss Cohen and I made the brisket," Olivia excitedly told them as they sat down to eat. "I helped mix the spices and rubbed them into the meat, and then put the onions and carrots on top, and then I put a whole lot of garlic on top of everything! Then we baked the brisket all night. It was a lot of hard work."

"I awoke to a most delicious smell the next day," Marvin said. "Unfortunately I was informed I couldn't eat any of it because it was being saved for the trip."

"The brisket is wonderful, Olivia. You did an excellent job preparing it," Lucinda told her.

Olivia looked up at Megan and spoke in a proud voice. "They like our sandwiches."

"Yes they do. It was really worth all our hard work."

"Yes it was," Olivia agreed.

"Carrie's mom sent dessert with us," Megan told them as she opened plastic containers. "We have apple, nectarine, cherry, and apricot tarts with whipped cream. I understand Carrie did most of the baking."

Megan tried one of the nectarine tarts. "This is delicious, Carrie. I'll buy the ingredients, but you have to teach me how to make these."

"I'd love to, Miss Cohen."

After Freddie had savored one cherry tart and one apricot tart, he declared, "Carrie lady, you can bake as well as you math!"

After dinner, Megan brought out a jigsaw puzzle for Carrie and Freddie. They sat at the dinette on the *My Meanderer* and worked hard to solve it. The puzzle began to reveal a man and a woman rowing a double scull. Across the top were the words Good Friends Row in the Same Direction.

"You bought this for us!" Carrie told Megan. "Thank you."

"My pleasure. I'm glad you two enjoyed it."

As the hour grew late, Carrie went back to the *Young Love II* and Freddie and Olivia went to sleep in separate bunks in the guest cabin.

Megan joined Marvin in the master cabin and found she enjoyed having him just like the first time, but this time he held her the entire night.

***

They anchored just outside the Butchart cove and boarded dinghies to travel over to the wharf at the Northern entrance to the gardens. Freddie and Jonah were briefly entranced by a float plane that landed and taxied up to the wharf to disgorge its passengers.

Their tour began in the Japanese Garden. Lucinda and Olivia were particularly fascinated by the efficient use of space and the beauty that could be found in every corner of that garden.

"The online description said it was a calm place to collect one's thoughts," Lucinda said. "They were certainly right on that one."

"It seems like they pack a lot of beauty in a small space," Olivia said as she videotaped the displays from as many angles as she could. Olivia carefully studied each display and how the beauty could be observed from many angles.

"Could we build a garden like this?" she asked her dad.

"I know nothing about Japanese gardens, Olivia. You'll have to read books about them, and then when you have a design completed, I'll help you build it."

"If you're willing to study and learn about them, I'll help you design one," Lucinda told her. "We'll have to visit the Kubota Japanese

Gardens in Seattle as well, to get more ideas. It's a lot of hard work to build, plant, and maintain a garden."

"Carrie always says if it's a lot of hard work then we can do this," Olivia said. "I think she's right."

Lucinda and Megan walked with her as the others moved on. Olivia seemed entranced by the textures and simplicity of each view.

***

They had just begun to talk about lunch as they walked past the Blue Poppy restaurant. Jonah read the menu displayed in a window next to the door. He saw a spinach salad that contained blue cheese, spiced cashews, preserved fruits, and champagne cucumber vinaigrette.

His mouth was watering. "I think I'm ready for a salad for lunch, troops," he announced.

But before they could go in and order their lunch, Jonah's cell phone started ringing. It was a ringtone reserved for very specific situations. In fact Holly had never even heard it before. He saw worry in her eyes as he answered the call.

He turned to Ryan while he listened to the message, and Ryan's face quickly went pale as he filled in the blanks.

The adrenaline kicked in and Jonah snapped his phone shut then shouted to Ryan. "Red ninety-one!"

Ryan then turned and shouted to Lucinda and Holly who had gathered together in anticipation of what the phone call meant. "We have to leave. Now!"

Jonah went up to Marvin next. "Listen, I'm sorry, Marvin, but we have to leave. Two people are meeting us in front of the visitor's center. You guys can spend the day and we'll talk to you later tonight."

Marvin looked worried. "Does this have to do with the work you and Ryan do?"

Jonah stared at him in silence. There was no answer he could give to that question.

"I served in the first gulf war with the hundred and first Airborne Division, Jonah," Marvin said. "I've recognized that you have serious-looking security people around you at times."

"All I can say is, we have to leave. Someone's been hurt. Never mind our boat—we'll arrange to have it picked up. Enjoy the gardens and the rest of the weekend, Marvin. It would be best if Carrie stayed with you, if that is all right."

He dropped his keys into Marvin's hand. "Here are the keys to my boat so you can get her things. I don't know where we'll be spending the night. I'll call you when I can."

Marvin took the keys and nodded. "Good luck and keep your heads down."

Jonah stepped over to Holly and pulled her aside.

Lucinda's expression became even more concerned when she saw the look on Jonah's face. She turned to Ryan. "What's going on?"

"I don't know any details and we can't really talk here," he whispered, "but that code means that someone in our group, or someone we know, has been attacked and there have been injuries. We're being met by local police who will get us to an airport where a military plane will pick us up. I don't know where we'll be going from there."

"Ryan Rifkin, I don't need this excitement now and it's not good for the baby either."

"I know," he said sadly, putting his arm around her. "I'm sorry."

Jonah, Ryan, Holly, and Lucinda left the others and hurried to get on the military jet. Once they were barely settled, Jonah received another call.

He listened for a minute and then he swore. Holly's eyes widened in shock—Jonah never used profanity. He looked at the floor for a moment and gathered his courage. He turned to Holly.

"Something happened in Meridian." "My family..."

Chapter Ten ~ An Incident in Meridian

WHAT'S GOING ON?" CARRIE asked.

"We're not sure," Marvin told her. "Something's happened, but that is all I know. You are going to stay with us tonight, Carrie."

"What should we do?" Megan asked.

"All we can do—let's try to have a nice rest of the day. We'll head home tomorrow morning. How about eating lunch guys?"

Megan called Anna Levin to tell her what had happened and that Carrie was with them, safe, and they would bring her home the next day.

***

When Anna related what little she knew about the situation to Michael, he stood up and announced that he was going shopping.

"Michael, we've talked about this."

"Yes we have and I should have done this a long time ago. I'm calling Meyer Minkowski. Hopefully he'll have some time to go with me."

He called Meyer immediately and he agreed to accompany Michael to the gun store.

"I'm going to buy a couple of pistols and rifles with Mr. Minkowski," he told David Linn. "And then we're heading out to the gun range to meet his friend, Gene, for some shooting lessons. Want to come with me?"

"For sure!"

"Michael—"

"Anna, I know you don't like guns, and I'm sorry, but if something happened and I had nothing to defend my family or my neighbors with, I would die of shame."

"Please be careful, Michael. You be careful as well, David Linn. Learning to shoot is not a game."

***

Back on the *My Meanderer*, they conducted a brief *Havdala* service to mark the end of *Shabbat* on Saturday evening. They said a prayer for those who had been injured.

"Do you think anyone was killed?" Freddie asked.

"We don't know. We certainly hope not," Marvin told him.

"Life is so fragile," Megan said. "We never know when we might be taking our last breath."

Olivia and Carrie shared the bunks of the guest cabin that night, while Freddie slept on the sofa in the salon.

Marvin and Megan spent the night holding each other, both seeming lost in thought as to what their future might look like.

***

Seeing as it was Saturday, Ruth and Oliver Holt had invited their son Drew's half-sister, Nancy, to come along with Drew and Beverly to their home in Meridian, Idaho. They were going for an early morning run followed by breakfast at the Holts'.

Nancy seemed to love the runs and the weekend family activities. They had made sure to include her in everything since she'd moved in with Drew. True to form, both Ruth and Oliver went out of their way to make her feel as if she had always been a part of their family. She especially seemed to look forward to talking to Ruth, who couldn't wait to hear the latest stories about Nancy's work at the senior center.

Oliver was nervous that morning. Being father to not only Drew and Karen, but Holly and Lucinda too, he remained on alert for threats arising from Holly's and Lucinda's husbands' jobs.

During his daily runs that week, an inordinately high number of cars passed him, always having two men in them. Each time they passed, the passenger looked directly at him and the driver ignored him.

"Probably just my paranoia," he said to himself.

Due to his son-in-law's classified military work, he, Drew, and Beverly carried concealed weapons and regularly practiced with them.

"Let's let Nancy lead and set the pace today," Drew suggested. Nancy agreed and they set out on their thirty-minute run.

Fifteen-minutes into the run, a brown compact car passed them for the second time. It went through the intersection ahead of them and parked on the side of the road.

"Do you see them?" Oliver asked Drew.

"I do. That's the second time they've passed us."

"Nancy, proceed right at the intersection," Oliver said. "Then go up half a block and turn right and go down the alley. Go up four houses and proceed left through the yard. When you get to the next street, turn right again."

He turned to Drew. "Let the girls run in front. When we turn down the alley I'm going to duck to the right and get behind cover. You continue a short distance and find cover on the left. If you hear me yell or shoot, come out of your cover with your gun ready to fire."

As they turned into the alley Drew looked back and saw at least one of the men had left the car and was running toward them. "Someone's following us," he reported.

They turned into the alley. Oliver ran past a garage and got down behind a garbage can. He pulled out his pistol and checked to make sure he had a round in the chamber and moved the selector off safe. Drew had concealed himself about ten yards farther down the alley.

A thin man wearing a brown ski-mask ran past Oliver. He carried what Oliver recognized as a silenced semi-auto pistol in his right hand. The assassin seemed to notice a movement to his right and he brought his gun to bear in the direction he was looking, just as a bullet from Oliver's gun began its destructive path through his brain.

Oliver immediately moved to pick up the assassin's gun. Drew had come out of his cover as soon as Oliver fired his shot.

They both turned their heads as a second man entered the opening to the alley and crouched into a firing position aiming at Oliver. Oliver saw the direction Drew was aiming and dove to the ground as a shot sailed through the space his body had just occupied. Drew fired three rounds, the first two of which caused the shooter's body to jerk at each impact and finally sent him sprawling to the ground.

They heard an exchange of gun fire erupting from the direction the women had run and they took off running toward the sound.

***

As the three women had come out from between the houses and turned right to run up the sidewalk, Beverly saw an old lady coming up the street carrying a large bag of groceries.

She thought it was odd because the woman was walking tall and striding purposefully—like a man.

She looked away but turned back just in time to see the old lady reach into the bag of groceries and pull out a long-barreled revolver.

"Get down!" she shouted as she withdrew her carry-pistol and dove to the ground. She twisted into a position that allowed her to bring her weapon to bear on the shooter.

Just then, Ruth made the worst mistake of her life. Instead of doing what Beverly said, as Nancy had, she turned and asked, "What's going on?"

She was immediately hit in the lower abdomen. A second round went through her right thigh as she fell. Nancy rolled on top of Ruth to cover her and immediately jerked as a bullet entered her lower back.

Beverly opened up on the shooter. She hit him at least once as he moved to hide behind a parked car. Before he could get there, she heard the thunderous report of a shotgun from behind her. The glass of the car windows exploded toward the cowering assassin.

Beverly looked back and saw her neighbor, Betsy, with her twelve-gauge Remington 870-Tactical-shotgun firing a second round at the shooter. She ran past Beverly and out into the street. Her husband, Kevin came screaming out of their house carrying a 7.62X51-carbine which was similar to the one he used in Iraq and a first-aid kit, just as Oliver and Drew ran up.

Kevin dropped the first-aid kit near Ruth and ran to provide covering fire for his wife.

"Drew, load a full mag in your pistol and go back them up," Oliver shouted.

Drew dropped the partial magazine out of his pistol and stuffed it into his front pocket, then slammed a full magazine into the well, chambered a round, and took off at full speed to cover his neighbors.

***

With fear and trepidation, Oliver gently moved Nancy off Ruth. "Beverly, use my cell phone. Hit speed-dial nine. When someone answers say 'Call Grandma Sonya'. Ignore what they say next and tell them, 'Lanes Delta Red Ninety-One'. After that, tell them where we are."

They heard Betsy yell, "Go ahead and reach for the gun, hockeypuck. I've only got five-shells left."

Kevin entered the street and spun his head in the direction of a small car on the far side of the road. A man was bringing a gun to bear in their direction, so Kevin began firing at him as he ran toward the small car. He proceeded around it. "I got him!"

Down the street a small compact car sped away from the scene, as sirens rang out.

Kevin ran back to help Oliver.

Ruth looked in tremendous pain and she was bleeding profusely. Oliver applied bandages as quickly as possible to try to stop the bleeding.

Then Nancy began moaning, a deep guttural sound.

Kevin looked and saw the small red entrance wound in her back. He quickly tore open a sterile dressing and applied pressure with it. He turned Nancy's body to look for an exit wound but there was none. He smiled at Nancy who looked up at him with eyes that seemed to be glazed over.

"Help is on the way, Nancy. Hang in there."

"How's...Ruth?" she struggled to ask.

"Oliver's working on her. I'm sure she'll be fine. Just keep breathing and try to stay calm."

The sirens sounded as if they were getting closer as Drew and Betsy returned from the street.

"Drew, Betsy, and Beverly, keep looking around," Kevin said. "There might be more shooters."

"Are any of the shooters alive?" Oliver asked Kevin.

"I don't think so. The guy in the street bled out and the other guy has a huge hole in his head."

"There were two shooters in the alley, but we stopped them," Oliver told him.

Ruth didn't make any sounds and she was starting to look pale. "Hang on, Ruth. Help will be here shortly," Oliver told her.

"Thanks, Sis, for covering Mom," Drew said as he held Nancy's hand.

Nancy looked at him. She seemed in too much pain to do much else.

Police, paramedics, and five men Oliver recognized as security officers from the agency his son-in-law Jonah worked for arrived with anger on their faces, carrying assault weapons.

The paramedics hurriedly put Nancy and Ruth in ambulances. Oliver traveled with Ruth. Drew and Beverly stayed behind and told the police and security officers what had transpired.

As the ambulance sped along, Ruth squeezed Oliver's hand and tried to say something.

Oliver patted her hand. "Save your strength, Ruth."

She reached up and pulled her oxygen mask aside and whispered something.

Oliver tried to put the mask back in place, but she stopped his hand.

"No. Let me...speak. I don't want you...to be...alone."

"I'm not going to be alone. Drew and Beverly will be at the hospital in a short time."

Ruth shook her head. "Not what I—if I die, I want you to find someone else."

Oliver shook his head.

"Oliver Holt...if you don't promise...I'll come back and haunt you."

"That's not funny." "Promise."

"Ruth, you're going to be fine."

Ruth coughed once and blood sputtered out of her mouth. Oliver tried to keep his face neutral, but that wasn't a good sign.

"Oliver," she rasped, "promise me."

"Okay, okay, Ruth. I promise."

"I love you." Ruth closed her eyes just as the ambulance pulled into the hospital.

Thank God she was still breathing, just unconscious. They rapidly whisked her away to the ER.

***

Back at the scene of the shooting, Drew's sweat suddenly felt cool on his skin and he started to shiver.

Kevin and Betsy walked over to him. "That was awfully precise shooting, Drew. You saved your dad's life."

"I was scared beyond belief. Look at me. I'm still shaking. I don't think I planned any moves. I just reacted."

"That's why you two attended IDPA matches at the range with your dad and us," Betsy said. "You and Beverly both did great."

"When I saw the old lady," Beverly told them, "I remember thinking she walked funny, not like an old lady but more like a guy. I had a bad feeling and when I looked back, he was taking a gun out of the grocery bag he was carrying. If I had looked sooner I might have stopped him before he opened up on us."

"If you hadn't realized he was walking funny," Betsy told her, "he probably would have shot you as well."

"Come on, guys," Kevin said. "I'll drive you to the hospital." Beverly hugged Kevin and Betsy.

"It sure is nice having Marines in the neighborhood," Beverly told them.

"Those hockey-pucks picked the wrong neighborhood," Betsy said angrily. "I was more furious at them than I was at the Taliban I fought in Afghanistan, because these clowns were invading the neighborhood where my children play."

When they arrived at the hospital, Oliver met them in the ER. "Both of them are in surgery," he told them. "Mom was unconscious by the time she arrived here. She has severe internal bleeding. Nancy was conscious, but in terrible pain. It will be a number of hours before we know anything."

"I should have looked sooner—taken action sooner." Beverly's whole body started shaking as she cried.

"You did great," Drew told her as he wrapped his arms around her. "No one knew who they were or where they were going to come from."

Beverly sobbed into Drew's shoulder for a number of minutes. "I should call my folks," she said wiping tears off her face. "I don't want them to hear about this on the news."

One of the security people who had accompanied Oliver to the ER handed his cell phone to him.

"Hello? Hi, Holly. Nancy and Mom got shot up pretty bad. The rest of us are okay. They're in surgery now. Where are you?" Oliver listened for a moment before speaking. "The four of you take care of yourselves."

He turned to everyone around him. "She couldn't tell me where they are, other than they're at a secure facility. The security folks don't want her to come down here until they know who is responsible for the attack and have them neutralized. Right now, they have no idea who these guys were, or who sponsored them. We're going to have a security escort the next few days including a detail staying around my home. It would be best if the three of us stay at my house the next few days."

A grim-faced doctor approached them and asked for Oliver Holt.

Oliver turned to him.

"I'm sorry to have to tell you this, Mr. Holt. We did everything we could…Mrs. Holt's wounds were too severe and she died on the operating table."

"No! Please! No, don't say that!" Oliver's eyes filled with tears and he looked as if he might collapse.

Beverly screamed, fell to her knees, put her hands over her face, and began sobbing hysterically.

Then, in the midst of his own anguish, Drew did his best to comfort them both.

Chapter Eleven ~ Heading Home

IT WAS A SAD Sunday morning cruise back to Hunts Point on the *My Meanderer*. They were all worried about who had been attacked.

It was also sad because Megan was leaving the next day.

"Do you have to go back to that other place?" Olivia asked her.

"My home and my job are there."

"But we're here and we won't see you."

"I'll come back some time and spend a weekend with you."

"Who's going to help me put together my outfits?"

Megan stared at Olivia with a heavy heart. "I'm going to give you my phone number so you can call me anytime."

As the GB forty-six had a planing hull, they cruised home at a rapid twenty-seven knots and were back in Hunts Point in a little over three hours.

When they were alone, Megan spoke with Marvin. "I love your children. You can't imagine how much it hurts to leave them," she confessed. "The time I've spent with them has been one of the happiest times I've ever had. I never surmised someone else's children could make me feel this way."

"I'm glad that's the case," he said. "I've had a pleasant time with you, but truthfully, it's emphasized how lonely I am. I'm going to have to do something about that."

"I had a pleasant time with you as well," she said.

"But not an exciting or can't-wait-to-see-you-again time."

"I know. I've been hurt so bad and made to look like a fool so many times, I just can't seem to allow myself to get close to anyone."

***

When Megan returned to work in LA, she smiled every time she thought about sweet Olivia and Freddie. She kept fantasizing about becoming their mother.

She was just getting back into the rhythm of her job when her boss, the company owner, entered her office. "Good afternoon, Megan."

"Hello, William."

"No sense mincing words, Megan. I was hoping to take Todd's place at one of your weekly meetings."

"Which one are you referring to?"

"His every-Wednesday meeting. The one where he enjoys your pretty body."

"Excuse me?" Her stomach twisted. He couldn't possibly know. Could he?

He threw some photos on her desk. She didn't have to look at them to know what they displayed.

His eyes darted between Megan and the photos as he grinned lasciviously at her. "If you want to keep your job—as well as that fancy condo you brag about—and you don't want these sent to your parents with a note stating that you were accompanying a married man, I suggest you be ready for my arrival at your apartment this Wednesday, say...around six."

He chuckled and left her office, grinning sardonically.

The bastard was blackmailing her. She couldn't believe it. But what choice did she have? If she tried to deny him, she could lose all the trappings of success she had worked so many difficult years to attain.

***

Resigned to her fate, as soon as she arrived home on Wednesday, Megan dressed in a sheer robe and tiny lace panties. She figured the more quickly he became aroused, the sooner it would be over.

As she expected, he arrived with the same derisive grin on his face.

Megan took a deep breath and allowed him to have his way.

His love-making consisted of what could best be described as licking, poking, and prodding. It had all the sexiness of copulating with a rutting buffalo.

She tried to separate her mind from her body, her brain struggling to retreat from the sensations his hands, toys, and mouth were generating. He was trying to humiliate her—that much was clear.

When he was done, he rolled off, a sweaty, disgusting excuse of a man. "Thank you, Megan. That was most satisfying. Let's make this a weekly event, shall we?"

Pig.

Megan made no reply as her boss dressed and left. Then she dragged her used and abused body into the bathroom to scour his filth from her skin. She adjusted the temperature of the water to come out of the spray head as hot as she could stand it in an attempt to wash the vulgar experience from her body and mind.

Her body was bruised, inside and out, but more than anywhere else, her mind had absorbed the most pain. After the beauty of the last few weeks with Marvin and the children, the ugliness of what just happened was almost more than she could bear. Megan began vomiting violently as the shower pelted her aching body. Was this a preview of her future? Was this all she was good for?

Chapter Twelve ~ At a Secure Military Base.

JONAH'S PHONE RANG. EVERYONE looked at him as he spoke. "All right. Thanks for letting us know, Drew."

Jonah was sitting next to Holly on a small couch. He closed his cell phone, turning his head toward her, his brow furrowed, his lower lip quivering, and his eyes filling with tears.

An unsettling knowing filled her with dread and Holly began shaking her head from side to side.

Jonah tried to put his arms around her but she pushed him away. Then he said the words she did not want to hear.

"I'm sorry, Holly. Your mom didn't make it."

"Oh no, not Ruth." Lucinda also began shaking her head in denial.

"This can't be true," Holly pleaded, her voice wavering as tears filled her eyes. "They must be wrong. Call them back, Jonah. Ask to talk to the doctor. Talk to my dad. Drew must be wrong. He has to be...I already lost her once. I can't lose her again. I can't! Jonah, please. You have to do something. Give me your phone. I have to talk to Dad."

"Holly..." Jonah hung his head in resignation then handed her the secure phone.

Drew answered.

"Let me talk to Dad, please."

"Just a minute." It sounded as if Drew had his hand over the phone, but she still heard him speak to her father.

"Dad, it's Holly."

Then Drew came back on. "I'm sorry, Holly, but he's sobbing too much to talk to anyone."

Holly slowly moved the phone away from her head, letting it drop to the floor. She covered her face with her hands and began weeping uncontrollably.

Jonah wrapped his arms around her as the sound of her pain mixed with Lucinda's and echoed off the walls of the room.

"It's not fair," Lucinda cried. Her body shook as she sobbed in Ryan's arms.

That was all that was heard for a long time, their emotional state precluding further conversation. Jonah and Ryan held their wives, helpless to do anything to fix this.

Once Holly had cried to exhaustion, she took a few deep breaths to try to get her emotions under control. Then she spoke. "We seemed so safe, Jonah. I was willing to become your partner in whatever you do, holding to the belief that we would be protected. My foolish thinking cost my mother her life. What have I done?"

"It wasn't just you," Jonah said. "I thought we would be safe as well—we all did. We did everything we could. But all our hours practicing shooting wasn't enough. We weren't there when she needed us."

During dinner, they all picked at their food, unable to eat. "I wish there was something I could do to bring her back," Holly said.

A despondent Lucinda looked down to her belly. "Our children will never know her," she shook her head. "That's just not fair."

"My cousin, Ari Minkowski, just called," Jonah said, returning to the table. "He's flying Karen and Benjamin back from Tel Aviv. They'll be in Meridian late tomorrow. Our security group is flying us out there tomorrow as well."

Chapter Thirteen ~ Acceptance and Hope

THE FOURSOME ARRIVED AT Oliver's home in Meridian. Holly greeted Drew and Beverly.

"Where's Dad?"

"He's in his room," Beverly said. "Lunch is almost ready. Why don't you go and tell him?"

Holly found him in his leather recliner reading a book. Jonah followed along but hung back at the door so Holly could speak to her father.

"Holly, I'm so glad you're here."

"Hi, Dad," she said as he stood up and embraced her. "How are you doing?" she asked.

"Okay, considering. I feel so damn lonely. Life just sucker punched me and I'm having a devil of a time dealing with this. How are you doing?"

"Managing. An obstetrician checked Lucinda and me, and the babies are fine." Holly shrugged and headed to the door. "Lunch will be ready shortly."

Oliver nodded toward Jonah and the couple left him to his book, a sad, despondent look on his face.

Karen and Benjamin arrived and Lucinda walked over to greet them. The two sisters didn't talk, but instead they wrapped their arms around each other and cried.

"She was so good to Ryan and me," Lucinda said to the others as they sat in the living room after lunch. "She realized immediately what a great couple we were...how good we were for each other. If she hadn't helped me develop a sense of self-worth, I might never have believed in us as partners."

She turned to look at Ryan. "Remember when she called us at your apartment and warned us about the snowstorm in Nome, Alaska as a way to let me know that it was okay if I wanted to spend the night with you?"

"I remember that."

She lowered her head for a moment and smiled. "I'll never forget the look in her eyes when she found out that you paid for my scholarship. It was a combination of joy for me, and pride that you would think to do that. Family was everything to her. She may not have been my birth-mom, but she never treated me any differently than her own daughter. I so looked forward to having her help me raise my own children. I'll raise them with her values...but I'll have a hole in my heart for the rest of my life."

"She took me in when I developed mono," Karen said. "From that day on she and Oliver treated me like their own child, too. How could this happen to such a kind and caring woman?"

Jonah began to speak. "Ryan and I want to say..."

He choked up and couldn't continue, so Ryan finished for him. "We want to say that we're sorry that our work led to Mom's death."

"Oh no! There'll be none of that," Oliver said firmly. "I have no doubt that what you do is important—important enough that someone might try to kill us to stop it. As sad as I am at Ruth's death, I expect you two to keep doing whatever it is. If you quit, the bad guys win and she wouldn't have wanted that."

Just then a call came in and Jonah answered it. He waved Ryan over and they stepped out of the room for a moment as Ryan's phone rang in for the conference call.

Ryan answered and the man on the other end spoke to them both.

"I'm glad I reached you both. We found them. The hit came from a group of gangsters whose operations were run from a building in one of the former Soviet Republics. They were financed by a terrorist group in Asia that was trying to prevent our maintaining leadership in the genemathematics field. During a meeting of some of their leaders this morning, a wayward drone aircraft happened to run out of fuel, accidentally crashing into their building. Unfortunately, the drone was loaded with explosives and the entire building, and everyone inside, was destroyed. The remaining leaders of that group are being arrested as we speak. So you know—they are also responsible for hiring the people who killed Mrs. Holt. If anyone asks, we'll keep watching, but the primary threat is over."

Jonah and Ryan thanked the man and hung up then Ryan told Jonah he would tell the others.

He went to them and told them what he could, but in their grief for Ruth, there was little sympathy for the perpetrators whose building exploded.

***

The mourners were gathered at the funeral home two-days-later. Jonah read a eulogy that Holly had written but was too distraught to present, while Benjamin read a combined eulogy from Karen and Lucinda. Drew, as well, read a few lines of his prepared speech but couldn't continue, so Andy Schulman read it for him.

Then as Ruth's casket was lowered into her grave, Oliver was the most visibly distraught. He had just lost his life partner. As he grieved, his entire body shook. Drew had one arm around him and held Beverly up with the other, while Holly, Drew, Karen, and Lucinda did their best to console each other.

"Each of them know," Jonah said to Ryan. "They've lost not only their mother, but best friend as well."

Jonah overheard Mrs. Schulman talking to Anna Levin.

"I've been to funerals before, but this time, I feel like I've lost a sister," she said.

Anna nodded. "Me too."

"I loved her so much," Dell Beckham added.

"Poor Oliver," Mr. Schulman said to Michael and Jonah. "He and Ruth were so close. I don't know how he'll manage."

As Jonah drove them to Oliver's home following the funeral, Holly turned to him. "Lucinda and I need to know if our mother's death had any meaning, Jonah. She died because of what you and Ryan do for a living and we want to know why someone would try to kill us to stop whatever it is."

"Holly, you know I can't talk to you about that."

"If you two can't convince us that it's something that might save the world," Lucinda added, "why should we continue putting ourselves, and soon our children, in harm's way?"

"We told you, as honestly as we could, about the risks when we started this work," Ryan said.

Jonah looked in the rearview mirror at Ryan. "Later we'll drive over to the airport so we can have a private talk in a secure room."

***

They arrived at the military side of the airport, went into one of the secure meeting rooms, and sat around a small table.

"We do research into the mathematics of genetics and it has huge implications, both positive and negative," Ryan explained. "Jonah's dad found certain mathematical algorithms that have the ability to predict gene expression. We've continued that research and we're known as genematicians. We have a number of experiments going on. You've seen that Freddie Lipinski's right leg and hip are getting better?"

The two women nodded.

"That's because we, genetically speaking, gave instructions to his knee and hip to begin reforming in a normal pattern. We have a little three-year-old girl who was born with a deformed hip socket and she was on her way to a lifetime of crutches, but after six- months, our treatment has her walking a handful of steps without support and we're hoping for a full recovery. We've been involved in Anna's sister, Chela's psychotic break. She hasn't healed but sits up on her own now and seems to notice people coming in her room, whereas she was in a near catatonic state previously."

"Why would someone want to stop your research if so much good comes out of it," Lucinda asked.

"The problem is that our research can also be used as a weapon," Jonah replied. "We have to continue the research and stay ahead of the others trying to duplicate our work. Someday someone might invent a genetic combination which, for instance, would attack by causing people's red blood cells to mutate into forms that would kill them. If we don't do the research, we wouldn't know what to look for and hopefully have an antidote before it was too late."

Jonah and Ryan both silently implored their wives to understand the importance of their work.

Finally, a long silence was broken by Holly. "We've married soldiers," she said in a monotone voice, while staring down at her folded hands.

"We have," Lucinda agreed reluctantly. "I guess we knew that. I'm devastated that we lost Mom, but do you think she would want them to continue?"

Holly answered immediately. "If I asked her if Ryan and Jonah should continue to perform research that will help a three-year-old throw away her crutches and at the same time help our country fight evil—we both know what her answer would be."

"I know," Lucinda said, "but soldiers don't stop fighting until the war ends. It sounds like this could be a long war."

Jonah looked to Ryan and they spoke in unison. "It will be."

***

"Dad, you have to keep your strength up," Drew told him the next day. "You have to stay strong to help me support Holly, Karen, Lucinda, and Beverly. You're our only parent now."

"I know, Drew, but who is going to support me?"

"I will."

"I know you will, but a partner provides a special kind of support. I don't have that anymore. You can't imagine how painful losing your mom is." He leaned forward, putting his elbows on his knees and his hands over his face.

After a few seconds he stood up and put an arm around his son. "I'll manage. It will be hell, but I'll manage."

Then, two-days-after the funeral, Oliver insisted that everyone get back to their own lives, as normal a life as possible. Once they left, loneliness took command of his life and he found himself nearly drowning in sorrow.

***

Back to reality, Beverly and Shelly arrived at the hospital with Mrs. Corbett from the senior center.

"Hello, dear," she said cheerily as she was wheeled into Nancy's room. "I was told you were under the weather and just knew that a visit from a famous actress would cheer you up."

"Mrs. Corbett," Nancy said just as cheerily. "A visit from you is just what I needed. That is so kind and considerate of you."

"We actresses have to keep our public in mind, dear. All my fans and I miss you terribly, Nancy. We are looking forward to your return. We brought these flowers and a card for you. Many of the people who signed aren't famous like I am, but I explained that you were ill and probably needed a good cheering up, so they were happy to sign your card."

"Please relay my best wishes to everyone."

"I will, dear. I'd like to stay longer but my good friend Dorothy needs a visit as well. You take care of yourself, my little angel."

"Thank you for visiting, Mrs. Corbett. I'll be seeing you soon." Shelly wheeled Mrs. Corbett off to deliver cheer to her friend.

"Lots of the seniors are asking about you," Beverly told her. "Since you started working with Mrs. Corbett, the other caretakers imitate how you treat her and she's been a delight to be around."

"I can't wait to get back to work. Taking care of those people is so rewarding."

"How much longer will you be here?"

"I won't be out until the end of next week, but I won't be allowed to return to work for a number of weeks after that. My doctor stops in to see me twice-a-day at least."

"Honey," an elderly nurse said to Nancy as she came into take her blood pressure. "You are getting the most attention I've ever seen Dr. Christen give anyone. The nurses on this floor have a pool going to see how many days he'll wait after you're discharged to call and ask you out."

"What? He's nice and all that, but ask me out?"

"Child, he has patients all over this hospital that he sees once a day. You're the only one who he manages to find time to visit twice a day."

"Wow," Beverly said. "A doctor! Nice going, Nancy."

"This is silly. He doesn't even know me."

"Nancy Grace," the nurse said, "did you ever hear of a doctor showing up right at dinnertime—bringing his own dinner no less—so he could eat and talk with a patient like he did last night? I've worked here for more than twenty-years and I've never heard of it. Until now, that is! You take it from this old nurse. That kind young doctor is single and he has *plans* for you."

Chapter Fourteen ~ Discovering Purpose

OLIVIA CALLED MEGAN ON the following Wednesday, just as she was preparing for the next session of humiliation with her boss. She had just dressed in her sheer robe when the phone rang.

"Miss Cohen, Dad is sick. He's sleeping a lot and seems sad. Would you call him?"

She did and learned that Marvin had been sick and stayed in bed the entire day.

"I've got some kind of pain in the right side of my abdomen," Marvin told her. "It's not too bad if I lay down, but it doesn't seem to be getting better. I'm sure I'll be okay by morning. I have to make breakfast for the kids, and if I'm still in pain then I'll go see a doctor."

He thanked her for calling. Megan immediately called Sheryl and told her to check on Marvin and the kids.

***

When Sheryl and Ethan arrived, Ethan looked in on Marvin. He was covered in sweat and shaking. He could barely respond to Ethan's questions.

"Sheryl, I'm calling nine-one-one. Take the kids over to our house. I don't know what he's got but if it's contagious they shouldn't be here."

Sheryl called 9-1-1 and then Megan. She told her that an ambulance was coming for Marvin.

After Sheryl got off the phone, Olivia declared, "I'm not leaving my dad."

"I'm riding with him to the hospital," Freddie stated.

"Kids, your father might have something that you could catch," Sheryl said. "Please, kids, you need to come with me so we don't take a chance on you getting sick as well. Be nice, and please, come home with me."

"No way," Freddie said as he sat down on the floor. "I'm not going anywhere," said Olivia.

Sheryl looked to the side and wondered what Megan would do. She immediately duplicated Megan's ice-lady expression and, imitating the voice Megan used when she was angry, declared, "Olivia start moving right now."

Olivia, of course, knew she wasn't looking at Megan, but the expression and voice Sheryl pulled off must have been identical because she starting moving to the door. Freddie was still frozen on the floor with his arms defiantly folded across his chest when the rafters started shaking from a thunderous roar emanating from a few steps behind Sheryl.

"Get up!" red-faced Ethan thundered at Freddie.

As Freddie leaped into the air from fright, he had the good sense to get his legs under him and start moving toward the front door.

"Thank you, Ethan," Sheryl said, as she turned and smiled at her beloved partner.

They heard the ambulance's siren as Sheryl drove the children over to her home.

***

"I can't believe Mom's gone," Holly said on a Saturday morning, two-weeks after the shooting. They were sitting on their patio, gazing out at the lake.

"I know what you mean," Jonah told her.

"Oh-oh," Holly yelled.

"What happened?"

"I think our daughter wants to make an appearance a couple of weeks early. My water just broke."

When Holly's contractions were close enough, they notified their obstetrician and headed to the hospital.

A number of hours later, Ruth Maureen Kaplan made her entrance with a cough and a few cries. She was quickly given a pink knit hat and wrapped in a blanket.

"We've been looking forward to meeting you, and I have a song for you," her father told her. "*Shíí Naashaa...'ahaa lá...'ahaa lágóó naashá*," Jonah sang to Ruth Maureen as he held her and walked her around the delivery room.

"He's singing her a Navajo song we learned some time ago," Holly told the nurses.

Four-days-after the birth, Holly had the baby-blues. Between grieving over her mom and her body's chemical changes after childbirth, she had a few days of crying spells. Jonah was constantly at her side during this time, and did his best to keep her spirits up. The moment she arrived home from the hospital, Michelle was there to help take care of her and Ruth Maureen.

From meals to household cleanup, Michelle was constantly making things easy for her. Her bright spirit helped Holly get over her blues, and by the end of the second week she was almost back to her usual self, although she realized it would be a long time before the pain of losing her mother would ease.

***

Ryan's grandmother, Cora Rifkin, arrived on Monday, the day Lucinda came home with newborn Rachel Lana Rifkin.

"Ryan," said Cora, "I have some things in the trunk of my car. Would you bring them in for me?"

Her trunk was full of groceries, plastic containers with frozen meals and a few ready to eat meals.

"Grandma, you've got enough food in there for a month!"

"Please, it's nothing. I had a little time on my hands just after Rachel was born and I made a couple of things. Besides, your wife must be exhausted from her labor so she needs some good meals to help get her strength back."

"We don't have enough space in our refrigerator's freezer."

"Don't worry. The truck with the freezer is right behind me. It'll be here in ten-minutes."

"Grandma, a freezer?"

"What? We're playing twenty questions? Go! Empty the car please."

"Grandma—"

Lucinda cut him off. "Could you please help me, Grandma? Would you mind holding Rachel while I shower?"

"Please, darling, let me have her and you go shower. *Oy. Oy, Shayna Madela*, what a beautiful girl," she said as she cradled Rachel in her arms, singing to her as she walked around the room.

"Your middle name is that of my mother. She was a wonderful person, a great cook, and a great parent."

Grandma Cora looked at Ryan, who wasn't moving but just standing and smiling at her.

"Normally, your father is a hard worker, Rachel," Grandma Cora said to her. "Maybe you need to tell him to get busy and empty the car."

Ryan walked over and kissed Grandma Cora on the cheek. "Thanks, Grandma."

"What's the big deal? A little food and a freezer. I'm teaching Rachel a song, so I'm sure you have other things to do, like decide where you want the freezer."

"I'll get busy."

***

Shortly after Sheryl called, Megan's boss arrived. As she opened the door for him and his hungry eyes looked up and down her body, she realized her life had changed. There was a family in Seattle that needed her. The condo, the expensive car, the job—all of it meant nothing now. Only that family mattered.

"We're not doing anything tonight or any other night," she said.

"I guess I'll have to send out those photos."

"You go right ahead and do that. And I'll explain to my lawyer how you're an expert at Photoshop. Besides," she lied, "I have hidden security video cameras all over my condo, so keep pushing and I'll be sending some video of last week's event to your wife."

"I don't believe you."

"You don't think I'm enough of a techie to record our session and store it on a remote terminal?"

"You wouldn't dare. Look how you're dressed. You're ready for me."

"I dressed like this so you'd remember what you're going to be missing."

"You'll lose everything if I fire you, and I'll make sure you never get another job in research!"

"I have family that needs me and I couldn't care less about this stupid condo or my stupid job. I quit. I'm leaving and I won't be back."

With a menacing look in his eyes, he started toward her.

"Don't even think about getting physical," Megan said laughing, "or Freddie will be over here in an instant and he'll shove your head so far up your rectum, you'll have to open your mouth to defecate."

He abruptly stopped moving. He'd never heard such threatening words come out of her mouth. Those words, combined with Megan's confident demeanor, demonstrated that she didn't fear him. The way his facial expression changed from anger to fear, Megan reasoned that he must have thought this Freddie person might actually show up in the next few moments.

"Go to hell," he angrily raged as he stormed out of the condo. Megan hurriedly threw some clothes in a bag, drove out to LAX, and got on the next flight to SEATAC. As soon as her plane landed, Ethan picked her up and drove over to Swedish Hospital.

She lied at the front desk, saying she was Marvin's wife. They guided her to a waiting area as Marvin was still in surgery.

"His appendix burst," his doctor said. "We got the appendix out, but his body is septic. We're trying to see what antibiotics we need to use. He's in rough shape and may be in the hospital for more than a few days. He's in a lot of danger, Mrs. Lipinski, and his prognosis is not good."

Megan smiled when the doctor called her Mrs. Lipinski, but it was short-lived, knowing he was in danger and his children needed him.

***

Marvin was asleep when he left critical care and was wheeled into his hospital room, around lunchtime the following day. His skin tone matched the dull white sheet he was lying on. Three different antibiotic drips were feeding into an intravenous line.

Megan held his hand. "Get well, good friend," she said. "The kids need you."

It was another six hours before he opened his eyes.

"What are you doing here?" he asked in a weak voice. "What happened? Am I in the hospital? Where are the kids? Who's watching my children?"

"I thought you might need your temporary partner until you feel better, so I flew up here. You had surgery last night to remove your appendix, you are certainly in the hospital, and the kids are with Sheryl and Ethan."

"Sheryl doesn't know their schedule."

"I know their schedule and I'll tell Sheryl, so you don't have to worry about Freddie and Olivia. You need to save your strength and get better."

Marvin gently squeezed her hand. "I think I need to sleep some more. Thank God you're here. I'm not so frightened now." He took a few deep breaths.

"I'm not worried about the kids," he mumbled as he stared at her with an expressionless face, his eyes drifting closed. "I don't have to worry about the kids now. Thank God, Megan's here to take care of them."

He took a deep breath, let it out slowly, and with the slightest smile repeated, "Thank God, Megan's here to take care of them." He drifted off to sleep.

"Rest easy, gentle man." Megan looked at him and silently asked the Lord to heal this kind and caring man, whose children needed him. She was beginning to realize she might need him to be a part of her life, as well.

Just after dinner Ethan picked her up at the hospital and drove her over to his home. "You need to talk to Olivia," he told her. "She and Sheryl are getting along well enough, but she's a basket-case with worry right now. She was so upset she couldn't fall asleep last night. Sheryl stayed up with her and didn't send her to school this morning." Megan entered their home and saw Olivia reading a book, sitting on the floor next to Sheryl.

She looked up and yelled, "What took you so long to get here?" "I'm sorry, princess," Megan said as Olivia ran over and threw her arms around her.

Olivia cried for a while. "Moms are supposed to be here when someone in their family is sick."

"I'm here now. Your father needs some time in the hospital so the doctors can make him better. I can spend some time with you now, but I will need to go back and stay with him."

"Can I go with you?"

"I'm sorry, but young children can't visit the hospital. Sheryl and Ethan will take care of you guys and I'll be here to visit each day until Dad comes home."

"Will you go back to that other place when he's better?"

"Let's not worry about that now. Your father's hospital room is boring so you should get busy and make a nice drawing for him."

"Will you and Aunt Sheryl help me?"

"I need to shower first and put some clean clothes on, but then I'll be happy to help you. Aunt Sheryl will help you get started."

Olivia followed Sheryl to get drawing supplies. Megan saw Ethan talking to Freddie about his father's condition. Freddie listened intently and then walked over to her.

"Thanks for coming. Olivia really needs you." He hugged Megan. "I'm happy that you're here as well," he admitted.

"Thanks, Freddie. How are you feeling?"

"I'm okay. It was a long day at school today, wondering how Dad was doing. I didn't sleep much last night. It's been rougher on Olivia. Mrs. Kaplan kept her home from school, which was probably a good idea. This kind of stuff is harder on girls I think.

"Is your homework done?"

"I have about fifteen-minutes of reading left."

"Why don't you go to sleep as soon as you're finished reading?"
"I'm not tired."

"It's been a wild day, so at least lie down and rest, even if you don't sleep."

"Thanks for coming," Freddie said as he gave her another long hug and proceeded to the guest room to finish his homework.

After they made a quick drawing of the *My Meanderer*, Megan reached over and placed her hand on Olivia's shoulder. "It's bedtime now."

Olivia looked at her with sleepy eyes. "Will you tuck me in?"

"I will as soon as you have your pajamas on."

When Sheryl and Megan went to tuck her in, Olivia looked confused. "Who's going to get my separates together tomorrow?"

"Aunt Sheryl will drive you over to your house tomorrow morning and help you pick out a nice outfit."

"Can Aunt Sheryl style my hair like you do?"

"I'm sure she would love to do that for you."

"I think I should wear my make-you-feel-better ribbon in my hair. I think I'll need it to feel better at school tomorrow."

"That's a great idea, Olivia," Megan told her.

"Sleep well, sweetness," Sheryl said.

They sat with Olivia until she drifted off to sleep and then checked on Freddie who was also sound asleep.

Megan collapsed into a large leather chair in the living room. "They respond to you like you're really their mom," Sheryl said. "The minute Olivia called me, I knew I had to get up here. It was suddenly completely apparent—I was needed and there was no choice. I knew they all needed me, and I knew that I could count on you and Ethan to help me and take good care of the kids while I was with Marvin. I hope it hasn't been a strain for you."

"I was scared at first, when we saw how sick Marvin was," Sheryl admitted. "I was also worried about how the kids would respond to us. I did my best to emulate the way you are with them and as soon as I started interacting with them like that, they became comfortable with us. I did my best to keep Olivia busy today with reading and grocery shopping. I have to tell you, when that little girl called me Aunt Sheryl the first time, I considered telling her that I wasn't really her aunt, but I was suddenly so happy to think that I was someone's aunt I couldn't get any words out."

A broad smile appeared on Sheryl's face as she relived that moment. "In truth," she continued, "I was more worried about what I would do with Freddie, figuring I would know how to comfort a little girl as opposed to a teenage boy, but I shouldn't have worried. Ethan decided to come home early from work so he was here when Freddie arrived from school. They went for an hour-long walk. I don't know what they talked about, but by the time they returned it was obvious the two of them had bonded, and Freddie seemed much more at ease. He and Freddie made Olivia's favorite spaghetti dinner for us, although, Olivia insisted on setting the table."

Megan knew how Sheryl felt. "When Olivia called me Mom the first time, we were sailing on the Comedy Craft. I was overwhelmed. I mean tears and everything. I feel so fulfilled when we do things together. That little girl is too young to understand, but she saved my life."

Sheryl appeared puzzled.

"I don't have the strength to tell you a long story tonight, dear Sister, but I promise I will when we get through this. I can't thank you and Ethan enough for what you've done."

"Hey, that's what sisters are for," Sheryl said as she embraced Megan.

***

Over the next two-days, Marvin mostly slept. On Wednesday evening, just after Megan arrived back from her visit with the children, Marvin started breathing in rapid shallow breaths. Megan called for help and a team entered the room to monitor him.

On the instruments, Megan saw that his pulse was approaching 170 and he couldn't seem to catch his breath. He was sitting up and in obvious respiratory distress. His lungs had been filling with fluid.

Megan did her best to smile at him, but she was frightened. As soon as they put him on oxygen, his breathing slowed and his heart rate decreased.

"That was close last night." Marvin told Megan the following day.

"I know. I was frightened that we were going to lose you."

"If I don't get better, who's going to take care of the kids?" "Do you have family?"

"I don't. Elisabeth had a sister on the East Coast, but we've never been close. I haven't talked to her in years." He reached out and took her hand. "If anything happens to me, I want you to take Freddie and Olivia."

"Nothing is going to happen, other than you getting better."

On the following Sunday, it was determined that Marvin could go home, but he would continue to need antibiotic medication fed into his intravenous line twice a day. Megan was instructed by the hospital staff on how to perform this.

Ethan and Megan brought Marvin home from the hospital. He was still worn out, so with Ethan's assistance, he climbed the stairs to his bedroom.

Megan laid out the medical instruments and medications she would use to give Marvin his antibiotic drugs.

Then, on Monday, Olivia sat down next to her in the kitchen to eat her after school snack.

"Now that Dad's home are you going back to that other place?"

No, sweetness, I'm not. I'm going to stay up here."

"With us?"

"I'm going to help your father get better. I'll sleep in the spare bedroom for now. After that, he and I can talk about our future."

"Will you get a job up here?"

"Not right away. I have enough investment income to live on for now."

"I was talking to Freddie the other night and he said that Mommy Elisabeth must have sent you to be with us so you can be our new mom."

"Olivia, my dear, that is the most beautiful thing I've ever heard."

"Maybe I should tell Dad so he'll know and ask you to stay with us. Do you want to stay here?"

"You guys are what I live for. I want to stay, but if your father and I discover that we don't love each other then it's not fair to you and Freddie to have two parents who are just playing house."

Olivia walked over and put her arm around Megan. "I think I'm happier when you're here, because you have so much love to give us. I'm sure Dad will see that."

"Thank you for saying that, Olivia," Megan said as she returned Olivia's hug.

***

On the first *Shabbat* after she was born, Ruth Maureen's cousin, Rachel Lana Rifkin was being held by her Aunt Karen when the doorbell rang.

The Levin family, with Freddie and Olivia, the Minkowskis, Kaplans, Holts, and, Goulds all arrived over the next hour.

"All the family is coming for *Shabbat*," Lucinda said to Rachel.

"If she grows up to have a body like us, I might need to have a private talk with her," Carrie whispered to Rachel's mom.

"It would be an honor for me if you did that," Lucinda said. "I think Karen needs a break. Why don't you sit in the rocking chair and hold Rachel for her?"

"Hi, Rachel." Carrie sat in the rocking chair and cuddled her in her arms. "I'm your neighbor and we're going to have lots of good times together. If you think like your dad, we can spend hours and hours doing math." She looked up at Lucinda. "Would that be okay?"

"I'm sure she'll love that."

"But what if she wants to know about plants?" Olivia said. "Then I'll get to teach her."

"Rachel is certainly lucky to have you guys for neighbors," Lucinda told them.

"Why don't you hold her, Olivia?" Carrie said.

"Can I?" she asked Lucinda. "Of course."

Carrie stood up. "Sit down in the rocking chair." She gently placed Rachel in Olivia's arms.

At that moment the room became brighter from Olivia's glow. "Wow! I could hold her like this forever," Olivia said as she gently rocked Ruth.

"See what joy a new baby brings?" Grandma Cora said.

"How's the first week been?" Holly asked Lucinda.

"With Grandma Cora here, it's been pretty easy. Whenever I'm unsure of something, I ask her and she shows me what to do and reassures me that I'm doing things right. I still have a midnight feeding, but with Grandma Cora's help I'm getting enough rest. She brought so much food I haven't really cooked all week. She wanted to cook for the big crowd tonight, but Ryan and I insisted on a caterer. It's been reassuring having her helping this week."

"I know what you mean. Jonah's mom, Michelle, did that for me," Holly said. "Even with all the books I read about taking care of a newborn, it was a huge relief to have someone experienced helping me. Dad is going to stay with us for a few days. I'm looking forward to that. He's really been quiet since Mom died."

"He's not doing too well. His perpetual smile is gone. I want to get a picture of him holding his two granddaughters."

"Dad," Holly called to Oliver. "We want to get a picture of you holding your two granddaughters."

He sat in a large leather chair with his granddaughters in his arms. As the first photo was taken he was smiling. By the third, his eyes were filling with tears.

"Please, somebody take them," he mumbled.

Carrie and Esther Minkowski were closest, so they each took one of the babies from him.

Oliver stood up and walked out of the house. Lucinda, Karen, and Beverly followed him.

"It should be your mom holding them. Not me. You can't imagine how much I miss her. Sometimes I want to tell her something, so I yell out her name, as if she was still alive. The only response I get is silence, which depresses me."

"I think these guys want to tell you something," Lucinda said with a huge grin.

"Beverly and I were going to announce something at dinner, but I think we should tell you now," Karen said.

"We're both pregnant, Dad," Beverly told him with a big smile.

Oliver hugged them both. "Congratulations! Thanks for telling me. Until you're a grandparent, I don't think you realize how much it means to have new additions to the family."

He embraced his two daughters while smiling at Lucinda.

"I know, Dad," she said. "If only Mom could have lived to see her grandchildren."

Oliver tearfully nodded in agreement.

***

Anna and Carrie drove over to the institutional home where Carrie's birth-mom, Chela, was living. Carrie was nervous but at the same time curious. She brought a short story to read to her birth-mom. The story was about a daughter's love for her mother.

"Carrie, I don't want you to get your hopes up, but there has been a change in Chela's condition. She had an experimental treatment a year ago. In the last year, she's started to look at people who come into her room. She hasn't talked to anyone but does seem to notice when someone is in her room. She still hasn't shown she recognizes anyone."

"Maybe she's getting better."

"We don't know, and after twelve-years it would be something of a miracle if that happened."

Anna remembered meeting Ryan and Jonah when she came to visit Chela during the previous summer. At the time, she'd thought it was odd they were there but quickly put it out of her mind.

They walked into Chela's room now, and Anna saw that Carrie didn't have a connection to the person they were about to visit, but was mostly just curious at this point. They entered a plain-looking room and Chela was sitting upright in a chair, staring out the lone window in the room.

"I look more like you than Chela," Carrie said to Anna.

An orderly told them, "We put her at the window every day hoping she'll see something she likes. One of the nurses thinks she's watching the birds fly by the window."

"This is your birth-mom, Carrie," Anna told her.

Carrie walked over and picked up Chela's hand. "Hi, Chela. I'm Carrie. I have a story to read to you. It's about a little girl who lost her mom."

Chela slowly looked up at Carrie, with no sign of recognition.

Anna moved a chair next to Chela. Carrie sat down and began reading her the story.

When she finished reading the story she turned to Anna. "Is this what she's been like since she got sick?"

"This is exactly what she's been like, except she's looking at people now. Her body is fine, but her mind changed."

"I hope she liked my story."

As they walked back to her car, Anna could see that Carrie was distraught.

"I feel so sad for her," Carrie said. "Nobody should have to live like that."

A huge downpour was in progress as they hurriedly climbed into their car. Just as Anna was about to leave the driveway, a rain- soaked nurse came running up to the car and started pounding on the window.

"Mrs. Levin," she yelled, "she's asking for you!"

***

As Megan setup the medication for Marvin's IV, he spoke. "We need to talk about our future."

"I've been thinking about that, Marvin. If it doesn't work out between us it will be a nightmare for the children. You know how much I love them. Freddie and Olivia are the light of my life. One of the happiest moments in my life occurred when she called me Mom for the first time. Freddie is always excited to tell me about his school day and his relationship with Carrie. He makes me feel I'm an important person in his life. He's been asking me things about what a boy needs to do to keep a relationship going. If I can follow my own advice, you and I may have a chance to enjoy a nice relationship. I do have a question, though. What do you think Elisabeth would think?"

"What would she think about you becoming a mother to her children? A woman with a graduate degree in chemistry who will understand what I describe about my work, be able to help Freddie with his mathematics and have the unbelievable patience to meet Olivia at her level, plus teach her the six- or seven-million things you have in the few weeks you've known her?"

Marvin took Megan by the hand. "Wherever Elisabeth is, she's smiling. To tell you the truth, Megan, after we went on the cruise to Vancouver and I saw how you took such excellent care of the kids, I began wondering if Elisabeth had somehow arranged to put you into their lives."

"That's what the kids said, too. I've always dreamed of becoming a parent," Megan said. "How do you feel about me and our relationship?"

"I realize I should be able to tell you how I feel—but that's not me. Airplanes I can describe and understand. People and feelings, I can't. I don't know where that leaves us."

Megan dropped her head and closed her eyes in disappointment. "If you don't have feelings for me, I'm not sure where we are."

He ran his hands through his hair. "We should just keep going like we have been and see what happens."

"I don't know how long I can do that, and as I said before, one of my important goals is becoming a parent."

"That's how the kids see you. The problem is me, and I don't know what to do about it. If I get emotionally attached to you and I lose you...I couldn't take that again. I don't know what I would do if that happened."

"Marvin, what should we do?"

He looked to the side as if trying to avoid the question. Megan remained silent. He roughly rubbed his chin with the back of his hand. Without looking at her he said, "Let's tell the kids you're going to live with us."

"That's okay for now, but we need to make a permanent decision."

After a long sigh, he finally looked at her. "I know." They brought the kids into the room and sat them down.

"I'd like to continue to live here with you guys, if that's okay," Megan said.

"Yes!" Olivia yelled.

"For sure that's okay with me," Freddie agreed.

"So this will be a test to see if we can get along together, like a family," Marvin added.

"I know we can," Olivia said.

"We'll be fine. I know we'll be fine," Freddie said with firm conviction in his voice.

"Your father and I have some things to work out, so we can't promise anything."

"If you need someone to talk to, you can talk to me, and I'll try to help you guys," Olivia volunteered.

Marvin and Megan began going on walks around the neighborhood so he could get some of his strength back and they decided to sleep in separate rooms for the time being.

***

As the nurse ran back into the hospital, Anna threw the car into reverse and backed into a parking spot. While she and Carrie ran up to Chela's room, she called Michael to tell him the news. Just before they entered, one of the nurses said it might be better if Carrie waited outside. Anna quickly proceeded inside the room.

"I want to see her!" Carrie yelled.

An orderly stepped in front of Carrie, putting his hands on her shoulders to restrain her.

"Let's wait to see what the doctor says," the nurse told her as she stepped out of the way.

Carrie felt a massive sense of rage welling up from deep inside her. "This is not fair," she said angrily.

She took two-steps-backwards, and with all the strength she could muster, raced at the orderly who was separating her from her birth-mother. The man put his arms up to grab Carrie's shoulders again. Just when his hands were on them, Carrie threw her forearms between the orderly's arms and used an outward motion to knock them aside. Carrie then lowered her head and slammed it into the orderly's midsection with all her weight.

The man grabbed his mid-section and doubled-over. He started gasping for air and dropped to his knees as Carrie ran full- tilt into Chela's room. The nurse put a hand on Carrie's arm.

Carrie knocked the hand off her arm and in a fierce voice screamed, "Jump back, Jack, or I'll have Freddie come over here and he'll shove your head so far up your ass, you'll have to open your mouth to take a crap."

The nurse didn't move and the orderly stayed on the floor.

Chela looked at Carrie. "When I was your age, I could get angry like that," she said.

She turned toward Anna. "Who is she?"

Her sister didn't reply, her face reflecting shock at Carrie's verbal outburst.

Carrie walked over to her birth-mother and gently held both of her hands. "I'm Carrie. I'm your daughter and I'm twelve-years-old." Chela's jaw dropped slightly and she tightened her grip on Carrie's hands.

In a very calm and deliberate voice Carrie explained. "You've been kind of out of it for twelve-years, so I need to tell you who I am. I love watching birds, just like you do, and I can tell the difference between a Rufous Hummingbird and an Anna's Hummingbird. I saw my first Golden Eagle two-weeks-ago, and people tell me I'm a math prodigy. I'm taking a special class at the university for precocious junior high math students. I would rather do math than almost anything else. I have a very good friend named Freddie Lipinski, who is also in my special math class. Jonah Kaplan, if you remember him, is teaching Freddie and me swimming and sailing every Saturday, and his wife, Holly, has been teaching me Italian since I was a baby. I'm going to have my *Bat Mitzvah* in six- months and I hope you'll join us for that."

"Anna…where's my baby?" Chela asked in an unsteady voice. "This is Carrie. She's your daughter, Chela." Her mother put her hand on Carrie's shoulder. "You've been in a sort of vegetative state for twelve-years."

"Twelve-years? A what?" Chela's tears welled up and started running down her face. She looked at her sister, who also had tears running down her face. She put an arm around Chela as they cried. "Where's Warren?" Chela asked about her husband, Carrie's birth father.

There was nothing but silence in the room until Carrie spoke. "He's traveling on business."

"Oh…"

***

"Michael is coming over. He'll be here in ten-minutes," Anna said, as a doctor walked into the room.

"Good Morning, Dr. Mitchell." Chela said in a weak but cheery voice. "I want you to meet…my daughter."

The orderly that Carrie had flattened stood outside the door.

Carrie looked at him. "I'm sorry that I knocked you over, but you were trying to prevent me from seeing my birth-mom and I kind of lost it."

"Carrie Levin, I'm shocked you did something like that," Anna said. "We will have a serious talk when we get home young lady."

The orderly looked at Carrie. "Apology accepted. I thought about it and realized that if someone had tried to prevent me from seeing my mother after twelve-years they'd still be on the floor."

"How do you feel, Chela?" the doctor asked.

"I'm a little confused but I'm also happy." She slowly turned her head to look at Carrie. "Look at my beautiful daughter. How else could I feel?"

The doctor began examining Chela while she continued to have a tight grip on Carrie's hand.

Michael ran into the room. He was out of breath and a huge smile formed on his face the minute he saw Chela.

"Michael, it's so good to see you!" Chela called out.

Carrie helped her as she slowly stood up. Michael walked over and embraced her.

"You're back!" he said.

"I think so."

Dr. Mitchel asked Chela some questions and then suggested she get some rest.

"I'm going home with them," she announced.

"Chela, you could have a relapse," Dr. Mitchel told her. "This can be overwhelming. Twelve-years is a long time. It may be a strenuous and difficult adjustment."

"I'd much rather have difficulties with my family around me, thank you."

"You could suffer a relapse," he repeated.

"Then I certainly want to spend as much time with them as possible."

"We live about a fifteen-minute-drive from here," Michael stated. "If something happens she would be in a safe environment and we could bring her back if needed."

Chela was becoming angry. "This is not *frijoles refritas* you are debating over. It is my life and I've just missed twelve-years of it. If I have to, I'll sign out AMA."

Dr. Mitchel smiled. "Her sense of logic seems okay. She's not a threat to anyone's safety, but I'd like to observe her for a few days before she goes home."

Chela seemed to be getting more upset by the moment. She tightened her grip on Carrie's hand and clenched the other. Her jaw was tight as she spoke in a voice loaded with fury. "I am going to observe my daughter for a few days and then I may let you observe me. Besides, if I don't get to go home with them, I'll have Carrie bring over—what's his name?"

Carrie laughed. "Freddie."

"Yes, Freddie will come over and you won't like where he'll put your head!"

Michael started laughing. "She sounds like the Chela I used to know. She's coming home with us."

"Anna, help me get dressed," Chela insisted. Michael, Carrie, and the doctor stood to leave.

"Don't try to give her too much information at once," the doctor said to Anna and Michael. "She'll probably tire easily. After a couple of days it could be a good idea to get her out for a short walk each day. Gradually lengthen it. I would like to see her in few days, but right now she looks and sounds great."

"So what do you think happened?" Michael asked.

"Let's just be happy it did happen."

As the doctor walked out, he added, "If you see Jonah Kaplan or Ryan Rifkin you might want to say thank you to them."

"That's odd," Michael said as his gaze followed the doctor out the door.

"Why do you think he said that?" Carrie asked. "No idea."

Chapter Fifteen ~ Oliver and Sierra

IT HAD BEEN A year since he'd lost Ruth and he was doing his best, at his children's insistence, to move on with his life. Indeed, Ruth herself had insisted he move on if he lost her. So, on this clear and cool November day, Oliver walked to his favorite coffee shop near the big mall in Boise.

Two sloppily-dressed males, who looked to be in their late teens, were in front of the shop arguing with a woman who looked to be closer to his age and whose head was covered by a tan floppy hat. They were trying to take a picture of her, but every time one of them raised his cell to take her picture, she tried to knock it away.

"Knock it off, assholes," she yelled.

"C'mon, lady," one of them said. "I want to remember your striped face for Halloween."

"I earned these stripes in Iraq during a fire, you ungrateful little bastards, so get away from me," she said.

"Leave her alone," Oliver called out menacingly as he approached them.

"Get lost, old man."

"She's a soldier like I am, so unless you two want to crawl away from here with your balls stuffed down your throats, I suggest you walk away while you can."

The teens nervously glanced at the shop windows behind them. "Hey, man, we were just joking," one of them said. "We didn't mean anything."

The woman turned to look at Oliver, as the teens slinked away with their heads bent down and their shoulders rounded. A very different display than the bravado they had been demonstrating when Oliver had walked up to them.

He then noticed that the right-half of the woman's face and neck were covered in ugly, uneven, alternately colored scar tissue, some of which reached onto her eyelid. Her exposed hands, which showed below a long-sleeved tan sweatshirt, also had extensive angry-looking red-and-purple scars. She had tears running down her face.

"I'm Oliver," he said as he shook her roughly textured hand.

"I'm Sierra."

"How about a coffee?"

"I'm going home. I tried this. It's just not for me. I've had enough outdoor adventure for the day."

"Surely you have time for a fellow soldier. I was in Iraq as well." She eyed him suspiciously but then shrugged her shoulders.

"I guess I do owe you for chasing those punks away. Sure. Why not?"

"What can I get you?" he offered as they walked inside, up to the cash register.

"Iced tea would be fine."

Oliver ordered a drink for each of them and joined her at a little table in the corner.

"I was an infantry soldier during my tour of Iraq," he told her.

"I was in charge of a transportation company. Nothing much happened during my first-three-tours in Afghanistan, until this," she said as she pointed to the scared side of her face.

"How many people were out with you when it happened?"

"There were twenty-nine of us. Transport people and security. We were moving cargo to a new base, like we always did."

"How many survived?"

"Three of us survived, if you can call my looking like this surviving."

"There were only two of us who survived from my squad in Iraq," Oliver told her. "I'm the only one, after many years of counseling, who is leading a fairly normal life—although I've been depressed the last year because my wife died."

"Sorry to hear that," Sierra said as she sipped her drink.

"Thank you."

She talked about her life before the burns. She had raised two children, loved dogs, and had dreams of being a trainer of rescue dogs.

"Are you still going to pursue that?"

"I took some courses to do that before I got hurt, but I don't feel like pursuing anything right now."

"You're actually luckier than I am," Oliver said.

"Are you nuts? What could possibly be lucky about this?"

"As soon as people see you, they know you have a problem. With me, however, everyone expected normal behavior because I came home and appeared normal. As we both know, it's the scars inside that hurt the most. I certainly remember how painful it was. Sometimes I had headaches that nearly disabled me. If not for Ruth, my wife, I may not have made it."

Sierra sat in silence staring at Oliver. Her chin began quivering and tears slowly formed in her eyes then began rolling down her cheeks.

"My Lord...someone who has felt the same pain I live with," she said, trembling. She leaned forward, covered her eyes with one hand, and quietly cried.

Oliver watched her tears for a while. He then shed his own as he told her about Ruth and how much he missed her. Sierra talked about her children, and how her mental pain made it difficult to have a relationship with them.

"I'm so busy thinking about the people we lost that day that I can hardly hear what my own children are saying. Thanks for rescuing me," she said as she finished her iced tea.

"I can tell something else about you," Oliver said.

"And what would that be?"

"As my son Drew tells me when I am depressed about something, I think you'll feel better if you have a cinnamon roll. Let's walk over to the mall. I know a great place to buy them."

"I haven't been to the mall in a long time. I can't stand how people look at me."

"As far as I'm concerned, if they don't like how you look they can go to hell."

"What?"

"They can go to hell if they don't like how you look," he said as he stood up, "because we're going for cinnamon rolls."

"Yeah, cinnamon rolls and letting people..."

A smile began building on her lips. "Just what I need."

"The new Sherlock Holmes movie is out," Oliver said pointing to the marquee as they walked over to the mall. "Want to see it after our sweet and sticky lunch?"

"I don't know."

"I hear it's a fun movie, and once it's dark in there people won't see your outside scars."

"Thanks," she said. "You really do get it."

After a warm, doughy, cinnamon-and-sugar treat, they watched the entertaining movie, and then walked back to their cars.

"Here's my number, Sierra," Oliver said handing her a card. "Call anytime if you'd like to talk."

"Thanks again, Oliver. It was easier to spend time with you than I had expected. It's been great being with someone who, you know, gets it."

"You are certainly welcome. It was fun for me as well. You really improved my day. This is the first time since my wife died that I didn't just spend the day thinking how much I miss her. It was most kind of you to do that."

"I'm glad I could help," she said. "Maybe we could meet for coffee again, tomorrow, if you're not busy."

"The only thing I have planned for tomorrow is my everyday eight-in-the-morning run. If you want to join me, my address is on the card. If not, give me your number and I'll call you afterwards."

***

She smiled and stuck the card in her purse. She climbed into her car, while Oliver waited like a gentleman for her to drive away before he climbed in his own.

She had gone out that day as a final attempt at having a normal life and things got ugly when those two punks had harassed her. She'd tried to stand up for herself, but honestly, she had been ready to call it quits just when Oliver had arrived. He'd saved her. In more ways than he could know. She'd ended up having a good day— better than she could have ever hoped when she had left the house, but now, the demons in Sierra's head were surfacing again as she started driving.

She arrived home, made herself some dinner, and tried to watch TV, but the more the elevated mood from her few hours with Oliver wore off, the more depressed she became. One thought was keeping the worst of the demons at bay, however. It was Oliver's remark that she had improved his day.

I did that for him. The thought kept her on the right side of her struggle.

However, as she got ready for bed that night, she looked at the pill bottle on her night stand. She had held that bottle in her hands before she had gone out earlier. Had even taken the time to count them, make sure there would be enough.

Pills or a run tomorrow?

No hurry. She could decide in the morning. They'd be here when she needed them.

Chapter Sixteen ~ Olivia's Otter

ON SATURDAY MORNING AFTER breakfast, Olivia was with Megan. "What's the Comedy Craft doing at our dock?" she asked.

"Ethan and Sheryl are buying a bigger sailboat, so I bought it from them. It's yours, Olivia."

"What?" she said slowly, as her eyes widened.

"When you're older, I'll explain in detail, but you saved my life."

"I did?"

"Yes, you did that for me, sweetness. Let's walk down to the dock and look over your new sailboat."

She took Olivia's hand as the girl bounced up and down, all the way to the pier. Olivia's face was aglow as she looked over the little Ensign sailboat, running her hand across the polished wood seats, flooring, and trim. She walked to the back of the boat and looked at the transom.

"Mom, you changed the name."

"Do you like it?"

"Olivia's Otter. I love it." Her eyes sparkled as she put her hands on her hips. "We're going sailing until the snow flies!"

"The boat is in wonderful condition after all these years, but your father is going to purchase a few replacement parts from Ensign Spars in Dunedin, Florida. Also, you and I need to refinish the tiller, and your father will help us refinish all the wood, so the boat will look like new."

"Wow, we'll be doing woodworking just like Dad, but on my own boat. You know what I think? When you and I get together we can do everything! When can we take it out?"

"Let's get our Saturday-morning housecleaning out of the way, and then we'll make a picnic lunch to eat while we sail."

***

Oliver walked out of his house like he did every day at exactly eight o'clock. He was pleasantly surprised to find Sierra sitting on the concrete step in front of his home.

"Good morning, ma'am. You're going to die of heat stroke wearing sweats on a sunny day like this, even if it is November."

"I know." She briefly crossed her arms across her chest. "I have running clothes underneath, if you think you can stand to look at my disgusting body."

"You're right on that one, Sierra. I'd much rather see you die of heat stroke than see your scars."

For the first time, Oliver heard Sierra laugh. She avoided his gaze as she took off her sweatshirt and pants. The mottled and unevenly scared skin on her legs, arms, and shoulders looked awful indeed.

"I need to wear sunscreen," she said taking a tube out of her sweatpants.

"With your permission, I'll help you with that," Oliver volunteered, taking the tube out of her extended hand. He quickly and gently applied it to her legs, arms, neck, and face.

"Thank you," Sierra said placing the tube back in her sweats. "That's the first time since the fire that a man has put hands on me, that weren't latex covered."

Oliver opened his cell phone and speed dialed a number. "Aunt Marne asked me to call," he said.

"TL zero, sir," was the reply.

Sierra looked puzzled, raising her shoulders and tilting her head.

"It's a little security ritual I engage in before I run every day," Oliver said.

"Does it have anything to do with your having a gun under your sweatshirt?"

"Yes it does." Oliver nodded and they headed out at a moderate pace.

As they completed a twenty-minute run and began walking to cool down, they saw five-year-old Timothy, Oliver's next-door neighbor, playing in his front-yard. When he saw Oliver he waved and excitedly ran up to him.

"Hi, Mr. Holt," he called out, smiling broadly.

"Hi, Timothy. This is my friend, Ms. English."

"Hi, Ms. English. Nice to meet you." Timothy held up his hand to shake hers.

"It's nice to meet you as well, Timothy."

"What're you guys doin'?"

"We just finished our run so we're walking to cool down," Oliver told him.

"My mom says I can walk to the corner if a big person walks with me."

"Let's do that," Oliver said.

Timothy moved to stand between the two adults and held up his hands to hold theirs. He kept glancing at Sierra's legs while they walked.

"What happened to your skin?"

Sierra looked embarrassed and didn't respond.

Oliver sensed her apprehension and stepped in to answer. "Timothy, she has special camouflage skin so she can go into the forest and not be seen."

Sierra remained silent, as if waiting to see if the boy would accept the answer Oliver had given him.

Timothy did. While still holding their hands as they walked, he began jumping up and down. "Wow. That is so cool. I hope you'll be my friend, Ms. English, because you're really cool."

"I'd be happy to be your friend," Sierra said as she smiled at Oliver.

"I can't wait for kindergarten on Monday so I can tell all my buddies about my new friend, Ms. English."

When they returned to Oliver's home, he offered to let her shower and asked what she was doing the rest of the day.

"I have nothing planned," she said.

"I was going to go up to Bogus Basin. I wanted to hike some of the trails we cross country ski on in winter. The scenery is drop- dead gorgeous. I have a hydration pack you can borrow."

Sierra hesitated.

"It beats spending the day alone," Oliver said.

A small smile formed on her lips and her eyes started to sparkle. "You're right. I'll get cleaned up and we can head out."

***

One-hour and a bumpy Jeep ride later and they were hiking along ridges and valleys with magnificent views of the surrounding terrain. Sierra mostly walked with her head looking down.

"You're going to miss some gorgeous scenery if you keep your head down like that."

"I guess I've developed the habit so that I don't see people staring at me."

"This place is practically empty. Take a chance and glance around."

Sierra did, and the tension in her shoulders and face eased as she absorbed the beauty surrounding them like a sponge soaking up water. The natural beauty really seemed to elevate her mood. She was now smiling and relaxed.

"Oliver, this is drop-dead gorgeous. Thanks for suggesting a hike up here. And thanks for making me look. To think I would have missed as this." She took a deep breath of the cool mountain air. "I can't imagine how beautiful it must be when it's covered with snow. Can we stop for a while and just stare?"

"Sure we can."

They sat quietly on a ridge overlooking a meadow as Oliver pointed out a few birds flying over and around them.

Sierra turned to him. "I'd like to tell you what happened to me. You know, when I got burned."

Oliver wrapped his arm around her. "And I would be happy to listen."

Sierra put her arm around Oliver, too, leaned her head on his shoulder, and cuddled against him. She took a deep breath and began telling him the story.

"We were in a convoy, riding in a Humvee," Sierra said. "I'm sure you remember how rough they rode."

"I remember it was like riding in a buckboard going over boulders, especially in that desert terrain."

"There were fuel tanker semi-trailers two vehicles in front of us and one fuel tanker behind. Our unit was moving down a gravelly and deeply pitted road, to a new base of operations. There were twenty-nine of us in total, between drivers, my unit, and the security team. We'd traveled that route may times before but never with fuel tankers."

"How far apart were the fuel tankers?"

Sierra glanced up at Oliver briefly, and then put her head back on his shoulder.

"You're right. Not having a problem on this route previously,we were too confident, too close to each other."

Oliver looked down and shook his head, "You get complacent in wartime, and you die."

"We had just driven into an area that had rising terrain to our right, accented with occasional large, car-sized boulders. The terrain to our left was flat and fairly featureless, except for a few bomb craters."

"Great terrain for an ambush," Oliver said.

"I have no memory of the sound of the first explosion. I remember seeing the tanker in front of us soar into the air, and then a huge column of burning fuel, with yellow-and-black flames, arced high above us and began falling on our Humvee. We heard an explosion of gunfire and RPG rounds coming from our right, so I grabbed my rifle and ran out of the Humvee to the left side of the road to try to find some cover. The air was thick with the acrid smell of burning fuel. I had to run through the flames to get away. I believed I was out of them," she swallowed hard and forced herself through the horrific memory, "when I collapsed in utmost agony. I don't know how to describe it, except to say I was in excruciating pain all over my body."

Oliver tightened his embrace. "I can't begin to imagine how agonizing that must have been."

"A guy and girl picked me up and dragged me farther away from the vehicles and into a bomb crater. A new scent entered my nose as the odor of burning fuel had been partially replaced with the smell of burned flesh—my own. I remember hearing people screaming and asking for help in between the gunfire and explosions."

Sierra's eyes began filling with tears. "The two soldiers that rescued me ran toward the second tanker to save more soldiers...that's when the second tanker was hit by an RPG and—"

She started to choke on her words. "It exploded, Oliver. It just—"

"Shhh." He rubbed his hand on her back. "You don't have to continue."

"No." She shook her head. "I need to. I've never told this to anyone, but I feel safe telling you."

She tightened her arm around Oliver, and after a heavy sigh to get her emotions under control, continued.

"My rescuers were instantly saturated with burning fuel. For the rest of my life, I'll be haunted by the picture of them trying to run, falling to the ground...writhing in what must have been an agonizingly painful death. I mean, from what I felt, getting burned like this." She gestured to herself. "I can only imagine…"

Now Oliver's eyes were filling with tears.

"One of the security people ran over to my crater. He was carrying a scoped M-fourteen rifle."

"He took one pitying look at me and told me to stay calm and keep breathing. I was in so much pain—it took all my concentration and energy just to get air in my lungs." Sierra grasped at her chest, feeling as if she was struggling to breathe. Whenever she remembered, it hit her like this, as if she was reliving the pain, as if she had cursed herself to never forget, never stop hurting.

"He began shooting and talking on a radio. The enemy would pop up from behind a series of boulders, fire a burst of rounds at us and then duck back down. Bullets kept hitting around us. My crater-mate began firing at them as their heads popped up. It was like a life-and-death version of that carnival game, where there are a bunch of holes and an animal pops his head up and you have to hit it with a hammer. He noticed someone firing at us from a long way off. After adjusting his scope, he fired one round. We didn't receive any more shots from that location. His disciplined fire kept any bad guys from advancing on our position."

"Thank God, he showed up."

"I'm sure it was only a few minutes, but it seemed more like hours to me, a flight of A-tens arrived, and with guidance from my crater-mate they began strafing the enemy's position. That ended the firefight. Helicopters began rumbling in, carrying medics and security forces. My pain was getting more intense. The faces on the medics that were transporting me to the hospital didn't exactly encourage me either. I knew it wasn't good."

Oliver nodded and neither one of them talked for a while, but they both cried quietly.

Finally Oliver spoke. "I can't imagine how long and painful your recovery must have been."

"Thank you for listening, Oliver," she said as she kissed his cheek. "It feels wonderful to have a man, a fellow soldier to boot, having his arm around me, understanding what I'm going through."

"My pleasure, Sierra."

"The worst part though, the survivor's guilt thing, didn't really start ripping me apart until later. During my recovery, the hero who shared my crater stopped to see me, and he told me we were the only survivors."

"And gradually you began to feel guilty as you thought about the people who didn't make it. The more you thought about them, the deeper you sunk into depression."

She nodded as they looked at each other with tear-streaked faces.

They held each other for a number of minutes, and then, holding hands they walked silently for another hour-or-so. After that they returned to Oliver's place and went their separate ways.

Sierra was feeling good about herself, having opened up to Oliver. She desperately tried to imagine them as a loving couple, but sadly realized it wouldn't happen yet—she still had too many demons that were eating away at her soul.

***

Oliver received a frantic call from Sierra when he was at work the following Thursday afternoon.

I'm sorry to bother you at work but I'm having a real bad day.

Is there any way you could find some time for me?"

"See you at the coffee shop in twenty-minutes."

At the speed Oliver drove to the coffee shop it only took him ten-minutes, as opposed to the normal twenty, which meant he spent an agonizing ten-minutes waiting for Sierra.

"Please, Lord, make sure the little lady shows up so we can talk," he prayed quietly. "I'm doing my best to support her. She is such a wonderful woman, but I need You to help me find the right words to say to her."

Sierra walked in, looked around, then briskly walked over.

Oliver stood up to greet her. As she approached him, her eyes were puffy and her cheeks tear streaked. Instead of greeting him she threw her arms around him and started to quietly cry. He put one arm around her and used the other to hold her head gently against his chest.

"What's wrong?" he asked as he guided her to a small couch.

"I haven't been able to sleep. Two-nights-ago I had this awful dream that I was running through a fire and couldn't find my way out of it. I was engulfed by huge yellow flames and black smoke. My legs were getting heavier and it became more and more difficult to run, but the harder I tried, the bigger and more painful the fire became. I could hear my troops yelling my name, calling me to help them, but I ignored them because I was occupied with saving myself. I haven't slept since then because I'm terrified that I might have that dream again."

She hung her head and took a deep breath. "I kept thinking about a bottle of pills I have and ending this nightmare of a life once and for all. I nearly took them but decided to call you instead."

"I'm glad you did. Maybe you should call your VA doctor."

"No. I don't want to talk to him. He'll just give me another damn pill to make my head feel all fuzzy," she said and started crying again.

"You seemed happy after our hike last weekend."

"That's just it. I was happy—for a few days—but then the bottom dropped out. I feel like I'm trying to climb out of a slippery well. As soon as I make a little progress my demons show up and drag me back into the black, cold water."

"So you were happy, and then you weren't. Why do you think that happened?"

"Oliver, I have absolutely no clue." Sierra gazed into Oliver's face. "You know why this is happening to me," she said, wiping away a tear.

"I do. It happened to me."

"Is it because of my survivor's guilt?"

"It is. You're not allowing yourself to become happy because of your sense of guilt."

"What should I do? I can't take this much longer."

"I think you need a cinnamon roll." He smiled. "Then we'll go for a walk and talk about this. After which we go by your place to throw out some pills and then we need to meet some friends of mine for a hamburger dinner."

"Oliver, I couldn't stand meeting strangers, having to explain why I look like this and having to endure their pitying stares."

"Trust me, Sierra, the people we're going to meet won't care about your scars. Cinnamon rolls, a little walk, pitch some damn pills, and a hamburger with my friends. Let's stay together and see if we can knock out some of your demons."

She stared at the floor for a moment then looked up at Oliver. "I dread the thought of being alone."

Oliver stood up and held out his hand. She took it firmly in both of hers as if she was grabbing a lifeline. They started walking over to the mall. He was deeply saddened by the pain and frustration he knew she was going through. After all, he had been down that tortuous path himself. Tears began forming in his eyes. He looked to the side, away from Sierra, and steeled himself, quickly wiping away his tears. He was determined to be strong for her.

They sat in silence as they consumed their cinnamon rolls. "Why can't I get over this?" Sierra finally asked.

"Do you think about the friends you lost?"

"Sure. I think about them every day."

"If you could ask them what kind of life they'd like you to live, what do you think they'd say?"

"I haven't got a clue."

"Do me a favor and think about that."

She nodded as they climbed into his antique 1955 Mercedes 300 gullwing, two-seat-coupe and began the drive over to her apartment. Everyone who entered the Mercedes' gullwing doors commented on them. Not Sierra. Oliver realized that she really did still have huge demons to slay before she could resolve her pain.

She stood by the entrance to her apartment as if she didn't want to go any farther inside. She seemed to be shaking as she pointed down the hall. "The pills are on my nightstand."

Oliver found and flushed the pills. When he returned to the front door, she took a deep breath then stood on her toes and kissed his cheek.

"Now for a burger," he said giving her a brief hug. They drove across town to a small airport.

"Are we going to have a hamburger at the airport?" Sierra asked as they arrived.

"Not exactly this airport." Oliver parked the car. "I almost forgot." He removed a couple of black baseball caps from the glove compartment. "I bought one of these for myself and one for you."

Each hat was emblazoned with the Screaming Eagle emblem of the 101st Airborne Division.

"My old unit," she said.

"And mine," Oliver reminded her.

"Thank you," she said as she removed her ever-present floppy hat from her bald head and proudly put the new hat on.

They walked across the tarmac. A man and a woman about their age waved at them as they approached. "Hey, Oliver," the man called out.

"Hello, young lady," the woman said to Sierra. "We've heard good things about you."

"And that's in spite of the awful things Oliver probably said about you," her husband added with a hardy laugh. "I'm Wilson Beckham and this is my wife, Dell. We live a few doors down from Oliver."

She reached out to take his extended hand. "Hi, I'm Sierra English."

Wilson shook her hand with both of his. "First of all, thank you for your service to our country."

"You're welcome," Sierra said shyly, reaching over to shake Dell's hand as well.

"My husband and I were part of the Eighty-second Airborne," Dell told her.

"Fellow vets...thanks for your service as well," Sierra said. "Shall we head out?" Wilson asked.

Sierra looked surprised that Oliver had been right when they acted as if they didn't even see her scars.

The foursome walked over to a rather large and proud-looking high-wing, single-engine airplane that had a large round engine in its nose. It was an old tail dragger-type airplane originally built in 1935 and had a large interior with comfortable seating for five. It looked like the epitome of a 1930s businessman's aircraft. Sunlight reflected off its glossy-red finish.

"We just completed rebuilding it last summer. It's called a Howard DGA," Oliver proudly told her.

He opened the rear door to reveal a wide three-person couch at the back and two single seats up front for the pilot and copilot.

Sierra and Oliver initially sat at opposite ends of the couch but she moved to the center as the mighty radial engine rumbled to life.

As soon as they were airborne, Sierra pulled Oliver's arm around her, held his hand in both of hers, and promptly fell asleep leaning against him. She slept soundly for the duration of the forty- five-minute flight.

"Welcome to Sun Valley," Oliver said as they touched down. Sierra stretched.

"Feel better?" Oliver asked.

"Yup, I do."

"This is a gorgeous area," Sierra said as she climbed out of the plane and gazed at the surrounding mountains, whose peaks were lightly dusted in snow.

"I have a letter from an ancestor of mine," Wilson explained, "written not long after they settled in Boise, after crossing the Oregon Trail. She and some neighbors came up here to camp and she wrote a letter to my great-aunt describing the magnificent views. It took them a train ride, plus two-days on horseback, to get up here. The train ride cost twenty-five-cents and the horses, pack animals and supplies cost three-dollars-a-person." He chuckled. "We made it the same distance in forty-five-minutes."

"Not only that," Dell added, "but the hamburgers we're going to eat will cost us over a-hundred-dollars-each."

"How much?" Sierra asked incredulously as the other three laughed.

"That's pilot humor," Dell explained. "Pilots look for any excuse to go for flights in their airplanes. When you include the cost of the plane and gas to get here, it can easily cost over-a-hundred- dollars for a hamburger."

* * *

"There's a dinner at our home tomorrow night," Wilson explained while they ate. "We belong to a group that helps wounded veterans get readjusted to civilian life. We would really appreciate it if you could attend."

Sierra's face went completely blank as she sat back in her chair, as if trying to put distance between herself and the request.

"Honey," Dell told her, "even if you've been having a rough time, you would be a wonderful inspiration for the vets who are coming home with terrible physical and mental problems that they have to deal with. They're scared to death, some of them. We try to get them to relax by being around former military people so they can ease back into civilian life."

"I couldn't inspire anyone."

"Bull," Wilson said. "You inspire me, Sierra, and I just met you. I can only imagine what hell you went through recovering from those burns—and that doesn't even consider what mental pain you went through, or may still be going through. If the recently wounded vets have a chance to talk to you, it will give them hope. Sometimes their family members abandon them and we fellow vets are all they have. Just talking to you might add enough to their hope so they can start adjusting to their condition."

"I know it won't be easy," Oliver told her as he grabbed and held her hand under the table, "but please consider coming out and meeting some of the men and women. They could use your support."

"Will you be there?"

"Oh, yeah. I hadn't gone for a while after Ruth died, but these guys talked me into going again the last few months," Oliver said. "At these events, I try to spend my time talking to the quiet ones. Sometimes they're the ones in the most pain. After I talk to them, I try to make sure they're getting the help they need."

"You don't have to decide today," Dell said. "But please think about it. We could really use your help."

They headed back to Boise, and when they arrived at the nearby airport, Sierra thanked the Beckhams for the plane ride.

"I'm afraid to sleep at my place tonight," she told Oliver as she got into his car. "I know it is a lot to ask but can I sleep on your couch or something?"

"I have a perfect room for you," Oliver said.

When they arrived at his home he took her upstairs. "This was my daughter, Holly's, room. See that teddy bear over there. His name is Jonah and he watched over Holly nearly all the years she lived with us. He didn't let anything happen to her and he'll keep an eye on you just like he did for Holly. If that's not enough, I'll be right next door. I sleep with a twelve-gauge-shotgun under my bed so if anyone tries to interrupt your sleep they'll be picking buckshot out of their ass for a week."

"I'll be okay, Oliver," she could barely say through her laughter. "And thank you for meeting with me today," she added. "I have a special favor to ask."

"Go ahead and ask."

"I know we're just getting to know each other but I'd like to hold you for a while."

He opened his arms to her and she wrapped herself around him as tightly as she could. She took a deep breath and after slowly letting it out, she wore a contented expression that made Oliver smile.

"I feel so much better when you're around," she said. "Do you think you might have time to spend with me tomorrow?"

"I don't work on Fridays anymore, so the entire day is ours to do with as we please."

"Good night, Oliver. Thanks again for today."

***

The next morning was cool and clear as they went for a run. It looked like it would turn out to be a lovely fall day that begged for outdoor activities.

"I'll have to wear the same clothes today," Sierra said.

"Don't worry," Oliver said. "My daughter Lucinda leaves clothes here. I'm sure she wouldn't mind if you borrowed an outfit." Sierra glanced down. "I have awfully big girls. It's tough to find clothing that fits."

"You look about the same size she is. Let me show you her room."

She changed and then they sat in the kitchen and ate a simple breakfast.

"I've been thinking about what you asked me to consider, Oliver. I think the soldiers who died in my old unit, who were also close friends, would have wanted me to have a life that was as happy as possible."

"I can't tell you what will work for you, but every morning I start my day by thanking the Lord for letting me have another day with my children. I ask Him to take care of my lost buddies and I ask that he guide me to act in a way that would make them proud of me."

Sierra stared at him.

"I also used to thank him for putting Ruth in my life. As of this morning, I've begun thanking him for putting Sierra in my life."

"Oliver..."

"I mean it, Sierra," he said as he took her hand in a firm grip. "We're not kids. I know what I like, I know what I need, and I love when we're together. I haven't had a moment's peace since Ruth died...until you showed up. When we were out at Bogus Basin, sharing the gorgeous scenery together, I had my arm around you and I realized I was starting to feel some real peace of mind. You put your head on my shoulder and I can't begin to tell you how comforting that was. Prior to our getting to know each other, I had trouble sleeping, and if I did get to sleep I was waking up three or four times every night. You changed that. I think our shared experience in the military has given us a jumpstart—a foundation, if you will—to build a great relationship on. That is, if you think the same way."

"I had a good marriage...until this stuff happened," Sierra said quietly. "Not a great one but a good one. He couldn't handle my problems. We divorced three-years-ago. My kids call occasionally, but they live in Texas and are busy with their own careers and families. I'm frightened, Oliver. Trying to add building a relationship on top of all the unresolved emotions I have—well, it may be overwhelming, even if I love spending time with you."

"Has the time we've spent together seemed like work?" She shook her head.

"So we spend more time together and see what happens." He leaned over and softly kissed her lips.

"You're taking a big chance, Oliver. I may not be able to get over this."

"I'm willing to take that chance because I enjoy our time together. Besides, there are two of us in this fight now."

She pulled his head down to her shoulder and placed her cheek against his, wrapping her arms firmly around his neck, and held him like that for a few minutes. Then, pulling away slightly she said, "I actually got a decent amount of sleep last night. Maybe there's hope after all."

He tightened his embrace. "I'm sure there is."

***

Sierra spent the morning reading while Oliver researched some civil war maps. She occasionally glanced at him, wondering if all this was too good to be true.

Just before lunch, they heard a gentle knock at the front door.

Oliver opened it and Timothy was standing there. "Hi, Mr. Holt. Is Ms. English home?"

"Timothy wants to see you," he cheerfully called to Sierra. "Good Morning, Timothy."

"Good Morning, Ms. English. I wanted to show you my new camouflage jacket. My dad bought it for me from Cabela's. Now we can both go out in the forest and hide."

"Deep-woodland camouflage-pattern. Perfect for hiding, Timothy," Sierra said smiling at her young friend as she ran her hand over his jacket.

A UPS truck pulled up in front of his house. "That must be the maps," Oliver said. "What kinda maps, Mr. Holt?"

"They're from the civil war. They're very old and I'm going to put on cotton gloves to prevent damaging them when I touch them."

Oliver thanked the UPS driver and carefully placed the map on his large drawing table. Sierra picked up Timothy so he could look at it.

"Why do people need maps?" Timothy asked.

"If you're going someplace you haven't been before," Sierra told him, "then a map will tell you where things are and how to get there. They can also tell us things about people who lived a long time ago."

He nodded his head.

Oliver looked at Timothy and said, "Would you like to go to the zoo? I haven't seen the new red pandas yet."

"Wow, red pandas! I saw a picture of them at school. I'd love to go, but we have to ask my mom."

Oliver called and got permission.

"We have to draw a map of how to get to the pandas, Timothy," Oliver said. "Would you like to do that with me?"

"Oh yeah—oops, I'm sorry. I meant yes please. You're gonna find out I'm a pretty good draw'r."

Sierra watched as Oliver secured a two-foot-square paper to his drawing board and brought up the online map of the zoo on a nearby monitor. He quickly sketched the outline of the zoo and its walkways.

"When we get there we'll start in the parking lot by the Expedition Grill, so you need to draw some people eating over here. Then we'll walk past the primate house, which will need monkeys drawn here, and then a wallaby by the wallaby walk about over there. Then we turn north and follow the path to the red pandas."

"How do we know where north is?" Timothy asked after adding a monkey to the map.

"We'll use a compass. I'll put the word north over here in the corner of the map and an arrow to indicate where north is. By using the compass we'll know which way to go."

Oliver took out a compass which had a lanyard attached and he put it around Timothy's neck. He demonstrated how it always pointed north.

Timothy was enthralled with the compass. He carefully held it flat as Oliver had instructed and slowly turned right and left.

"It always comes back to point the same way. This is cool." He ran over to Sierra.

"Watch this," he said as he demonstrated the compass. "Isn't that cool?"

"That is amazing cool," she said.

Sierra couldn't contain her grin as she watched Oliver entertain Timothy. It didn't appear to take any effort on Oliver's part.

"Ms. English, would you like to come with us to see the red pandas?"

"Thank you for inviting me, Timothy. I'd love to see them."

They climbed in Oliver's Jeep and headed for the zoo. Every time Oliver made a turn he would ask Timothy where north was.

"Good thing I'm with you guys to tell you where north is."

"You are absolutely right, Timothy," Oliver told him.

"Were you always this good with children?" Sierra asked as they walked across the parking lot to the entrance of the zoo.

"Not always. Besides, he's holding your hand, not mine."

"Don't worry, Mr. Holt," Timothy chimed in. "I'm holding her hand just like you told me so she doesn't get lost."

"Is this a setup?" Sierra said laughing.

"Of course it is. I've got the map, and Timothy has the compass. If we get separated you need to be attached to one of us or you'll get lost."

"Just hold my hand, Ms. English, and you won't get lost."

"I'll hold real tight."

After Timothy used the map and compass to find the red pandas, they stopped for a fresh-fruit snack. Oliver took Timothy to the washroom to clean up, after which Timothy had a question for Sierra.

"My pee looks yellow when it comes out. Does yours?"

"Actually, yes it does," she said, giggling at his innocence.

"I don't even remember eating anything yellow today."

As they chatted about the pandas, Sierra leaned over and whispered to Oliver, "No demons bothering me today." She kissed Oliver's cheek.

"Why did you kiss him?" Timothy asked.

"He's most kind to me and helps keep some awful demons from bothering me."

"If those demons bother you again, Ms. English, tell me. I'll use my camouflage jacket to sneak up on 'em and I'll scare 'em away."

"I'm sure you would, Timothy."

***

Oliver and a most-nervous Sierra arrived at the Beckhams' party for the wounded vets.

Sierra was introduced to a woman named Dinah, who had lost her arms.

"My body went one way and my arms went the other," Dinah said.

"How do you manage?" Sierra asked.

"Not well, at least at first. My initial thought was one that devastated me. I realized that I would never be able to hold my children. I wouldn't even be able to hold them so they could nurse.

My second thought was that my husband wouldn't want me. We had only been married for a month when I was sent overseas. On top of losing my arms, when I was in the hospital they told me I was pregnant. I was a basket-case. I sent my newlywed husband Bill a letter telling him what had happened and that if he wanted out of the marriage, I would understand. As soon as he got the letter he managed to call me. He told me that he loved me and that nothing had changed between us."

She shrugged and shook her head. "I didn't believe him. After weeks of healing and therapy, both mental and physical, I returned to the States. I was so worried, I hadn't slept in days. Bill was standing on the runway with a sign welcoming me home. When he saw me he ran over, picked me up, spun me around, and put kisses all over my face just like all the other guys did for their girls. When we got home, he had a romantic dinner waiting. I kept apologizing for his having to help me. He finally told me to quit apologizing because he was happy that the Lord had given him the opportunity to demonstrate how much he loved me. My head started spinning when he said that. Bill made me so happy. Another special thing...that first day home, he made it obvious he couldn't wait to get me in bed."

"Quite a guy," Sierra said.

"You realize he has to help me with everything from showers to cleaning me when I use the toilet, plus feeding and dressing me. I'm not going to tell you it was always easy for him. It wasn't. Sometimes my mom comes over for a few days to give Bill a break. Eventually though, all the things that he had to do for me simply became part of our lives. We laugh and joke and tease each other and have arguments just like any other couple. That was exactly what I needed. Within a few months I started to feel whole again. A specialist from the VA showed us how to arrange the house in a way that would allow me to do many things on my own. I remember about a month before I delivered our baby, Bill arrived with a sling I could use to hold our baby against me while she nursed. I lost it that day. I was so happy and full of love for him, I must have cried for an hour. I can't tell you how supportive he was, and is. He is absolutely the rock of my life. If all that isn't enough, I'm pregnant again."

A little girl of about four-years-of-age ran up to Dinah and pulled herself onto her lap. She hugged her mom, and turned to Sierra. "My mom doesn't have arms to hold me, so I have to hold her with *my* arms lots of times every day."

"That's lovely that you do that for your mom," Sierra told her.

"Oliver said you didn't think you could inspire anyone," Dinah said. "Look around. Your body may not look as good as it did, but at least you have all of your parts. You don't have to inspire anyone.

Just go talk to them."

Sierra was still worried about the wounded vets' reactions to her, but after listening to Dinah, she became determined to try. She walked around introducing herself and talking to people, and she noticed a female burn victim who looked to be in her early-twenties sitting alone, off to the side of the room, sipping a drink. Sierra walked over to her, partially rolled up her sleeves exposing her extensive scars, and extended her hand. "Welcome to the zebra club."

She shook hands and sat down next to the woman who introduced herself as Susan. Her mildly surprised face was easily as disfigured as Sierra's was.

"Come on, I'll introduce you to some of the other vets." Susan didn't move.

In a bitter voice she spoke. "My folks pushed me to come here tonight. I didn't want to...who's going to want to have anything to do with a woman who has a face like this? I can't even walk down the street without people staring at me."

For a moment Sierra had no idea what to do. She felt every bit of Susan's pain. From her own experience she knew there were times when words weren't enough, but she also knew Susan needed to meet people and begin learning to live in a world of pitying stares. Sierra realized that only action, not words, would make a difference.

"Watch this," Sierra said.

She walked across the room to Oliver who was standing and talking to Alex Schulman, plus another vet.

"Kiss me," she told him as she walked up to him.

"What?"

"I need one of the girls to see you kissing me."

Sierra slid both of her hands behind Oliver's head and brought his lips down to hers in a most passionate and lengthy kiss. He slowly wrapped his arms around her, holding her tight.

"Thanks," Sierra said winking at him as she walked back.

Oliver's expression indicated that he must have had the same fireworks going off in his head as she did. She hoped no one besides her would notice the sudden bulge in his pants.

"Did you see how he kissed me?" Sierra said as she returned to Susan's side. "He likes to kiss me and hold me. You'll find someone mature enough to look past your scars, but you have to be willing to meet people. And screw 'em if they don't like how we look."

"Maybe..." Susan said slowly. "I'd love to have someone who cared enough to see past these damn scars. Getting kissed like that...that would help lots of things."

Susan stood up, took a deep breath, and said in a nervous voice, "C'mon, let's meet some people."

Sierra walked around with her, introducing her to the guys and girls, until one guy kind of got in front of them and kept nervous Susan engaged in conversation. Sierra excused herself and when she looked for them twenty-minutes-later, she found them laughing and enjoying a meal together.

Sierra had been worried that Oliver's neighbors would be angry with her for taking Ruth's place. But then Dell introduced Sierra to Sherry Schulman, another of Oliver's neighbors.

"I'm so glad you find time to spend with Oliver," Sherry told her. "We all are. He was so lonely after Ruth died. We used to hear him calling her name. There wouldn't be a reply, of course, and then we'd hear him crying. There is no way Ruth would have wanted him to be alone. He smiles so much when you're around him. Wherever Ruth is, she's smiling because you make him happy. Thank you so much for what you've done for him."

"You're welcome," Sierra said. "I've found that spending time with him is a warm and healing experience—for both of us."

Sherry smiled and briefly hugged her.

Sierra realized she had nothing to worry about. She felt welcomed and appreciated. Then at the end of the event, Susan walked up.

"I'm so glad you were here this evening," she told Sierra. "I didn't want to do anything with anybody until you talked to me. That guy is an engineer and he wants to see me again. We're going out tomorrow for dinner and a movie."

"Susan that's great!"

"When we were saying good-bye, he told me he was sure glad I made it to the event so he had someone interesting to spend the evening with. He even kissed me good night."

Susan's eyes began filling with tears as she reached out and embraced Sierra. "Thanks, Sierra. That guy may not be the one, but at least I know there are guys who can look past my scars. If I can ever do you a favor, just let me know."

"I'm happy for you and I'm glad you had fun tonight. We zebras should stay in touch."

"We will," Susan said emphatically.

They exchanged cell phones and punched in their numbers. "I know we will," Susan repeated.

After all the other vets had left, Dell Beckham was saying good night to Sierra and Oliver. "Next month is your turn to host, Oliver."

"I can't do it. It's the Christmas party and it's just too big of an event for me to handle."

"We'll be fine, Dell," Sierra told her as she wrapped her arms around Oliver's left arm.

"What?" Oliver said, shock written all over his face.

"I made a new friend tonight. Her name is Susan Collins and I'm sure she'll be glad to help. I'm certain Mark Ginsburg and his fiancée will help me put holiday items together for the Jewish vets as well."

"I'll be looking forward to the evening you two put together. If you need any help, Sierra, or have any questions ask me or Sherry anytime."

***

Oliver and Sierra walked back to his place after the party. They could see their breath in the cold, dry air indicating that snow might be on its way. They had an arm wrapped around each other as they walked. They stopped in his driveway to look up and watched tiny snowflakes silently and slowly falling out of the black sky. He wrapped his arms around her and kissed her lips, then placed his cheek against hers and held her tight.

"I'm not someone who can describe his feelings, but I want you to know you've repaired a hole in my heart. Your laughter, your smile, and your warmth do that for me."

She put one of her hands behind his head and gently brought his lips down to hers.

When their embrace ended, he saw she had tears running down her cheeks.

"Hey, lady, those tears are going to freeze in weather like this."

"Then we better go inside so you can light a pretty fire."

After he lit the fireplace and the logs began to pop and crackle, they enjoyed its warmth and light by sitting together in a large bean-bag chair. Sierra pulled a vintage Pendleton Indian Trade Camp blanket over them. She curled up against him, tucking the blanket around them.

"I feel so much better when we're together," she said.

"You don't get over survivor's guilt overnight."

"I know. I'm going to talk to my doctor. I think I'm at a point where I can start working things out."

"I'm glad to hear that."

"I think I may have helped someone tonight," she said at they discussed the evening. "I'm really feeling good about that."

"That surprise kiss sure made me feel good," Oliver said. Sierra laughed.

"I liked it too. I needed to prove to Susan that I found someone who could look past my scars."

"Why did you volunteer to put together the Christmas party?"

"I've had nothing to look forward to for the last-three-years. Now I look forward to spending time with you, and I'll be looking forward to putting together an event for the wounded vets to enjoy. I can't do anything for the people I lost, but I can try to do something for these folks. I'm certain the soldiers who died would have liked me to do that."

Oliver leaned over and gave her a long kiss.

"I want you to consider something," he said. "I'm going on a two-week vacation to southern New Mexico at the end of this week. I'm traveling to meet a professor friend of mine and go over some antique civil war maps he just received. I was going to take my motorhome and drive down. I dread going alone. Would you consider coming with me? We haven't known each other long and it's a lot to ask of you, but I think we'd have a nice time."

Sierra softly kissed his lips and put little kisses slowly across his cheek and neck.

"We'd have a wonderful time. I've never traveled in a motorhome so you'd have to teach me how to use it."

"You don't have to answer now. Think about it."

"Two-weeks with you, day and night. I've thought about it. I'd love to."

They kissed and hugged like teenagers for a while.

"Are we far enough along in this relationship to sleep together tonight?" Oliver asked.

Sierra tensed. "I want you, but I'm frightened of what you'll think of my body."

"Scars or not, I think you have a lovely body."

"You haven't seen it. The nipple on my left breast nearly burned off and I have no hair, Oliver...anywhere."

"We'll leave the lights off and get undressed in the dark."

Sierra sighed. They watched the fire for another hour then she took his hand and they proceeded to the bedroom.

Oliver got out of his clothes on one side of the bed and Sierra on the other. He slid under the blankets. In the darkened room he could see she was just standing next to the bed. She turned on a small bed-side lamp, which dimly illuminated her scared and hairless body.

"No one could think this body is sexy."

"Sierra, I think we need an impartial interest indicator. Wait a minute! I think I found one." He pulled back the covers and pointed at his fully erect interest indicator.

When she finished laughing, she pushed him onto his back and straddled him, taking him inside her. "Lie still and let me do the work," she said as she began moving on him.

Afterwards they did their best to wrap themselves around each other like hugging octopi.

"What do you think Ruth would think about me?"

"Who do you think put such a kind, compassionate, loving woman in my life to end my loneliness?"

They drifted off to sleep and when they awoke the next morning, Oliver greeted Sierra with a smile.

"Welcome home, soldier," he said

"I am home," Sierra agreed, gently kissing his lips. "Anytime, any-place, as long as I'm with you."

Chapter Seventeen ~ Tough Times for Megan and Marvin

MARVIN HAD DECIDED TO take a year-long sabbatical from work to do some woodworking and write some research papers at the house.

One day a process server came to the house and asked for Megan. He handed her a notification that she was expected to give a deposition during a divorce proceeding involving Todd Portman and his wife. Her past was catching up with her.

When Marvin arrived home after a trip to the university's library, she showed him the notification.

"Why do they want you to appear?"

"I had an affair with a married man."

"Did you know he was married?"

"I did."

"Did you destroy his marriage?"

"Our affair did. Someone took photos of us on a nude beach when we took a trip to an island in the Caribbean. It even ended up with him in the hospital as he had been repeatedly stabbed by his wife when she saw the photos. My affair has left scars on my soul, which is as painful as broken bones, but unlike broken bones it won't heal and will always be there."

"How could you have done that?" he asked while grave disappointment was etched into his face.

"I didn't have anyone and I was a lonely, bitter person. I justified my actions based on the fact that I was lonely and deserved to have someone."

Marvin just stared at her.

"Marvin, I didn't have to tell you."

"What if the kids find out?"

"I'll tell them the truth and explain how wrong it was."

"What if I decided to have an affair with someone I work with?"

"I'll have to assume that I'm not taking good care of you."

"I need some time to think about this."

"Marvin, I care about you and I love the kids.

"I know you do, but I never thought I'd be confronted with something like this. I can't think through emotions like you can. I'm sorry but I don't know what to think."

He walked into his study and closed the door behind him.

Megan ran to her bedroom, closed the door, collapsed to the floor, and sobbed. She wondered if this could ruin her chance of ever having a close relationship with Marvin.

Marvin barely talked to her the next few weeks.

Just after the kids left for school one day, a powerboat towing a sailboat without a mast and rigging pulled up at their dock. Megan called to Marvin about the arrival.

He walked down to the dock and helped the men from the powerboat tie the sailboat to the dock. After signing some papers, he walked back to the house.

"That's my afternoon project for the next six-months-or-so. It was a lovely fifty-three-foot sailboat once, but the owners weren't careful and had a fire in the kitchen that ruined much of the interior. I bought it for peanuts, but it'll be a lot of work to restore it to its previous splendor."

"If you show me what to do, I'll be glad to help you."

"Thanks for offering," Marvin said in a non-committal voice.

As this was the often-rainy Northwest, Marvin built a tent over the boat and part of the dock to keep the rain off. Each afternoon he spent three- or four-hours tearing out the old interior. It was exhausting work and each piece of the old interior he tore out required him to break it down to a size that could pass through the companionway. It was a small and narrow, raised and windowed, hatchway in the ship's deck, with ladder-like steps leading below the deck—it didn't make for easy removal of construction debris. At the end of every afternoon, he had to use a wheelbarrow to move the damaged material from the dock to the dumpster he had placed in the driveway.

Four-weeks into the sailboat restoration project, and having endured mostly silence from Marvin, Megan put on a raincoat and walked through the mist-like rain to the dock to view Marvin's progress.

"When they build a boat," he told her, "they put the interior in before they put the deck on. I've had to get everything in or out of the boat through that little companionway. Either that or I'll have to cut a big hole in the deck which I'd rather not do."

Without being asked, Megan started loading broken and burned bits of the interior into the wheelbarrow. She wheeled it up to the driveway and emptied its contents into the dumpster.

When she returned to the dock to get another load of refuse, Marvin handed her a pair of work gloves. "You're going to need these if you're going to help me."

It wasn't exactly encouragement, but it meant that Megan would be working with him nearly every afternoon the next couple- of-months.

If they talked, it was only about the work on the sailboat or the children. Marvin still seemed confused about Megan's previous life. The Megan he had come to know must have seemed little short of an angel to him.

Olivia noticed the chasm between them. "Are you guys mad at each other?" she asked at dinner one day.

Marvin and Megan stared at each other for a moment. "We have some issues to work out," Megan explained.

"That's not true," Marvin said. "I'm the one who needs to work some things out in my mind. Unlike your mom, who is brilliant when it comes to feelings, I'm an ignorant fool."

"Marvin..." Megan said.

"It's true, Megan. Any man with one-eye and half-a-brain would see that you're one of the world's best moms and a mighty fine partner. For the first time since Elizabeth died, I don't have the pressure of raising the kids alone. You give me four-hours of silence every morning so I can work on my research and help with the woodworking I love in the afternoon. I apologize to you, for not being a better partner. I apologize to you kids for not working things out for all of us, and not letting you know how much I want Megan—your mom—to be a permanent part of this family. I promise all of you, things will get better."

After dinner she sat in a chair in his office, while Marvin sat at his desk. The kids were in their own rooms doing their homework. "I was thinking," he said. "I would like to rearrange the office to include space for a desk for you. I'd appreciate your help with that."

"I'd be glad to. Are you sure you want to give up your privacy?"

"A small price to pay to have you closer to me when I'm working."

He stood up, walked over to her, put his hands on either side of her face, and kissed her.

"It's not easy for me to talk about feelings," he said. "I know."

"But I want you to know, having you up here since we took the kids for a boat ride has been a blessing. Anyone who sees our family can see the aura of happiness surrounding us. You did that for us. I have an angel living here and I'll never know how I deserve that."

"I'm certainly not an angel."

"Should we ask Olivia and see what she thinks?" Megan smiled briefly and Marvin kissed her again.

"With your permission," she said, "we sleep together tonight."

"I'm a bit overwhelmed."

"Does that mean yes?" Megan reached up and pulled his lips down to hers for a long kiss.

"We sleep together tonight."

Megan smiled, thinking that they would work things out.

She became an expert in treating her and Marvin's blisters and sore muscles. In late-October, Marvin came home with matching insulated coveralls for each of them.

"It'll be getting awfully cool out there before we can get the heat going again," was all he said to her, but he smiled as he said it.

"Fixing that old boat is a huge amount of work," Freddie said.

"Why don't you just pay someone to repair it?"

"Some of us get a sense of pride when we repair something by doing it ourselves. In addition, doing this kind of work also gives me time to think."

"Can we help?" Olivia asked.

"I can find something for you kids on the weekends, but during the week your job is school work," Marvin said.

***

A few days before Megan was to fly to LA, she told Marvin that she would stay at her condo so the only cost would be meals and airline tickets.

It was mid-morning when she arrived at her LA condo, and Megan took the keys to her Mercedes CLK to see if she could get it running. It started right up. Then she called a neighborhood store and had food sent over. The condo had been recently cleaned, so it looked nice for her visit.

She gazed out the living room windows at the lovely view of the pacific. She knew the kids would love to visit LA and see the parks here, not to mention having an ocean nearby that was warm enough to swim in.

They'd have a place to visit when it's cold and gray during the Northwest's winter. Though the place had nothing but bad memories for her, she thought if they did bring the kids down there, they could start building some happy memories. She could invite Sheryl and Ethan and they could stay in the second bedroom—the kids adored them.

She imagined seeing Olivia's joy around Sheryl's new baby. "Dear Lord, why are the kids so good to me? Even Marvin was until recently. I know I don't deserve the warmth they bring to my life, but could I please have a second chance?" she prayed. "I'll do my best to turn off that sensation of not wanting to get close to anyone. Please let me keep trying and I think I'll work things out. Marvin and I might even find that we love each other one day. I'll take my time and be as kind and patient as I'm capable of. With your help, I honestly believe we'll find a place in each other's hearts."

After a few minutes, Megan called Olivia, whose first question was, "When are you coming home?"

"I'll be home in a couple of days. I want to talk to you about something. What would you think if we used my condo for winter visits when it's cold and rainy in Seattle?"

"A winter home? Does it have a swimming pool? Does it have a place for Freddie and Dad to do their workouts? Is it really warm there in the winter? Is it near Disneyland? How far is Universal Studios?"

Megan laughed. "Yes to all those things and it's about three-point-five-miles from the theme parks."

"When can we see it?"

"I'll let you know. We have to talk to Freddie and your father before I decide anything."

"Mom, Leah Minkowski called and she needs to talk to you."

"Thank you for relaying the message, Olivia. I'll call her tomorrow."

Feeling stressed and wondering what kind of questions she would be subjected to, Megan drove across town to the attorney's office. She was ushered into a conference room which had a large oval shaped table in the middle of the room and individual chairs lining the outside walls. Portman's attorney asked her for identification and directed her to sit at the end of the table. Mrs. Portman was still in jail, so she wasn't present. Todd Portman weakly smiled at Megan from the other side of the table. She ignored him.

Mrs. Portman's lawyer spoke. "Something has come up the last-few-weeks. A police detective is going to say a few things." He gestured to the detective.

"Good morning, folks," the police detective said as he and his partner showed them their badges. It was the same detectives that had been to Megan's condo earlier in the previous year.

"Mr. Portman, do you know Douglas Raines?" the detective asked.

"He's CEO of a small company in San Diego. I worked there three-years-ago. Why?"

"We've had a suspicion that there was someone else involved in your stabbing since the beginning of this sorry mess. We put a snitch in Mrs. Portman's jail cell and learned about Raines. Since you worked at his company, your wife has been having an affair with him. As part of a plea bargain, she told us that she had planned to attack you before she received the photos. He supplied her with the knife and he disposed of it after the attack. She thought by attacking you in LA, we would think Ms. Cohen was responsible."

Mr. Portman's lawyer sighed and looked at the other attorney. "I don't see any reason to continue."

Mrs. Portman's lawyer nodded in agreement. "Thanks for coming down to LA, Ms. Cohen."

Megan called Marvin as soon as she was out of there. "So his marriage didn't breakup because of your affair."

"My behavior was still wrong, and I'll go to my grave with the guilt of that affair weighing on my soul."

"Well, I guess if it weren't for the affair, we might never have met," Marvin said grudgingly.

"That's probably true. I certainly had no plans to visit Seattle. I'd like to talk to you about my condo. I think it would be a great, winter home for us."

"No discussion on that today, please. We'll talk when you come home. I have some sailboat things I need to discuss with you."

***

Megan returned Leah Minkowski's call and learned that she was planning a cool-weather-party at her home.

"We'll be there, Leah. Please let me know what I can bring and how I can help."

"I'm making lists now so I'll get back to you on that. Sheryl told me you're visiting LA. How are the kids handling your absence?"

"They're okay, but when I told Olivia about using this place for a winter-home, she immediately wanted to know when she could see it."

"Today's Thursday. I'll call Ari and ask if he can setup a flight for Marvin, Olivia, and Freddie to come down after school on Friday."

"Last-minute tickets will be way too expensive."

"Not on Ari Air," Leah told her.

"Ari Air?"

That's what we call it in the family. Ari gets flights on private jets for the business all the time, so when someone in the family needs to get somewhere quickly we call Ari Air." "I couldn't possibly afford that."

"Ari Air is free to family. You're Sheryl's sister and she married Ethan, whose mother is Michelle, who always refers to Ari's father as her big brother, so I think that makes you family. They'll be coming down in a jet that seats six-to-eight people. Think about it and let me know."

"I will. I'll call the kids and see what their schedules are like."

***

Freddie had plans that weekend, so only Olivia flew down to LA. As she walked across the tarmac holding a flight attendant's hand, Olivia called out, "Hi, Mom! I had that pretty jet all to myself."

"You can send that little angel on my plane anytime," the attendant said. "She entertained us all the way down here."

Olivia and Megan played tourist. On their visit to Disneyland, they watched an artisan hand-form glass figures. They discovered a tiny piece of glassware in the shape of an old-time pushcart with colorful flowers on it.

Megan was pleased to observe Olivia's appreciation of its beauty and the workmanship it took to create it.

"It must have taken a huge amount of work to make the little flowers," she said.

"Not everyone appreciates that tiny piece," the artisan said proudly.

"That being the case I think it should go to a home where it will be appreciated," Megan said as she opened her wallet and handed over her credit card.

"Are you buying that for our house?" Olivia asked.

"I think it should be displayed in your room. Do you think you can find a safe place for it?"

"I'm sure I can. Thanks, Mom!"

"Thank you, Olivia, joy of my life."

***

Three-months into the restoration project, Marvin was in his workshop creating some of the pieces that would go back into the boat.

"Megan, I have some interior pieces that are going to need stain and finishing. Before we start working on the boat today, I'd like to drive over to a woodworking store to choose some stains for the interior. If by some chance we can work out a relationship, it's important that you like the interior's appearance. I'd appreciate if you'd come with."

Megan was happy to go with Marvin to choose stains, and by early spring, the restoration of the sailboat was nearly complete. There were only a few more detail items to finish.

They were both working at the forward edge of the main cabin. As Marvin climbed down a ladder he slipped and fell against the thin-walled eight-inch-diameter pipe that would eventually support the dining table.

Marvin grabbed his side and fell to the floor.

Megan kneeled next to him in an instant. She opened his coveralls and lifted his shirt to see if he was bleeding. Instead, a nasty scrape and an angry red welt were beginning to appear. "I'll get some spray antiseptic from the house to put on that," she said.

He looked up at her as tears formed in his eyes. She tried to stand up but he grabbed her arm to keep her close. "You are more precious than words can express."

"No, I'm not."

"You absolutely are. I heard what you told Freddie about his relationship with Carrie. It was brilliant. You are without a doubt his mother. You've been a godsend for Olivia. She looks up to you as her mom and her role model. She hangs on your every word. You are her mom and she is blooming into a fine young lady because of your guidance."

"Marvin, please."

"I love you. More than you can imagine. Megan Cohen, you have to stay with us and you have to marry me, because I love you and I need you. You've brought more joy and happiness to our family than any of us deserves. I'm sorry about what happened earlier in your life, but that's then and this is now."

He wrapped his arms around her and he softly kissed her lips. "More importantly, I know you love me and you've loved me for a long time, even if it was difficult for you to admit it."

"Marvin, I couldn't love anyone, because I didn't love myself. How could anyone else love me? I know I love you because you've taught me how to be happy. My anger prevented me from seeing that. I thought being a person who just takes from other people would make me happy by preventing any pain. Instead, my relationship with you has shown me I am supremely happy when I am a giving person. I thought I had everything that made me happy in LA—money, expensive things, a well-paying career."

She rested her head on his chest. "But Olivia, Freddie, and especially you have shown me that happiness in my case has no cost. All I have to do is love and take care of my family. I couldn't be happier than when I'm doing that. I should have seen it before—I was so happy just after we met when I was teaching Freddie and Carrie about chemistry. I certainly should have seen it when I received so much joy from doing things with Olivia. But it wasn't until I was taking care of *you* that it finally hit me. One day I woke up and realized that I hadn't been angry in months. My greatest desire is the opportunity to love you and the children for the rest of my life. I know that nothing will make me happier."

Marvin wiped a tear off Megan's cheek. "Let's get cleaned up and go shopping."

"Shopping for what?"

"Shopping for an engagement ring, precious Megan."

***

At dinner that night, they had all just gathered at the kitchen table when Marvin kneeled next to Megan and presented her a ring. "Megan Cohen, will you become my wife?"

"It would be an honor to become your wife."

He slipped the ring onto her finger and they kissed.

Olivia slid off her chair, ran over to Megan, threw her arms around her, and began crying.

Megan wrapped her arms around Olivia too, and held her close.

"I'm sorry I'm crying, Mom."

"I understand, sweetness. Sometimes things can make us so happy we cry."

Olivia looked up. "You're crying too."

"That's how happy I am."

Chapter Eighteen ~ Carrie makes a New Friend

Carrie's friend Ann had begun showing seventeen-year- old Carrie how to swing dance during her freshman year of high school and Carrie simply loved it. Her parents said they could hear her practicing almost every day. Even as she traveled through the house, she was dancing, and repeating, "Rock step, one, two three, rock step."

She taught David Linn the basic step and she had found her first dance partner.

When school started that fall, she tried to convince Freddie to go with her to a dance lesson. "We get to dance with lots of different partners and meet a lot of friendly people from around Seattle."

He looked at her as if she were insane. "I realize I haven't seen you that much lately, but Carrie, I still need to use a cane. I'd look like a fool on the dancefloor trying to dance while using my cane."

"You could come one time and try."

"Forget it! I'd look like ridiculous. I don't think we're even friends anymore!" Freddie turned and stormed away, limping every step.

Carrie was confused and hurt. She knew that she and Freddie had been drifting apart for the last couple of years as their interests seemed to diverge, but Freddie had never turned his back on her like that. She thought she had done the right thing by inviting him to take part in an activity that she enjoyed. Obviously Freddie didn't think so. Conversations between them became few and far between after that.

***

Carrie was becoming quite skilled at swing dancing. Many of the dances started with instruction so she was continually learning new steps. As usual, there were more girls than guys in attendance, so the guys changed partners every dance. She had danced with a number of them when a particularly cute one with a pleasant smile asked her to dance.

As she whirled around the floor with him she thought that his voice, laughter, and facial expressions seemed familiar. She had a lot of questions she wanted to ask him, but as soon as the dance ended he thanked her and asked someone else to dance. Carrie noticed that he occasionally glanced at her while he danced with some of the other girls.

Carrie wondered if he recognized her too. She lost sight of him for a while then he suddenly appeared next to her with two cups of soda in his hands. He offered one to her.

"Thirsty?" he asked loudly over the sound of the band.

"Thank you," an immediately nervous Carrie said while trying to think of something to say.

"I know it sounds like a pickup line," he told her, "but you look familiar."

She giggled. "That's just a pickup line!"

While he laughed, she added, "I was thinking that you looked familiar as well. I'm Carrie."

"I'm Avram."

"I love swing dancing," Carrie told him. "Other than math it's my favorite thing to do."

"You should talk to my brother. He's a real math crazy. I'm a sophomore at Bellevue College. My folks sent me there until I figure out what I want to major in."

"I'm seventeen. I'm still in high school."

Carrie thought she saw disappointment on his face when she told him her age.

He turned and stared at the couples on the dancefloor.

She wanted to keep his attention and was wracking her brain trying to think of something to say. "I like the *mezuzah* you're wearing," she finally said.

His face lit up as he turned back to her. "Are you Jewish?" "Want me to recite the *Shema*?"

"How about another dance instead?"

"Sounds great."

He was a head taller than she was, with a slim dancer's body, which moved with smooth and fluid motions as he guided her around the dancefloor. His bright blue eyes seemed to laugh when he looked at her, which somehow made her feel good.

He also had a voice that, oddly enough, reminded her of Ryan Rifkin. That's when she remembered. She had met Avram at a double-wedding when Ryan married Lucinda and Ryan's middle- brother Benjamin married Karen. Avram, Ryan's youngest-brother, was just another face in the crowd that day.

"How are Benjamin and Karen?" she asked.

"You know my brother and his wife?"

"Lucinda's due to have her second baby this week, isn't she?" Avram stopped dancing and stared at her.

"Of course, you're Carrie—Carrie Levin. I met you at my brothers' weddings."

The rest of the dance, he mostly partnered with other girls, which was the right thing to do, but every third dance he managed to partner with Carrie.

At Lucinda's baby naming the following Sunday, for her newborn daughter, Shifra, Avram arrived and called to Carrie.

"Hey, dance partner!"

"Hi, Avram. This is my family."

"Hi, Mr. and Mrs. Levin, I think we met at my brothers' weddings. It's nice to see you again."

The Levins exchanged small talk with him for a while, until Carrie announced that David Linn just arrived. "Come on, let's say hi to my brother."

She turned around briefly to look at her parents, who were whispering to each other and grinning. She could only imagine what they were saying, but Carrie was sure it was about her and Avram.

***

With her parents' permission, Avram began driving Carrie to dances on a weekly basis. Just before the late "October Dance in the Sticks" in Maple Valley was to begin, Avram, Carrie, and Madi, the dance instructor, stopped for a coffee at City Perk in the same town. While they sipped their delicious drinks, Avram asked Carrie if she would like to attend a dance in Spokane the following Saturday.

"There are two other girls your age going along," Madi assured her, "and you'll all be driving and rooming with me."

"I'd have to miss a day of school. There's not much chance my folks would let me do that."

"I'm not driving out until one o'clock, so if you ride with me you'd only miss a half-day of school," Avram told her.

"I'll ask, but I doubt it. They're not going to let me travel halfway across the state with a college guy."

"I'll walk in with you when I take you home tonight. We can ask them together."

Carrie wasn't sure if that would help or hurt, but she agreed. "It's going to be a great dance on Friday night and then lessons all Saturday morning," Carrie said while pleading her case to her parents. "I'll be home by dinnertime Saturday."

"Spokane is a long way across the state," her mother said. "Who is going to drive you out there?"

"Avram will pick me up at school at one o'clock. That way I'd only miss a half-day of school. I'm going to be sharing a motel room with Madi, my dance instructor, and two other girls my age. I have her number so you can call and check with her. We have a half-day of lessons on Saturday morning and then Avram will drive me home."

"We'll also be stopping by a cabin near Lake Chelan on the drive home," Avram said. "My brother Ryan is giving me the keys to the cabin because he thinks it would be a great place to use for a base to go cross country skiing. We'd just be there for like ten- minutes so I can see the place, and then drive straight home."

Carrie knew her mother trusted her, but she looked unsure about trusting Avram, who she didn't know very well.

Avram must have noticed her look of concern too. "Mrs. Levin, if I did anything disrespectful toward Carrie, my brother Ryan would beat me to a pulp. And if Dad found out...don't ask. There's no way anything like that will happen."

"I'm sure you'll take good care of Carrie. I'm not worried," her father said. "I'll be there to sign Carrie out of school at one o'clock. You two will have a great time."

"Thanks, you guys," Carrie exclaimed as she hugged each of her parents.

Chapter Nineteen ~ Freddie and Dana

"AS I PROMISED YOU," Dana's father had said to her in late June, "here is the personal watercraft we promised if you got all A's in school during your junior year. We are most proud of your achievement."

Dana had been very excited. "Thanks, guys," she'd said as she ran her hand along the side of the shiny new boat.

"A man from the dealership will be over this afternoon to teach you how to run it safely and how to tow it. This is a fast watercraft so you need to use it carefully," her father had warned her.

Dana had been eager and had drifted off, already imagining high-speed dashes across Lake Washington.

Her father had placed his hand on her shoulder. "Dana, are you listening to me?"

"Oh...sure, Dad. A guy's coming to give me lessons."

After a long safety lecture, which Dana had barely listened to, the dealer's PWC expert had left Dana on her own.

Her first time out, she'd moved away from the dock, gradually squeezing the throttle. The little engine had growled as the hull of the boat resonated with a steady tattoo as the little craft had ripped its way across the surface of the lake.

Dana had had a great time. She'd leaned into shallow *S* turns while she'd felt a sense of pride well up inside her as she'd enjoyed the seemingly complete control of the little craft. She'd experienced a sense of freedom unlike any she'd had before, as she cruised around the lake.

"Who needs boys? I've got *speed*!" she'd yelled into the onrushing wind.

Now, on an inordinately warm late-fall day, seventeen-year-old Dana was on the personal watercraft as she had been most of the summer. It gave her mobility like nothing else in her life. The little two-seat machine could turn and stop on a dime. It accelerated quickly even with her substantial bulk—at four-feet-eleven-inches, she weighed well over one-hundred-seventy-pounds.

She had been overweight as long as she could remember. Physical education class was generally a humiliating and exhausting experience. She wore baggy clothing in a vain attempt to cover her massive body, but she loved food and especially sweets. Dana was uncomfortable at social gatherings as she was almost always the widest person in attendance.

Her parents had sent her to weight reduction camp many summers. "Other kids are sent to camp to have a good time but I get sent to the fat farm to have a good sweat," she always said.

She had a pleasant group of friends who thought of her as a loyal friend, but that group was shrinking as the girls started spending most of their time with their boyfriends.

Dana spotted Olivia's Otter on the lake and cruised over to say hi to Olivia and Freddie, who was in her senior class at school. As she pulled up alongside the sailboat, she greeted the two of them. Olivia was at the tiller and Freddie was tending the jib.

"Hey, you guys, that's a nice sailboat!"

"Thanks. If we have another warm day like this, you'll have to go sailing with us," Olivia said.

"Let's plan on that, but seeing as it's November there may not be too many nice days left."

Dana waved and roared off as her craft knifed its way across the water's surface.

Among other activities with her watercraft, wake-jumping was one of Dana's favorites. She had just lined up on the stern of a large yacht and was heading for the wake at high speed. Unfortunately, the large yacht obscured her view of the much smaller Olivia's Otter until her boat was in the air and was headed right for the area of the sailboat between Freddie and Olivia. Her boat came down crossing the rail of the Otter, shot under the boom, and into the water on the other side.

Dana tried to duck by dropping her head and turning it to the left. She saw a flash of light as the right side of her face crashed into the boom. As she was knocked off the watercraft, her knees slammed into the far rail, and she hit the water facedown twenty-feet from the sailboat. She struggled to get her face out of the water, as her life vest didn't help her remain faceup. Dana lifted her head and took a breath but also took in water as she felt things going hazy.

The side of her face was beginning to ache. Trying to yell for help, she found the right side of her jaw caused enormous pain when she tried to move it and the vision in her right eye was blurry. Her heart started pounding in her head as the realization came that she was severely injured and needed help.

She heard loud rapid splashing in the water behind her. Someone wrapped a large, muscular arm around her neck in proper water-rescue technique. Dana grabbed her rescuer's arm with both hands.

"I've got you, Dana. You're going to be all right."

That was the last thing Dana heard before her body went limp and she lost consciousness.

***

Once they had the lightly damaged Olivia's Otter tied up at the dock behind their house, eleven-year-old Olivia ran inside and found her parents, where she screamed, "My brother was the hero!"

"What happened?" Megan asked.

"Dana Jacobs, she's a friend of Freddie's from his class at school, she was on a personal watercraft kind of a boat and she jumped a wake, and her boat hit the Otter. It slid under the boom and flew into the water but her face hit smack into the boom. She landed face down in the water, hardly moving."

Olivia was gesturing wildly as she told the story. "Then Freddie threw a life ring over to her, but he had to dive into the water and swim over and grab her, to get her face out of the water. Then he started towing her toward our boat, which I had turned around to sail over to them."

"You handled your boat by yourself?"

It was a strict rule in the Lipinski home that Olivia couldn't go sailing by herself.

"Mom, it was this big huge emergency—and besides, I'm almost twelve. I couldn't wait for Freddie to come back to help me. After Freddie jumped off the boat and started swimming toward her, with a wake like a motorboat, I yelled, 'Coming About!' and started to reverse course. I released the jib and pulled it over to the other side. When I brought the Otter around, I guided it to bring it right alongside Freddie and Dana. I got next to them and let out the sails and helped Freddie get her onboard. She was out like a light, Mom, and she had blood all over her face, but Freddie and I ignored that and just did what we had to do, like you always tell us."

Olivia took a moment to catch her breath before continuing. "Then, I got out the first-aid kit and we put some bandages on her face to stop the bleeding. I mean her face was really tough to look at, but that didn't slow us down. A police boat with its engines roaring came over to us. Its siren was screaming, and it had big flashing lights, and everything. They put her on a stretcher and took her on their boat and zoomed away. Freddie told one of the policemen what happened. He said, 'Nice open-water rescue, hero,' to Freddie and, 'masterful boat handling, young sailor,' to me. Do you believe that? Nobody outside the family ever called me a sailor before."

Marvin looked at Freddie. "How bad was she hurt?"

"When she hit the boom with her face, it made an awful thud as it hit. I think her jaw was broken and most likely some of the bones in the right side of her face got crushed—I think her right ear got torn off."

"That's awful."

"You need to know," Freddie said proudly as he smiled at his sister, "Olivia looked like she'd spent her whole life sailing, as she got her sailboat turned around and brought it up right next to us. I was exhausted by the time I got to Dana, but within a short time, Olivia was right next to us and helping me get her on board. My sister is a first-class sailor."

Olivia smiled and looked at Megan, who said, "You're a hero as well, young lady."

"Really?"

"Who singlehanded the sailboat and brought it over to Dana and Freddie? Who helped get her on board and who helped Freddie with the first-aid?"

"I did all that stuff."

"Then you're a hero just like your brother."

"Wow," Olivia said with wonder and pride.

Megan smiled at Marvin. "Great children, sir."

Marvin smiled. "Don't you dare blame me, Megan. I am not the one who taught them first-aid and I didn't teach Olivia how to sail."

"You did that, Mom," Olivia said proudly. "All the stuff we do together just saved someone's life."

Megan smiled at them. "I'll accept that I taught you, but you two did it. I wasn't on the water today. You were. I couldn't be more proud of you. Freddie, please call Mr. Kaplan and tell him what his swimming lessons helped you accomplish today."

Then, they went out to lunch at the kids' favorite restaurant to celebrate the rescue.

Olivia said to Megan, "See all the happiness you brought to our house? I bet the family at Dana's house is happy as well, because we saved Dana with the stuff you taught us. Freddie was right. Mommy

Elisabeth sent you to us because you have so much love to give, you teach us so much stuff, and you make us all so happy."

***

The next day, Dana Jacobs' parents visited their home to give their thanks for being there to save Dana.

"We wanted you to know that she's going to be okay," her father said. "But she would have drowned when she lost consciousness if Freddie and Olivia hadn't gotten to her as quickly as they did. We can't thank them enough for what they did for our daughter."

Freddie shrugged. "We used what other people taught us. It was the right thing to do. But you're welcome, Mr. and Mrs. Jacobs."

"My mom made sure we were ready for an emergency," Olivia added with a big smile.

"We understand that your boat was damaged. We'd like to pay for the repair."

"It's a rugged boat," Marvin said. "It was designed before there was a complete understanding of fiberglass's strength, so they used more fiberglass than we would use today. There's not that much damage, so I'll be repairing it myself."

Olivia cleared her throat and Marvin smiled at her.

"I mean, Olivia and I will be repairing it ourselves. I'm going over to the marine supply store. How about if I let you know what the materials cost."

"That's the least I can do." Mr. Jacobs stood and shook Marvin's hand.

Olivia went to her room to read and Freddie approached his father. "I'm still sad my relationship with Carrie ended," Freddie told his dad. "I haven't found another girl I like."

Marvin smiled and patted his son on the back. "I'd love to help you, but talk to your mom. I'm not good at explaining this kind of thing."

Megan was pleased anew every time she heard Marvin refer to her as the kids' mom.

Freddie turned to Megan. "I still feel angry that I've lost a friend," he told her.

She wrapped her arm around his shoulder and brought him nearer. "What makes you think you've lost a friend?"

"She seems to be busy with her dancing and learning languages. I have no ability in either of those. Our interests just seem to be going in different directions."

"Sometimes people grow in different directions. It's part of life. You had a good time getting to know Carrie and learning how to get along with a girl. Maybe that will help you in your next relationship."

"Shouldn't I do something to keep us together?"

"Freddie, do you know what *Basher*t means?"

"I think I have an idea. It's kind of a legend that a person's partner is declared before they're born and we're supposed to spend our lives looking for that person. That's how I thought Carrie and I were. You know, like a real together-couple. The more I think about it, I realize I'm really getting angry about this. We spent a lot of time together and did so many things together."

"Becoming angry won't accomplish anything. Believe me I know. I nearly destroyed my life with anger at someone I thought was my *Bashert*. Consider for a moment—if you and Carrie are growing apart, is it fair of you to try pushing a relationship that won't work?

"I guess not."

"And anger won't help that situation. Try to remember the good times you had, and move on. As close as you two were, there's no reason that you can't remain friends."

Megan paused for a moment then changed the subject.

"I talked to Dana Jacobs' mom. She tells me that Dana is, as you can imagine, depressed. She has some horrid scars on her face. Why don't you see if you can visit her? Maybe you can cheer her up a bit."

"What can you do for someone who is disfigured like she is?"

"Do you know Meyer and Joan Minkowski?"

"Sure. I met them at Jonah and Holly's home over the summer."

"When Joan was in her twenties she had cancer, which resulted in some awful scarring after her surgery. She says that when she showed the scar to Meyer, he just kissed her there and told her, 'Joan, you still look great to me.' She still gets tears in her eyes when she retells that story. Maybe you could think of something to say to Dana if her scars become a topic of conversation."

"I don't have a clue of what I would say," Freddie shrugged, "but I'll think about it."

"And be sure to think about our conversation concerning you and Carrie. Be happy with the memories you have. If you want to talk about it some more, I'll absolutely make time for us. Also note that Dana could be harboring a lot of anger concerning her appearance."

Freddie decided to go spend some time thinking about what he could say to Dana.

Marvin smiled at Megan and told her what a great job she did talking with Freddie.

***

Avram and Carrie were ready to travel to Spokane for the dance.

When his brother, Ryan, heard about the trip, he'd insisted that his younger brother take his Infiniti Q SUV for their drive across the state.

Avram had complained, "I appreciate the offer, but it's a four-hour highway drive to Spokane. The Q has those huge knobby mud-and-snow tires you had mounted on it. They make a lot of noise on the highway."

"Okay, so those tires are simply one more reason to keep your speed down to a reasonable level. Besides, there's a snowstorm coming Saturday night, so you might need them when you're driving back over the Cascades. I left directions and a set of keys to the Minkowskis' cabin in the glove compartment of the Q. Like I said, consider it for a base for cross country skiing this winter."

Avram's little economy sedan had good fuel mileage but had a harsh ride to accompany its raucous engine noise, and it was hopeless in snowy conditions. At least with the Q, they would have a much more pleasant ride and serious winter capability if needed.

"You take good care of Carrie," Ryan said as he slapped his brother on the back. "She's one of my favorite people."

Looking at the azure-blue sky that lovely late fall day, Avram grinned at Ryan. "Believe me, with everyone warning me how I better take good care of her, I'm beginning to think taking care of Carrie will be the most difficult part of this weekend."

The brothers laughed.

As he said good-bye to Ryan, Lucinda came out onto the driveway. "One more thing, Avram."

"I know, I know. I promise I'll take good care of Carrie!" he said in a laughter-filled voice while he climbed into the Q.

"How did he know what I was going to say?" Lucinda asked Ryan.

***

"Nice wheels," Carrie said as she climbed into the Q after her father wished the two of them a safe journey. She was so excited thinking about their trip—she had hardly heard her instructors that morning.

"Ryan insisted I take this monster instead of my little car. It's got every option you can buy on it. This is mostly Lucinda's car. If he could have, I think Ryan would have mounted a radar set and a radar-controlled rocket-launcher on the roof to keep other cars from getting too close to her."

Carrie laughed. "They're an amazing couple."

"I agree completely—but why do you think that's the case."

"I think it's the way they take care of each other," Carrie said after a lot of thought.

"Most perceptive, Miss Levin. I couldn't agree more. They are such a together-couple. You would think those two were designed for each other. It is odd though, because he's this genius math guy and she's a botanist."

"I've never seen or heard of that getting in their way."

"I admire people, like my brother, who have a sense of direction. I really don't have a clue what I'd like to do for a living."

"What do you enjoy doing?"

He shrugged. "Solving problems. That's why I enjoy taking engineering classes...but I can't see doing that for a living."

"My whole life I've loved math. I can see myself spending a lifetime doing research in advanced areas of mathematics."

They both got quiet for a few minutes, then Carrie spoke up. "I've noticed some guys don't like to date a girl who they think is smarter than they are," Carrie asked nervously.

"It depends."

"On what?"

"On whether or not she is a Jewish swing dancer."

Carrie's heart skipped a beat. "Avram, are you teasing me?" "We've had lots of fun times dancing together. Now we're on a trip together. If we still enjoy each other's company after this weekend, we should talk about becoming more than swing dance partners...if you'd like to."

Carrie was silent but when Avram turned towards her she smiled and nodded.

***

When they arrived at their motel, Carrie was surprised at how much cooler it was in Spokane. She shivered, wishing she'd worn a warmer jacket.

Madi, Avram, Carrie, and a young Jewish couple from Spokane lit *Shabbat* candles.

"Good *Shabbos*, Avram," Carrie said as she hugged him.

"Good *Shabbos*, Carrie," he replied as he wrapped his arms around her.

They had a thimbleful of wine after Avram sang the *Kiddush* prayer, and everyone shared a lovely homemade *challah* that had been baked that day. The young couple insisted that they sing *Shehechianu*, as this was Avram and Carrie's first *Shabbat* in Spokane.

Swing dancers of all ages, from all parts of Washington, northern Idaho, and western Montana drove in to participate. There was a good balance of guys and girls. Carrie danced with many partners of varying skill levels but mostly danced with Avram. They were getting to know each other's style and timing. This made their dancing have a smooth and accomplished look. By the time the dance ended at midnight, they were both worn out.

Lessons the following morning were on the complex side, which would necessitate lots of practice to perfect.

"Some of those steps seemed so complicated, I felt like I needed extra feet," Carrie said.

Avram laughed.

"It would be a shame to forget what we learned today," she told him. Much to Carrie's delight, he said, "You're right! Besides going to dances, we may have to establish a weekly practice session."

***

Following Ryan's suggestion, on their return drive after lunch on Saturday, Avram took a beautiful route, following highway WA2 from Spokane to Chelan. They hadn't seen this part of Washington State and enjoyed the many gorgeous vistas the route provided.

The cabin had some history in the Minkowski family, Avram told her, where some members of that family had become engaged.

Many friends and relatives had visited over the years and even driven their RVs up there for family gatherings. It was located high in the mountains north of beautiful Lake Chelan in north central Washington State. As they drove into Chelan, a dusting of snow was on the ground and more snow began to fall.

While Carrie leaned back and relaxed, Avram drove them up a winding road that led into the mountains, and then finally turned into the one-hundred-yard-long, curving gravel-covered driveway, coming to a stop near the front of the cabin.

As they climbed the ten stairs leading to the deck in front of the cabin, a disappointed Avram eyed the cabin. "From all the stories I had heard about this place, I assumed it was some kind of gorgeous Alpine chalet. Not an old A-frame-style log cabin."

They entered and wandered around. A two-story-tall window-wall at the front of the cabin looked out over the deck and flooded the interior with light. The window-wall was separated by a two- story-tall stone fireplace. Two bedrooms on a second level at the back of the cabin were above the kitchen and eating area. The back of the cabin was nestled into a gently sloping hill.

"I don't know why people would get excited about this old place. It seems cold and lonely perched way up here on the mountain."

"I don't know either," Avram said. "It's not much to see. Let's get back on the road."

"Maybe if it wasn't a cloudy, gray day with an overcast sky, we would see a nice view," Carrie said.

As they returned to the Q, Carrie noticed that the weather had gotten still colder and she again wished she had a warmer jacket. She wrapped her arms around herself as she settled into her seat.

Once they returned to Chelan, Avram topped off the Q with gas for the return trip.

On leaving town, they found the highway blocked by a state patrol car. A patrolman asked where they were headed.

"We're heading back to Seattle," Avram told him.

"Not today you're not. All the passes between here and Seattle are shut down. See the heavy black clouds to the west?" The patrolman pointed to the sky. "That is the leading edge of a heavy snowstorm. The passes in the Cascades are already blocked with a huge amount of snow and the storm is heading this way. I heard one report that it may be more than a day until they can clear all the snow off the passes from this storm. If you need a place to stay, the high school gym is open for folks who are stranded."

As Avram turned the Q around to head back to town, Carrie turned to him with a thought. "Why don't we buy some supplies and plan on staying overnight in the cabin. I remember seeing a lot of wood stacked next to the fireplace, so we'll stay warm."

Avram was quiet.

"Avram, it would be a good chance to see if we can enjoy spending time together, even if we're not dancing."

"Okay, but if we have problems it's down to the high school."

"I agree. I better call my folks," Carrie said excitedly.

When her mother answered the phone, Carrie told her what the situation was. "We're in Chelan, Mom. The highways back to Seattle are blocked, so we're staying at a cabin in the mountains above town. It belongs to Meyer and Joan Minkowski."

"Carrie Levin, you be careful."

"I will, Mom. Will you please call Avram's family and let them know we won't be home until tomorrow."

Her mother agreed and then Carrie said good-bye, and she and Avram stopped at a grocery store in town.

"I don't have much money left," Avram said.

"I've got some. We should be okay. I know just what we'll need to stay overnight. We'll be just fine."

Avram seemed pleasantly surprised by her enthusiasm to begin their little overnight adventure. He also appeared quite entertained by the way Carrie knew exactly what she wanted in the way of groceries. Into their shopping cart went milk, sugar, eggs, baking powder, wheat flour, oatmeal, cornmeal, cooking oil, butter, blueberry jam, apples, orange juice, dried apricots, and dried blueberries. In addition she added one number-ten-can of freeze-dried vegetable stew with beef and a same size can of freeze-dried seafood chowder.

"Whatever we don't eat we can take home," Carrie said.

As they climbed back into the Q, it was obvious the temperature was still dropping. Carrie shivered as she saw that the dark clouds, which had previously looked distant, were nearly on top of them.

"I wish I had some warmer clothes," Carrie complained. "Me too," said a shivering Avram.

Light snow continued falling as they left town. By the time they were on the gravel road that led the last couple of miles to the cabin, the Q was crunching its way through six-inches of new snow. Avram parked it as close to the cabin as practical.

As they took their supplies into the cabin the snow had changed from small flakes to large, fluffy flakes the size of cotton balls and the air had a bitterly cold bite.

"Boy it's cold in here," Carrie said. "I can see my breath. We need to get a fire started."

After placing logs on the grate, Avram used the fire starter and matches located next to the fireplace to get a roaring fire started.

They turned on some of the cabin's lights. It was getting darker by the minute as the black clouds covered the sky and the wind began to howl.

"We'll be okay until tomorrow," Avram insisted.

As if to contradict him the electricity went out, and Carrie experienced her first pang of fear.

***

It had been a few weeks since the accident, and Freddie decided to visit Dana in the hospital. He stopped at the front desk to get a pass to visit Dana's room.

"I'm sorry young man but only family are allowed to visit."

Freddie was about to protest when he heard a commotion behind him. An employee in a white lab coat was being escorted out of the hospital by two large security guards.

"You assholes can have this shit job," he yelled as he took off his coat and flung it across the room.

It landed near Freddie's feet. He looked around and the nurse had her gaze firmly fixed on the commotion, so he bent over to pick up the jacket and saw that it still had a badge attached.

He checked around again and it seemed that everyone was staring at the man who was still swearing as he was being wrestled out the front door.

Freddie quickly tucked the jacket underneath his arm and ducked around a corner where he donned it. Then he sucked in a breath and headed for the elevators. There was a security guard there. Each person was showing him their pass as he let them on the elevator. Freddie calmly flashed his badge and offered a smile, directing the guard's attention to the front desk. "Crazy that," Freddie said.

The guard chuckled and agreed, letting Freddie on the next elevator without a second glance.

When Freddie started down the hall to Dana's room, he took off the jacket and stuffed it in a laundry cart.

As he approached her room, he heard her screaming. "Get out of here. I hate how you're looking at me."

Dana's mother was in tears and being supported by Dana's father as they left their daughter's room.

"I don't think she wants to see anyone, Freddie. Thank you for coming to visit," her father said as he guided his wife down the hallway to a visitor's sitting area.

Freddie walked into Dana's hospital room anyway.

Dana's tear-streaked cheeks indicated she had been crying for some time.

"What are you doing here? Have you come to have a pity party because I'm so messed up?"

She seemed really angry, but Freddie remembered what Megan had said to him. He took a deep breath. "I came because I wanted to see how you were doing."

"Well, I have ugly scars across my face and neck, my legs are screwed up, my whole face is twisted, and my right ear is gone. Oh, and I'm still a fat slob—how do you think I'm doing?"

He sat on the edge of her bed. "Look, Dana, we've known each other since kindergarten. We've always been nice to each other— except that time when I dropped a slice of cake on your dress in third-grade. I remember you trying to slug me, but I ducked and you hit Carey Mason right in the nose."

A tiny smile formed on Dana's lips. "I remember that day. She had it coming. Mason was mean to everyone. I did feel guilty afterwards, though."

"Because you are a good person, Dana. And you've always been pleasant to everyone as long as I've known you."

"So why did this happen?" She gestured angrily to her face.

Freddie looked at his shoes for a moment, thinking. "I don't have an answer for your question, but I think you still look nice to me."

She lifted her hair to expose the ugly red scar tissue where her right ear had been torn off. "I was never pretty—and now I'm hideous."

"You don't look hideous to me, Dana." He leaned forward and kissed her scarred cheek.

Dana's face showed anger just before a high-pitched clap echoed in the room as she slapped him.

Freddie rubbed his cheek then spoke in calm measured tones. "If you need to slap me to feel better, then it is okay with me, because I'm your friend."

Dana stared at Freddie's cheek. She put both of her hands up to cover her face and started crying.

Freddie let her cry for a while and then he pulled one of her hands off her face and held it in both of his. "When you get out of here, maybe we can go dancing. Carrie Levin told me she's having a lot of fun with that."

"Freddie," Dana said, her voice subdued and cracking, "I'm going to be on crutches for a long time until my knees are healed. If you want to dance, you need a different partner."

"I was on crutches for a long time, and when I was, there was this girl in my class who held doors for me and sometimes carried my books too."

"Lots of people helped you."

"Until I met Carrie, you helped more than anyone else. I remember that."

"Being on crutches, I won't be able to do much of anything for a long time."

"One time, back when I was on crutches, I told Carrie that I couldn't do anything to help her, even if she did something as simple as dropping her books. She said I could at least fall on them so no one could steal them."

A smile came back to Dana's lips and then she began laughing hysterically as if she was envisioning Freddie diving onto Carrie's books. "Carrie's a riot. How's your sailboat?" she asked.

"Olivia's Otter is fine. My dad called some people who own the same boat and it was an easy repair. I still owe you a ride on that sailboat."

"I don't think people on crutches belong on sailboats."

"When Mr. Kaplan started teaching me how to handle a sailboat, I was still on crutches."

"You're kidding! Really?"

"For sure I was. Sailing is rad to the extreme—just the sailboat, the wind and the water. There is this—I'm not sure what to call it—this calm kind of feeling you get as the wind catches the sails and they pull you across the water. Mom says that sailing can be mesmerizing. You combine your sailing skill with the wind and water to create motion. When I'm all crazy from school, a few minutes of sailing assists me in getting rid of my crazies."

"I could certainly use some calm after all this crap."

"As soon as you get out, call me. Olivia loves having people on her boat that are new to sailing. She actually keeps track of people who get introduced to sailing on her boat. She has them sign a square of cloth that she and Mom are going to make into a quilt."

"That's a cool thing to do. I see you're not using a cane anymore."

"My knee and hip are getting better. I still can't run but most of the pain is gone."

"I can't wait for all this mess to heal,." she said as she waved a hand at her injured body.

"So what else do you like to do? I mean, besides spearing sailboats with a jet ski?"

Dana's laughter echoed through the room again. "You sir, are indeed strange. No wonder you need to go sailing to get rid of your crazies."

"So, you're starting to understand me."

She laughed again. "I like poetry and especially Emily Dickinson."

Freddie thought for a moment. "In one of her letters, didn't she describe herself with the words, 'I am small, like the wren; and my hair is bold, like the chestnut burr; and my eyes, like the sherry in the glass that the guest leaves'?"

Dana's face brightened as she heard him recite the lines.

"I read some of her poetry when I was recuperating from my surgery," Freddie continued. "Her history is almost as interesting as her poetry."

"Maybe we could try writing some poetry together," Dana said. "Although I don't think I'd know how to begin."

"We could start with something familiar and silly. How about a poem with the first stanza of; My jet ski jumped the other day, but Olivia's Otter was in the way…"

Dana giggled. "I have learned, to my disdain, that spearing sailboats can cause great pain."

"That's a great stanza, Dana!"

They laughed together and high-fived.

"I'll be leaving here in three-days. I'd appreciate if you had time to visit again. It's nice to see a happy face. My family tries to be upbeat around me, but their attempts to cheer me up are failing miserably."

"Tomorrow's Sunday so I'll be here when visiting hours start. I'll bring a book of Emily Dickenson's poetry that we can use for some dramatic reading if you like. I have to leave for home now."

"Are you and Carrie still a couple?"

"Not anymore. We haven't been for a few years. We're still friends but our lives went in different directions. That happens sometimes. I was pretty angry at first but my mom explained it's part of life sometimes, and we have to move on without being angry about stuff like that, or it can become overwhelming."

"Your mom sounds pretty cool."

"Dana, you have no idea how cool she is. Olivia says she defines cool."

"Thanks for stopping by to see me today, Freddie. I'm sorry I slapped you."

"Forget about it. I think I was still fuzzy from having droning Mrs. Julienne for English last period yesterday. You probably helped me clear my head after her boring class."

Dana giggled. "I'll be looking forward to seeing you tomorrow."

Freddie waved as he left the room but he ran smack-dab into a nurse.

"Only family is allowed to visit," she told him.

Lucky for Freddie, Dana's parents were just on their way back in. "He's family," he quickly told the nurse. "And he's welcome anytime."

He winked at Freddie.

The nurse nodded. "I'll let them know at the front desk." She went into Dana's room.

"Thanks for doing that, Mr. Jacobs."

"Thanks for visiting her, Freddie. We were outside—we haven't heard her laugh since the accident."

He shook hands with Dana's dad and her mom gave him an embarrassingly long hug.

***

"Let's look for candles and flashlights," Carrie suggested after the electricity went out.

After some searching, Avram found a couple of flashlights and a box of candles, but they were Sabbath candles.

"These are expensive," Carrie said. "Do you think it's okay to use them?"

"This is an emergency. So, yes, I think it's okay."

"We have a problem. The water pump is run by electricity. We're going to have to melt snow to have water. Does the stove work?" Carrie asked.

"Oh no! I hadn't thought of that," Avram said as he hurried into the kitchen. He turned on one burner but couldn't hear any gas coming out. He looked behind the stove and opened the valve for the gas. Within seconds he had the burners going.

"I'm going outside to check the tank and see how much gas there is."

Carrie got dinner started. She took the largest soup pan she could find, filled it with clean-looking snow, and placed it on the stove. While the snow was melting she got out the flour and made dumplings to cook on top of the stew. She took some of the melted snow and put it in a pitcher, crushing a large handful of blueberries into it.

"This won't be much of a meal without a dessert," she told herself. She looked around the cabin and found a cupboard with spices and flavoring.

"What luck!" she exclaimed as she removed a container of vanilla extract. "Now we'll have cookies for dessert."

In a bowl, she used a wooden spoon to mix butter with sugar and flour then began beating them until they were smooth. Much to her surprise, her arm was getting sore from the amount of work the mixing took without the help of an electric mixer. She added an egg and other dry ingredients, and beat them into the mixture as well as her sore arm would allow.

Avram came back into the cabin. "We've got plenty of gas for the stove. What can I do to help?"

"We need more snow brought in for water. It might be a good idea to melt some of the snow in front of the fireplace to utilize the heat from the fire as well."

"On the way," he declared as he grabbed more pans from the kitchen and headed outside to collect snow to melt.

Carrie rolled the cookie dough into a quarter-inch sheet, cut out squares, sprinkled them with sugar, and placed them on a baking sheet. After some fiddling with a match, she managed to light the burner in the oven and in went the cookies.

She found a pan with a tight-fitting lid, placed a measure of the freeze-dried stew in the pan along with water. She tasted it and added a pinch of powdered garlic, powdered onion, and three- dashes of Tabasco sauce. When the stew was getting warm, she added some extra water, and once the mixture was hot, placed the dumplings on top. She closed the lid and checked her watch.

"It smells great in here," Avram called from the living room.

"Dinner in twenty-minutes," a proud Carrie called out.

She set the table and walked over to the front-window-wall of the cabin. "I can barely see past the deck," she said.

He gazed out the window too. "There's at least a-foot-of-snow on the ground and it's still coming down. I sure hope it doesn't keep accumulating like this all night, or it's going to be a nightmare trying to get out of here tomorrow."

"Well, let's just worry about dinner for now." Carrie directed his attention toward the table.

"Carrie, this is lovely. Are there blueberries in the pitcher?"

"It's blueberry water. Try it. The blueberries are so sweet, I didn't add any sugar."

Avram tried the stew and sipped the water. "I can't believe you did all this with the simple ingredients we bought."

"My mom is a great cook and a great teacher."

Halfway through the meal, Carrie put a kettle of water on a burner. As soon as the water was boiling she took a few foil-wrapped tea bags out of the cupboards. When the stew was gone, she served the tea with the freshly-out-of-the-oven sugar cookies.

"I know we're just dance partners, but that was an amazing meal. Can I give you a hug?"

Carrie looked down, but nodded her assent. Avram walked around the table and briefly embraced her. She enjoyed having his arms around her, even for a brief moment.

He stepped away from her. "Thanks for such a rich meal. I'll do the cleanup."

"I'd rather we do it together."

Avram shrugged. "Fine with me."

They quickly washed, dried, and put things away, then they sat on the couch and read by candlelight. They had each found books on the shelves in the back of the cabin. With each of them covered by their own large wool blanket, they were cozy and warm even as the storm raged outside.

"Do we have enough water to flush the toilet?" Carrie asked about the single first-floor bathroom.

"We do and I've got a few buckets of water in there already. I've left the top off the toilet tank so it will be easy to refill. If you want, just tell me, and I'll refill it for you."

"Thanks Avram. You've turned this pile of logs into a functioning house."

"I just turned the gas on and brought in water, plus logs. You cooked that amazing meal, so I'd say we turned this place into a functioning house."

They read for a few more hours, until Carrie announced that she was getting sleepy.

"I checked the bedrooms and each one has a down comforter on a feather mattress, so we should be warm tonight. We should sleep in our clothes just for the extra warmth," Avram suggested. "Also, we can take some extra blankets up with us just in case we need them."

The wind howled and rattled the windows as the snow began pelting against them with such force it sounded like sand hitting them.

The noise caused Carrie to shiver as she felt a second-pang-of-fear. "I hope this place can withstand this storm."

Avram tried to cheer her up. "I'm sure it must have been designed for this area and this kind of weather."

As if the cabin were disagreeing with him, a groan emanated from the rafters as the wind load on the cabin rose and fell.

Avram looked up. "I think we should go to our bedrooms."

They went to the bedrooms, said goodnight, and engaged in another brief hug.

Carrie remained dressed as she climbed into bed and slid under the down comforter. Within a few minutes she was warm and drifting off to sleep, but every time she seemed to be nodding off, the wind would pick up, rattle the windows, and cause the structure of the house to groan again. She shivered in fright as she began to imagine the windows in her room breaking, or the roof opening up, causing her bedroom to be filled with snow. One combination of loud noises occurred so suddenly, they caused her to jump with enough force that her bed moved.

Carrie wrapped herself in the down comforter and quietly entered the other bedroom. "Avram," she whispered. "Are you awake?"

"What's wrong, Carrie?" He turned on a small lantern.

"Do you have your clothes on?"

"Yeah, why do you ask?"

"I'm not scared or anything, but I'm cold...so I think maybe we should share the same bed so we can double up our blankets and be warmer."

He got very quiet again and didn't reply.

"It's okay, Avram. We've got our clothes on. Sometimes you hold me against you when we're dancing, right? So this is okay. We'll just pretend we're dancing."

The house groaned again and Carrie jumped. She was sure that Avram saw her quake with fear at the sound, because he lifted the blankets next to him, inviting her in.

She placed her quilt on the bed and crawled in. As she lay down, he had her lay on her left side, facing away from him. She snuggled her back against his chest as Avram turned off the lantern and pulled blankets over the two of them, then bent his legs until the tops of his thighs were against the backs of hers. He kept his right arm along his side until Carrie reached back and grabbed it, pulling it around her mid-section.

She intertwined her fingers in his and squeezed her arm on top of his, pulling his arm tight around her, in the process realizing that when Freddie had held her it didn't generate anywhere near as warm a feeling as when Avram did. And not just warmth either. She felt her mind, as well as her body, relax as Avram held her. Logically, she knew she was in as much danger in this bedroom as she was in the first, but the storm could rage all it wanted and the cabin could shake, rattle, and groan all it wanted, because Avram was wrapped around her. Carrie felt safe and secure and didn't care why.

She remembered stories of how her mother, Anna, felt the first time her father, Michael, had held her. Now she was sure she was experiencing the same feeling for herself. She wondered if she should tell Avram how wonderful it felt, but she was afraid he would just think she felt that way because she was a young girl.

With Avram's warmth surrounding her and his arm reassuringly holding her, Carrie quickly fell asleep.

At three o'clock in the morning, Carrie heard the alarm on Avram's watch.

"I'm going down to put more logs on the fire, Carrie."

***

When Avram woke up the next morning, he was on his back with Carrie lying across his body. Her head was on his chest and she had one arm and one leg on top of him. Avram thought he should move but then realized there might never be another chance in his life to have this kind, precious, and pretty girl holding him.

He realized some mighty lucky guy was going to marry her and be the one who would get to hold her for the rest of his life. Due to their age difference, he didn't consider that he might be that lucky guy.

He closed his eyes, listened to her breathing, and luxuriated in the sensation of her warmth as he fell asleep again.

When he awoke the next time, they were in the same position but Carrie was awake. The moment she saw him open his eyes, she quickly moved to kiss his lips. After a minute of receiving a kiss that seemed to bury itself in his soul, Avram pulled away from her.

"Good morning, Carrie," Avram said. "I don't think it's a good idea to keep doing that."

"I know. But I was thinking, what the hell, it might be a long time before I have another chance to kiss a guy like that."

Avram smiled at her playfulness and radiant expression. "Besides," she continued, "you're never going to do anything to hurt me. I know that."

"How do you know that?"

Carrie thought for a moment. "I don't know. I just do—and that makes me feel good."

They started preparing breakfast. "Thank you for holding me last night," Carrie quietly told him.

"Anytime. I enjoyed it as well."

"Remember that—you said anytime, mister."

"It will be tough, but I'll try to remember."

At Carrie's direction, Avram helped her prepare biscuits, scrambled eggs, and blueberry pancakes. This was served with tea, butter, and blueberry jam.

Avram thoroughly enjoyed the flaky biscuits and rich blueberry pancakes. Then they cleaned and stored the breakfast pans and dishes.

While they were looking out the front window, Carrie wrapped her arms around him. He held her gently, thinking that it was crazy that it felt so good just to hold her. He'd had girlfriends before and even had sex with one of them. But Carrie had carved out a place in his heart and firmly wrapped herself around his soul. He was concerned that, as young as she was, she might not feel the same way.

"Can you see the Q?" she asked.

"Vaguely," he replied. "I think it's buried in snow halfway up the doors."

"It's getting colder in here," Carrie said. "We need to do something about that."

"We may have to walk around wrapped in blankets. I didn't even bring a hat."

"Hey look at that," Carrie said.

She let go of him and walked over to an old treadle powered antique sewing machine.

"It's just a decoration. There's not even a lever to transfer the motion from the treadle to the flywheel—and no needles."

"It's useless then."

For the first time in his life, outside of school, Avram started thinking like an engineer. "Wait a minute. This is just an engineering problem." He examined the machine, opening a small drawer in the center. "Look, it still has a couple of bobbins and needles."

Inspired, Avram then searched the cabin and the large shed outside.

When he returned, he was shivering and his light jacket and pants were wet. He placed his jacket on a chair in front of the fire to dry it. He proudly showed Carrie the arm he made from metal he found in the shed. He quickly attached it to the treadle and flywheel of the old sewing machine.

While he was working on the machine, he saw that a name had been carved into the side cabinet. "Hey, this must be a good luck sign. The name Sarah Levin and the year eighteen-seventy-five are carved into it."

"If it was made for a Levin, then it must still work!" Carrie said enthusiastically. "But the only material to make something warm out of would be these wool blankets, and we certainly don't have any thread." Carrie stated as she looked around the cabin.

"We'll search for thread," Avram said. "Let's choose a wool blanket to cut up for a jacket and hat."

They searched the cabin. "We're going to catch hell for this," he said.

Carrie shrugged. "It beats freezing to death."

He watched as she picked out two identical blankets.

"Carrie, there is no way are we going to cutup those beautiful, Pendleton Yellowstone blankets."

"They are warm as can be, and the bright yellow color will make it easy to find our bodies if the cabin collapses on us from the weight of the snow."

"Not funny. Besides, we still don't have any thread."

"We're going to take the covers off some of the sofa cushions and pull the threads out of the seams. We can also pull the thread from the binding of the blanket. You'll use your Swiss pocket knife and I'll use a nail file."

"Carrie, you are a genius—a destructive genius, but certainly a genius."

It took many hours of tedious work to pull the thread that they needed.

"The first jacket and hat are yours, Carrie."

Carrie did some measuring and cut out a large rectangle. She cut a hole in the middle, put the rectangle over her head, and had Avram mark her sleeve length and circumference.

"I remember seeing my grandmother sew things," Carrie said. "She kind of made them inside out."

She cut a small rectangle of material from the blanket, plus an oval piece. These were sewn together to make a bright yellow hat which she immediately put on her head. It took her a bit of practice to get used to keeping her feet moving while she guided the cloth but the old sewing machine, with Avram's repair, was still ready to work.

After a while the material seemed to move easily and quickly through the machine creating lovely, evenly spaced stitches.

"It's so easy now, it's almost like the machine is assisting me," Carrie reported. "I'm getting a real sense of accomplishment as I do this."

Avram watched as Carrie's hands quickly and skillfully guided the material and then flew around the machine to get it positioned to start another row of stitches. She looked like she had been using the machine for many years.

"Maybe the spirit of Sarah Levin is helping you."

"I don't know," Carrie replied. "It feels as if I've been doing this for years."

Within a couple of hours they were adorned in their new bright yellow jackets and hats.

"Just in time," Carrie stated as the temperature in the cabin was dropping again.

Then they prepared a lunch with the savory seafood chowder.

Avram asked Carrie for one of the leftover biscuits to use as a base for the chowder. Carrie proudly gave him one which he split and then spooned chowder on top.

"If the snow doesn't stop falling," Avram said, "we may have to stay another night."

"My folks will be worried. I don't have cell service up here."

After lunch they wore their new clothing while they trekked through the gusting winds and blowing snow out to the old shed to see what else they could find that might help them. They discovered shovels and inspected a slightly used 900 series CAT bulldozer equipped with a bucket loader, but lacking an enclosed cab.

"If we can get this thing started, we can clear the driveway and get the Q out of its snowy cocoon," Avram said. "I'll check the fluid levels just in case."

They found a manual on the seat of the dozer.

"I better take this in the cabin and read through it if we're going to have any chance of starting and running it."

They examined the CAT but discovered that its battery was flat. They did find an old trickle charger.

"If the electricity comes back on we can try charging the battery," Carrie suggested.

They trudged back to the cabin through the still falling and blowing snow. It was only fifty-yards from the shed to the cabin, but each step through the three-plus-feet of snow punished and tired their legs.

Once inside, they brushed the snow off their new jackets and hats, placing them on chairs to dry near the fire.

They pulled a couple blankets over themselves, sat on the couch, and began reading. Avram began studying the bulldozer's manual. After a while he saw that Carrie kept glancing at him. "Can I help you?"

"Actually, yes you can, but I'm worried that what I want to do is something you'll think only a little girl would want to do, and I don't want you to think of me like that."

"When I was wrapped around you last night, I didn't feel like I was wrapped around a little girl. I'm not that much older than you. I've been thinking about our age difference. My parents have more years between them than you and I do. We have to be honest with each other. If you want to do something that I think is childish, I'll tell you. And if I do something that makes you uncomfortable or seems childish you have to tell me. You are more grown up than you realize."

"You think so?"

"Absolutely! I've loved every moment that we've been together this weekend. So tell me please, what would you like to do?"

"While we're reading, I want to sit in a way that we're touching."

Avram threw his blankets aside. She did the same and moved to sit on the end of the couch leaning her back against the arm rest. She placed her legs over Avram's thighs so they were touching.

"We can even share the same blanket now," she said.

Avram pulled a blanket over them. "Is that better?"

Carrie didn't say anything but just looked at him with a shy smile.

"I'm amazed how natural it feels to do things with you," he said.

Avram put his hand behind her neck, leaned toward her and softly kissed her lips—twice gently, and then a long, long kiss.

She brought her hand to the back of his neck to hold his face against hers. "Thank you, Avram. I love doing things with you. It makes me feel special."

They were quiet for a while and then Carrie asked in a quiet voice, "Do I sound like a little girl when I say things like that?"

"I love hearing that, and very much enjoy thinking that I can make you feel like that. Carrie, I love when our bodies are touching like last night, and right now. You can't imagine the sense of peace that comes over me when we do things like that. There is a special connection between us. I've kissed other girls before, and embraced them, but I never felt a closeness like this until you came along."

"Thank you for telling me. I feel close to you as well."

"There's an old myth that humans originally had two faces and four arms and legs, but the Greek god Zeus split them in half, so that now we have to find our other half. If our time together is any indication, I think I may have found my other half."

"That's a beautiful story, Avram. Please kiss me again, other half."

He did and they stayed wrapped around each other until they fell asleep.

When they awoke, it was dark again. They set about lighting candles and began preparing dinner. Avram brought more logs into the cabin and continued bringing in snow to melt.

Stew was served again with dumplings, and this time accompanied by cornbread with dried tomatoes, which Carrie had rehydrated, chopped and seasoned with smoke-flavored Tabasco.

They talked, laughed, and even danced while bathed in the light of the fireplace that night.

Avram wished he had a camera to have a picture of Carrie's radiant expression and also capture the sparkle of the crackling fire reflected in her eyes.

Around midnight the snow stopped. When they climbed the stairs to the bedroom level, there was not one thought of sleeping separately. Again, they remained dressed as they got into bed. When Avram put out the last candle, the room became pitch black. They snuggled together under the blankets.

"Do you think I'm too young to consider that we might be *Bashert*?" she asked.

"If we were, it would be most uncommon to have found our *Bashert* so young."

Avram thought for a while and added, "It happened to Ari and Leah Minkowski. They met as children and Leah said she knew before she was thirteen that she wanted to spend the rest of her life with Ari. I asked Ari about it and he started telling me about all the things they did together as youngsters. It included a number of instances when one of them was sick and the other took good care of them."

***

"You have a note from a sailboat," Freddie said when he arrived in Dana's hospital room on Sunday morning. With a big smile on his face, he handed her a large envelope.

She opened it and removed a photo of the repaired Olivia's Otter. The photo had a few lines written across the bottom, which read:

Ready to take you sailing. Get well soon. Your friend,
Olivia's Otter

Dana looked up and smiled at him. "Did you do this?"

"Nope, it was Olivia's idea. She hoped a message from her sailboat would cheer you up."

"Tell her the photo did cheer me up. In fact, I'd like to call her and tell her myself. Please let me borrow your cell."

He pressed speed-dial and handed her his phone.

"Hi, Olivia. This is Dana Jacobs. Thanks for sending the photo. Please tell Olivia's Otter it certainly cheered me up. I'm going to keep it next to my bed, so if I get sad I can look at it and feel better."

"I'm glad it cheered you up, Dana. When you're ready, that sailboat will certainly keep you cheered up. I promise that will happen."

"I'll be looking forward to the time when you take us out for a sail."

"Are you still in pain?"

"Not so much physical pain, but more mental pain, since I learned what I look like."

"I'll take you sailing and you'll even feel prettier. It works for me."

"Thanks again, Olivia."

"You're welcome, Dana."

She hung up and handed the phone back to Freddie. "Your sister's a little angel."

"That's certainly the opinion at my home," Freddie said as he opened the book of poetry he had brought.

***

On Monday morning, much to their joy, the cabin's lights turned on and they heard the hum of the electricity returning. Avram setup the battery charger for the bulldozer.

After lunch they trudged back out to the shed where they disconnected the battery charger, and using a checklist he found in the manual, Avram attempted to start the bulldozer.

The powerful diesel engine slowly attempted to turn over a few times before it came out of its winter slumber. With one cough, one smoky belch, the engine slowly rumbled to life with sufficient volume to let them know it was more than ready to begin work, even on that frigid day.

The two of them cheered their success and embraced, then Carrie slogged through the deep snow back to the cabin as Avram began using another checklist to verify the correct operation of the bulldozer's controls.

Within minutes he had learned enough that he rumbled out of the shed and began clearing the driveway. It was a tedious job for someone who had never controlled a machine like that, because he had to think about every input to the control levers to remove and pile the snow to the side of the drive. Gradually his muscle memory began helping him so that he didn't have to think about every action. Even so, it took over two-hours to clear the drive, plus a path to the Q.

Unfortunately it began to snow again, the wind picked up, and the electricity went out again. It seemed as if they just couldn't catch a break.

Avram tried to keep the snow cleared off his clothing while he worked, but he could gradually feel the snow melting its way through to his skin. He was shivering as he completed his task and returned the bulldozer to the shed.

"Thanks, old girl. You sure can work!" Avram told the bulldozer as he switched it off.

Avram had begun shoveling a path to the cabin when he noticed Carrie at the window, looking outside. She appeared concerned, as he had been out there for a long time and it was obvious his clothing was getting wet.

She came to the door and shouted to him. "Avram, come in the cabin already and warm up. You're going to freeze if you stay out there much longer."

He waved her off. "I just need to clear a decent path so you don't have to walk through deep snow."

An hour-later he returned to the cabin with almost all his clothing soaked through. He was shivering, and his skin tone appeared blue.

Carrie looked frightened. "Avram, you're freezing!"

"I didn't want you to have to trudge through deep snow again." She pulled him inside the cabin. "We have to get you out of those wet clothes. Come stand by the fire and undress. Wrap yourself in a blanket and I'll get a towel to dry you off."

While he did as Carrie asked, she hurriedly began drying off his shivering body. There was no sense of excitement or sexiness as she rubbed the towel all over him. Carrie only seemed worried about him and her only concern was getting him warmed up.

As soon as she had him dried off, he lay down on a blanket in front of the fireplace. Carrie placed a blanket and a comforter on top of him, tucking the blankets around him as best she could, and then she put a couple more logs on the fire and arranged his wet clothing on the fireplace hearth.

"I can barely feel my fingers and feet," he said through chattering teeth.

"I have to get you warmed up." She appeared to be thinking, when she sat on the floor next to his shivering body then rotated so that her back was to him. She pulled off her socks and shoes, stood up and removed her slacks, then pulled off her wool jacket and hat.

"No, Carrie!" Avram chattered.

Carrie looked over her shoulder at him. "I have to do this. Heating water will take too long. Just close your eyes, please."

He tried to say something but was shivering too hard to get the words out, so he did as she said and closed his eyes.

He heard the sounds of Carrie removing more clothing. Then, lifting the blankets, she slid under them and quickly lay on top of him wearing only her panties.

"Oh, Carrie, you are so warm. That feels wonderful."

"I wish I could say the same—I feel as if I am lying on a block of ice."

"I'm sorry."

"Don't be. You need to warm up. But I don't want to squish you."

Carrie put her arms on either side of him to lift her upper body weight off his chest, although her large breasts were still against him. He could feel his chest lifting her breasts each time he breathed, but he tried not to think about that sensation.

Gradually his shivering decreased and Avram began to sleep. At some point he noticed that she gently and slowly rolled off him, but stayed against his side.

When Avram awoke, Carrie was in her clothes again. Part of him wondered if it had been a dream, but the mischievous smile she wore, when he opened his eyes and looked at her, told him that it wasn't.

They were both exhausted from the strain of enduring the cold temperatures, so they enjoyed a quiet dinner that night, read briefly, and went to bed.

***

They woke up on a sunny and clear Tuesday morning, they carefully closed up the cabin, emptying all the water from the pipes and toilets, put the blankets away, emptied the ash from the fireplace, carefully stored all the pots, pans, and dishes, and took all their garbage out to the Q.

As Avram was locking the front door, Carrie pointed out the view that was finally visible. "Now that's a magnificent view— distant mountains across a wide valley and deep blue Lake Chelan down there. My mom loves scenery and she would certainly love that view."

They were sitting in the Q waiting for the engine to warm a bit before they left, when Carrie turned to Avram. "How will I ever repay you for the way you took such good care of me?"

"I didn't do that much. Carrie, you took good care of me. The meals you prepared were more than good. They were great. You even made clothing for us."

Neither of them said anything as they each proudly reviewed what they had done for each other.

With little difficulty, the Q, using its knobby snow tires and all-wheel drive, broke out of its snowy cocoon and clawed its way to the path the bulldozer had cleared.

As he started carefully driving down the mountain, Avram spoke again. "In truth, Carrie, we took care of each other."

"We did. We should be proud of that."

"Carrie Levin; thank you for great meals, helping me with everything around the cabin, making clothes for us, and especially doing what you did to warm me up. I know that wasn't easy."

"You're welcome, Avram. Remember when we first stopped by the cabin and I couldn't understand why anyone would get excited about that place?"

He nodded.

"Well, that cabin has been our home for over two-days and I'm going to miss every one of those silly, stacked logs. I'm going to remember that little place, and our few days here, for the rest of my life."

"I guess it changes from an empty cold cabin to a home," Avram said, "when you fill it with love."

"Stop the car," she commanded.

"What?"

"Please, stop the car."

He pulled to the side of the road, quickly bringing it to a halt. Carrie undid her seatbelt, came across the center console, wrapped her arms around his neck, and kissed his mouth for a long time. Then, in a shy voice she said, "I know I'm just a kid, but I love you, Avram."

"Carrie, there's no question in my mind that we're *Bashert*."

She slid back to her seat and looked out the passenger-side window. She didn't want Avram to see the tears of happiness his remark had elicited.

He leaned toward her and kissed her cheek. She turned back to him, wrapped her arms around him once more, and they engaged another long kiss.

As soon as they were out of the mountains and nearing Chelan, they had cell service, so Carrie called home.

"I'm so sorry, Mom. You and dad must have been worried. The storm kept us stuck in the cabin since late Saturday afternoon. Avram had to use a bulldozer to clear the driveway so we could get out. It was so cold up there—I even had to sew jackets and hats from this big blanket to help keep us warm."

A short while later they arrived at her mother and father's home to a warm greeting from Carrie's family.

As Avram was about to leave, Carrie turned to him. "Thank you for one great adventure, dance partner." She grabbed either side of his shirt collar and stood on her toes to kiss him, right in front of her parents.

When she released him, she noticed that the look of embarrassment on Avram's face had caused her mother and father to grin.

"Thank you as well, Carrie," he managed to say.

"Please join us for *Shabbat* dinner this Friday, Avram," her mother called after him.

"I'll do that, Mrs. Levin."

Carrie sat down with her mom and dad to tell them about her time at the cabin.

After detailing the struggle to perform ordinary activities while also trying to keep warm, she told them about Avram. "You can't imagine how Avram took care of me. We slept together in the same bed to stay warm—but with all our clothes on, so don't worry. We had to work together to do everything because of the snow and cold. When we decided to make jackets and hats from the pretty wool blanket, he insisted we make mine first so I would be warm. He fixed an old sewing machine so I could do it. It had the name Sarah Levin carved in the side."

"Sarah Levin?" her father asked.

Carrie nodded and continued. "We spent the entire time working hard to take care of each other. Your daughter might have frozen to death up there, but Avram made sure I was warm and secure. He even set an alarm on his watch to get up in the middle of the night to add logs to the fireplace, just to make sure the cabin stayed as warm as possible during the night." She smiled at that.

"The two of us made pancakes, oatmeal, dumplings, and biscuits just like Mom taught me. We had dried fruit, which I reconstituted to serve with the meals. I even baked sugar cookies to have for dessert. Whenever I became frightened, Avram held me in his arms and it reassured me. Remember, Mom, how you felt the first time Dad held you? I know how that felt now, because I know I just found my own Michael. I was scared to death the first night until Avram held me. But I was fine after that."

Her mother gave her a look of concern. "Carrie, you're just seventeen. You haven't known Avram that long. Are you so certain of your feelings?"

"We're *Bashert*, Mom. I know we are—and so does Avram. We should have been frightened to death up there. We hardly knew each other before this weekend. Yet we solved problems as a couple, did things to make each other laugh and feel secure, and it didn't matter what we were doing...we were happy. Cold at times, I have to admit, but happy."

"*Bashert* is a big jump from dance partner," her mother said, while clearly doing her best to ignore her father's grinning I-told-you-so expression.

Chapter Nineteen ~ Cabin History

JOAN AND MEYER OPENED the door and welcomed Carrie and Avram inside.

"I heard the cabin saved you two in that big snowstorm," Meyer said.

"It did. Thanks so much. There are a couple of blankets missing from your cabin though," Avram said. "We wanted to show you what became of them."

They put on the jackets and hats, which were made from the Pendleton Yellowstone Blanket.

Meyer pretended to be angry at first, but then started laughing, as did Joan.

"It must have been a huge amount of tedious work, to sew them together by hand," Joan said.

"Avram fixed the old sewing machine and I used it to stitch everything together."

"Stand still a moment. I need a picture of this," Joan said. "You resurrected that antique sewing machine?" Meyer asked incredulously.

Avram nodded. "I had to add a crank arm but it worked just fine. I found an ancient can of oil that was covered in rust in one of the drawers, so I applied a few drops to the places that looked like they would need a little oil. I noticed the machine had the name Sarah Levin carved into it."

Meyer nodded. "When I bought it at a flea market in Seattle, I noticed the name. The guy selling it said it was in good shape."

"It was really easy to use," Carrie said. "After a few minutes it wasn't a problem at all. I want to learn more about sewing with an old machine like that."

"I've tried to use old machines before," Joan said. "I thought it was next to impossible to remember when and which way to keep my feet moving and at the same time guide the material."

Carrie grinned. "I think the spirit of the old machine helped me."

"Carrie," Meyer said, "the next time I'm up at the cabin, I'm bringing that machine home for you. Seeing as it still works and you want to use it, it's a complete waste to have it as a decoration in the cabin. I'll get some other antique for us."

"Thank you so much. I'd love to have that old machine. It really did a nice job for us. I promise I'll take good care of it. We're sorry about destroying the blanket and the couch cushions that we used to get the thread for sewing, so we'll certainly replace them."

"No, you won't," Joan said. "Your punishment is that you have to stay for lunch and tell us everything that happened. Let's eat in the den in front of the fireplace."

With youthful enthusiasm Carrie and Avram began relating their adventure, all the time with Avram's hand firmly locked in Carrie's.

"I heard there were six-foot drifts out there. How did you get out of the driveway?" Meyer asked.

"We got the CAT fired up. I found the manual the second day and read through it. Once we started it running, I used a checklist to verify proper operation of the controls, and then used it to clear a path to the road. After the first-hour, the controls became pretty intuitive."

"I bought that dozer a few-months-ago," Meyer said. "I haven't even driven it myself yet. Next summer, Moshe, Ari, and I are going up there to build some small trails, cut out a foundation for an addition to the cabin and build a shooting range, all with the help of the CAT. I'd appreciate if you'd come with us. We could use an experienced operator."

"I'm only two-hours experienced." Avram laughed. "But I'd love to help."

"He can help," Joan said, "but only if Carrie can come as well so she can help us shop for antiques for the new rooms."

"I'd love to help with that, Mrs. Minkowski," Carrie said.

"Also," Joan added, "anyone who helps us improve the cabin gets to stay there whenever they want to." Avram and Carrie exchanged a broad smile.

As Joan and Meyer went to the kitchen to bring dessert to the table, she whispered in his ear. "Do you see how they relate to each other?"

"Not only relate to each other, they positively sparkle when they look at each other. They find the same joy in each other as Ari and Leah displayed at that age."

"They seem to have taken good care of each other just like Ari and Leah would have as well. We need to tell them about the cabin's curse."

Upon returning with dessert, Meyer said to them, "If I'm ever stuck in a snowstorm, I know who I'd want to have with me. You guys did great. I'm really proud of how you used whatever resources you had to take good care of each other. You should be proud of that as well. But we do need to tell you guys that the cabin has a way of putting a curse on couples who stay there."

"Meyer Minkowski," Joan said, laughing, "I've been telling you to burn down that cabin for years."

"Why would you do that? It's a great place," Carrie asked as Meyer laughed.

"What kind of curse are you talking about?" Avram asked. Meyer explained. "Every time a couple goes out there alone, they become cursed and end up getting engaged, then married, and being happy with each other for the rest of their lives."

Carrie and Avram gazed at each other with unabashed joy as they both blushed.

"Avram told me that story," Carrie said. "I thought he was joking."

***

Before they sat down to *Shabbat* dinner, Michael called Carrie and Avram over to see an aged photograph of an old woman in a long skirt sitting at a sewing machine. She had a warm smile and one of her hands was resting on its bobbin winder.

"It's my great-great-whatever-grandmother," he said. "Taken about the year-nineteen-hundred, I think, shortly before she died. The original photo was fading, so someone in my family took a photo of the original."

"She has a beautiful smile," Avram said.

"I don't believe it," Carrie said. "You can still see a name has been carved in the side of the machine's cabinet. I can barely read it. What was your great-whatever-grandmother's name?"

"Sarah Levin. I've been told she was tall and had a rugged, almost manly body. Sarah, along with her son, brother, and his family came across the Oregon Trail to settle in the Portland area. My grandparents knew her. They said she was intelligent, kind, fluent in Hebrew, and a real frontier woman. There is a family story that four ruffians were accosting her brother in his store. She picked up an axe handle and quickly dispatched them."

Chapter Twenty ~ Growing Together

THE DAY FINALLY ARRIVED when Dana was going to go sailing with Freddie and Olivia. She had been on a special diet since she had been in the hospital, and she had lost nearly twenty-pounds; but still looked heavy. After a tiring walk on crutches from the driveway, she arrived at the edge of the dock. Olivia's Otter sat there, slightly rocking, resplendent in her new coat of varnish.

"I'm frightened of killing myself trying to get on this boat."

Freddie handed Dana's crutches to Olivia, put an arm across her back and his other arm under her legs. He lifted her up, as if she weighed next to nothing, and stepped onto the boat.

"I'm sorry," he said, after gently lowering her onto the seat. "Would you repeat that? I didn't hear what you said."

"Thank you, Freddie," Dana said through gentle laughter. Freddie saluted her and began raising the sails.

Dana turned to Olivia. "Your brother is a prince."

"I didn't think that when I was little, but now, if I need anything, I can tell him and he makes it happen. I'm not allowed to go sailing by myself, and you wouldn't believe how often he'll go sailing with me, so I'm able to take my friends out on the Otter. If some of my friends don't know anything about sailing, Freddie patiently helps me teach them."

"How's the physical therapy going?" Freddie asked.

Dana shrugged. "I may never get these braces off my legs. The physical therapy I need to do every day is so painful I just can't do that much."

"If you like, after sailing we can go into the exercise room at my house. I work out with weights every day. I can put a routine together for you that is really simple and easy to do."

"Okay, Mr. Freddie, I'm willing to try with you, but when I decide it's enough we quit without argument. Do you agree?"

"No problem."

Freddie sat next to her as they left the dock. It was a partly sunny day with cool temperatures and just enough wind to make their sailing interesting.

Dana tilted her head back and closed her eyes. She drank in the scent of the lake and the feel of the breeze that tossed her short hair around her face. "Mmmm, I could get to love this," she said.

"Olivia, my dear, you are absolutely correct. This is so relaxing."

Olivia smiled, looking rather pleased she had just introduced another person to the serenity of sailing.

Freddie began teaching Dana little bits of sailing technique. Her legs were quite weak, though, but Dana appreciated Freddie's attempts.

She thanked him. "But what I really am enjoying is how calm and quiet this is."

When they returned to the dock, Freddie assisted Dana while she stepped off the boat and they proceeded into the family's exercise room. There were free weights and a weight machine in the middle of the room. Two of the walls had mirrors on them. A third wall had charts which demonstrated various exercises. Colorful drawings also had been placed around the room showing human musculature. Freddie had Dana sit on the padded bench of the weight machine and he handed her a pair of five-pound hand-weights.

"Will these help my legs?" she asked.

"They'll help you warm up," Freddie answered. He grabbed a pair of forty-pound hand-weights and began demonstrating some exercises. Dana followed him and was soon out of breath and straining to lift the weights.

"Excellent form, Dana. You're doing great."

"It doesn't feel great," Dana complained as her biceps, triceps, and forearms started aching.

Freddie setup the weight machine so she could simply straighten her legs from bent at the knee to a fully extended position while pushing against a bar which was connected to the weight stack.

"Ugh," she complained, barely moving her legs. "This is too much weight."

Freddie looked astounded as he glanced at the machine, and Dana realized he had no weight on the stack. Her legs were that weak.

He positioned himself to assist her by moving the bar with his hand and asked her to try again.

She managed to straighten her legs a few times, but it was a painful struggle. "That's enough, Freddie."

He looked pensive for a moment, as if he was wracking his brain. He shrugged. "One of the guys in our group said you would give up and not try hard."

"Who said that?"

"I'm sorry I told you. That wasn't nice of me."

"Freddie, please tell me who said that."

"Why don't you do five more, just to prove you can do it?"

Dana was furious. She took her anger out on the exercise machine, and with Freddie's assistance did the additional repetitions.

"Great work, Dana!" Freddie told her. "You're not a quitter!"

She wiped sweat from her brow. "I can't believe someone would say that about me. Let's see if I can do three more. I may have some bad habits, but being a quitter is not one of them."

She groaned and strained mightily but managed an additional three repetitions.

"You do a thirty-minute workout like this every-other-day and you'll be in great shape in no time."

She shook her head. "Be serious, Freddie. I haven't been in great shape anytime in my entire life."

Freddie ignored her remark. "So, every-other-day you come home with me and we'll do a workout together."

At school the next day, Dana's muscles were sore as can be, but she kept telling herself that she wasn't a quitter and that the soreness she felt was proof of that.

***

Eight-weeks-later and she had lost another twenty-pounds and the leg braces. Freddie had gradually increased the weights for her and she became so accustomed to her routine that he performed his own workout while she ran through hers. Their routine had gradually lengthened from fifteen- to thirty-minutes.

Dana said she began looking forward to the workouts. Occasionally she stayed for dinner at the Lipinski's and she and Freddie studied together, too.

"You keep working out," Megan told her one night, "and you're going to have a great figure."

Dana laughed. "On my best days, this figure never looked good, let alone great."

It seemed without a conscious effort on their part, Dana and Freddie started relying on each other. It started with simple things like their exercise routine, an occasional trip to the store, or a walk around Bellevue Mall on a rainy day. They didn't consider themselves boyfriend and girlfriend, but certainly the more they did together the closer they became.

Some of his friends had teased him about hanging out with the marshmallow, but Freddie would say that he and Dana were just friends.

At the end of their exercise routine in late April, Freddie suggested she join him on a hike. "Some friends and I are going to hike up Little Si tomorrow. Maybe you'd like to join us."

Dana smiled but looked to the floor. "Thanks, Freddie, your friends are nice but they don't want to have me around to slow them down."

Freddie shook his head and looked right at her. "All the time I was on crutches, I seem to remember someone slowing down to walk with me. Let me see...who was that? Oh yeah, it was you! If they want to go faster, then we'll let them. The views off that little trail are to die for. Bring your camera. You'll need it."

Megan had overheard them, and after Dana left, she asked Freddie, "How would you describe your relationship with Dana?"

"We're just friends. That's all."

"Maybe you need to rethink that. When we were buying your new suit last week, you mentioned at least three times that you wondered what Dana would think of it."

"I did?"

"In four-weeks, your senior prom will take place. Have you thought about who you will take?"

"No, I haven't given it any thought."

"So tell me please, just how good a friend is Dana?"

Freddie didn't reply as he was thinking about all the things they did together and how there was hardly ever a cross word between them. He realized that he rarely did anything without talking to her first.

"Dana is a good friend, but maybe she's more than that. She's kind and generous and she makes me laugh. We do so much stuff together." Freddie walked away from Megan as if he was in a trance. He proceeded into his bedroom and closed the door. He immediately dialed Dana's number on his cell phone.

When she answered, he went right to the reason he called. "Dana, if no one has asked you to next month's senior prom, I was wondering if you would give me the honor of being your escort."

She was quiet for a moment and Freddie wondered if she would turn him down. He held his breath until she answered.

"Thank you, Freddie. I would enjoy that."

"Thank you for saying yes."

***

They hung up and Dana dropped her phone, put her hands to her face, and began sobbing. She had never been invited to a school dance in her entire life and didn't think for a moment she would be attending her senior prom. Now, not only would she be attending the prom, but also the guy who was kinder to her, more than anyone else, would be her escort.

Through tear-filled eyes she looked around her room at the many pictures she had taken of the two of them—sailing, shopping, hiking, and doing so many other things together.

"This is too good to be true," she said to her teddy bear, which she had named Freddie. "He said he wanted me to give him the honor. It's more like he's giving me the honor to attend with him."

Once Dana had regained her composure, she walked into the family room, and in as casual a voice as she could manage said, "Mom, we need to go shopping this Saturday. Freddie just invited me to our senior prom. I'll need a dress for that."

"Shopping for a prom dress? Freddie? Sure. Saturday? Sure, Dana, we'll start at Neiman-Marcus. I'm sure we'll find something."

"Are you okay, Mom?"

"Fine. I'm fine—you're fine, Freddie's fine, we're all fine. Shopping on Saturday will be fine." Her mother stood and gave Dana a huge hug and when she stepped back, Dana noticed a tear on her mother's cheek.

***

Freddie loved baseball and he loved a chance to play softball with some of the neighborhood guys and girls. He was usually chosen last, which didn't surprise him. It hurt more than they knew that he wasn't in any way competent at his favorite sport.

Two-weeks before the prom, he, Dana and some friends got together to play. In the seventh inning with two runners on first and third and two outs, it was his turn to bat. Freddie's team was down by two runs. Another out would end the game. As usual his teammates looked disappointed to see him come up to bat. They were too nice to say anything, but it was obvious they felt that way. Generally, Freddie couldn't hit the ball hard enough to get a pinch runner to first base.

"Come on, Frederick! Convert some of that ATP!" Dana yelled to him.

He smiled at her, then swung gently at the first pitch but missed. Freddie couldn't get much energy in the bat as it usually hurt his hip to transfer weight from one leg to the other as in a proper swing. He was surprised that he didn't feel any pain this time, though. He shifted his weight from side to side and realized there was absolutely no pain involved.

He swung much harder at the next pitch and, while he missed it, he still felt no pain. Much to his surprise he'd heard a swooshing sound as he swung the bat. That had never happened before. Freddie glanced at his teammates who were now looking away from him. He stepped out of the batter's box for a moment to collect his thoughts and decided to swing at the next pitch with as much strength as he could muster.

He stepped back into the batter's box. His hands had a death grip on the bat as he prepared every muscle fiber in his six-foot-two-inch, two-hundred-and-twenty-pound body to try to produce the strongest swing he had ever managed. He stared at the pitcher who clearly thought one more fastball would end the game.

The pitcher wound into his mightiest fastball yet, which was headed right down the middle of the plate. Freddie took a deep breath and stepped into the pitch with his right leg. He extended that leg to rotate his hips, right side back and left side forward, which accelerated all his body's weight into the bat.

Freddie erased a childhood's worth of bad memories, failure, and pain during sports activities with one mighty swing, solidly connecting with the ball.

No one moved as the ball was following a forty-five-degree angle and still climbing as it went over the centerfielder's head.

Dana screamed. "Run, Freddie!"

He bent forward in the direction of first base and took off like a sprinter coming out of the blocks. One of the other boys was supposed to pinch run for him but Freddie was rounding first base and accelerating toward second by the time the pinch runner had only gotten halfway to first.

As he approached second base he looked out toward centerfield and saw the centerfielder had a long way to go to retrieve the still-bouncing ball. He felt a little discomfort in his right knee as he rounded third base, but the ball had gone far enough, he easily made it around the bases. He crossed home plate, standing up to receive the triumphal cheers of his teammates.

"Freddie, man," one of his friends said, "you took off like you'd been shot from a cannon!"

Freddie looked down at his shoes and, much to his friends' amusement, said, "It wasn't really me. I had my fast shoes on today." He looked over at Dana who had tears running down her face.

"Way to break off those phosphate molecules, Freddie," she screamed joyously.

***

The next day, Dana and Freddie were going through their exercise routines. Freddie did pull-ups every day. Dana wanted to try them too, but the bar was too high. Freddie stood behind her, put his hands on her waist, and lifted her while she jumped up to grab the bar. She managed nine pull-ups.

"Dana, do you realize how much your body has changed?" Freddie said. "All this exercise has slimmed and firmed your body."

"Freddie, you're a doll to say that, but my body still mostly resembles stacked marshmallows."

"Look in the mirror sometime when you're not wearing your baggy clothes. You'll see I'm right."

Dana had been in the habit of not looking at her body ever since childhood, as she was ashamed of her puffy figure. Following Freddie's suggestion, though, the next morning she decided to take a chance after a shower. She nervously gazed in the full-length mirror. The naked form that was reflected back caused her jaw to drop.

There were gorgeous curves in all the right places. Her average-sized breasts were nothing to brag about back in the days when her belly stuck out much farther than they did. But on this body, with her now-thin waist and tight abdominal muscles, they beautifully accented her feminine form.

She walked across the bathroom and bravely stood on the scale she always avoided. She sucked in her breath when it read one- hundred-and-fifteen-pounds. She got off the scale and stood on it a second time to see if it would read the same. It did!

"All that exercise with Freddie did this. I owe him big time," she said to her reflection. She began planning how she would show him how her body looked and how she would thank him.

***

Ari and Leah Minkowski had decided to have a pool party to celebrate the start of summer at their spacious home on Lake Washington. Family and extended family were in attendance. As it was Dana's eighteenth-birthday and the day after they would be attending their prom, Freddie invited her to join his family for the party.

They arrived together.

"How was the prom?" Leah asked.

"You should have seen the fantastic dress Dana was wearing!" Freddie said. "It was blue with sparkles all over it."

Dana smiled, remembering the form fitting dress and how many people did double takes when she walked in. "Frederick and I danced so much, it's amazing we woke up today."

She leaned towards him and whispered, "Frederick, do you have your suit on under your clothes?"

"Yeah, do you?"

Without answering, Dana looked around. Not seeing anyone looking in their direction, she grabbed Freddie's hand and pulled him into a bathroom. She locked the door and began taking her outer clothes off and Freddie did the same. She had a fluorescent green bikini on.

"I took your advice and looked in the mirror as I was getting ready for the prom. This is what I saw." She slowly rotated in a full circle.

"Wow, Dana, you look great. The guys at school will be excited and all over you now they realize what a great body you have."

Dana stepped toward Freddie and put her arms around his neck while placing her head against his muscular chest. He slowly wrapped his arms around her. Her body felt firm and warm as they embraced. Freddie had never held a nearly naked woman against him before.

Dana took a deep breath and quietly spoke. "The guy I'm holding right now helped me create this body and is the kindest man I know. He is the only one I want to be excited and all over me."

She dropped her arms and guided Freddie's hands under her bikini top.

"Frederick, it feels wonderful to hold you like this and I love your touching me." She stood on her toes and put one hand behind his neck, pulling his lips down to hers. "Thank you so much," she said, after a long kiss.

"You called me Frederick," a slightly dazed Freddie said as they walked out to the pool.

"Freddie is a name for a child. A child couldn't do what you've done for me, and a child couldn't make me feel this good. You saved my life and then hung around during the dark-days of my recovery. When I had no sense that I was going to recover, it was Frederick who kept showing up and taking me places and exercising with me. He laughed, joked, and cajoled me into this shape. Believe me— even in the places in my mind that you can't see, I feel pretty. You did that. I care about you, Frederick Lipinski, and I pray we keep doing things together."

"Believe me, Dana, that won't be a problem."

***

As they walked onto the pool apron, Lucinda did a double take and yelled to Dana. "Hey skinny! You look fantastic."

Her three-year-old daughter, Rachel, who was sitting on her lap, said enthusiastically, "She's looking fantastic!"

"*Lei è bella,*" her three-year-old cousin, Ruth, who was sitting on Holly's lap, said to Rachel.

"*Sì, lei è bella,*" Rachel replied.

"When did the girls start speaking Italian to each other?" Dana asked.

"We're not sure," Lucinda said. "Holly speaks to Ruth in Italian and Jonah speaks to her in Hebrew. At our house Ryan and I speak Hebrew to Rachel. When they were around two-years-old we found they would speak to each other in Italian at Holly's house and Hebrew at our house. Also, when Jordan and Pearl Levin come over later on, you'll see that Rachel speaks to Jordan in Hebrew and Ruth speaks to Pearl in Italian. Holly and her mom always spoke in Italian to Jordan and Pearl but only Pearl is fluent in that language."

"Since we noticed that, I speak to Ruth and Rachel in Italian and it's never a problem for either of them," Holly added. "We have a feeling they understand a lot of Navajo as well. Last week Jonah asked me in Navajo if he could take them to the bakery to buy snacks. They both looked at each other and smiled. Our mom would have been so proud of them."

"Thanks for what you guys said," Dana told them. "This is my body by Frederick. He started me exercising all the time. Now it's hard for me to skip-a-day."

Lucinda watched as they walked over to the pool. She leaned over and whispered to Holly, "Based on the tilt in Freddie's kilt, I'd say he's enjoying the look of that body as well."

Holly laughed hysterically.

"Aunt Holly thinks tilt in the kilt sounds funny, Mom," Rachel said in a playful voice.

"Freddie, are your folks coming over?" Holly asked.

He turned around at the sound of the patio door. "Looks like they're here now."

Everyone turned to see Olivia followed by Megan and Marvin walking out holding hands. "Sorry we're a little late," Megan said. "We've been on Marvin's sailboat."

Marvin smiled and placed an arm around Megan's shoulders. "We practically live on that thing."

Olivia nodded her head in agreement. "What did you name it?" Lucinda asked.

Megan smiled up at Marvin. "*We're Bashert*," she replied.

~ ~ ~ The End ~ ~ ~

Also by Richard Alan

Meant to Be Together series

Book 1 Finding a Soul Mate
Book 2 The Couples
Book 3 Finding Each Other
Book 4 Growing Together

American Journeys series

Book 1 American Journeys: From Ireland to the United States
Book 2 American Journeys: From Boston to the Pacific Northwest
Book 3 American Journeys: A Female Doctor in the Civil War

If you enjoyed this contemporary romance, please leave a review on the website from which you purchased the book. Thank you!

Don't miss out!

Visit the website below and you can sign up to receive emails whenever Richard Alan publishes a new book. There's no charge and no obligation.

https://books2read.com/r/B-A-XUNH-QSNX

BOOKS 2 READ

Connecting independent readers to independent writers.

About the Author

Richard is a 101st Airborne Division Vietnam veteran. After an education in mathematics, 17-years in manufacturing engineering then 22-years as a software engineer, Richard embarked on a career in writing. His debut series, Meant to Be Together, is a tender and heartwarming, multigenerational family saga about relationships, love and life. This was followed by a series of historical fiction novels, set in 1847 – 1900, about the predecessors to the characters in his Meant to Be Together series. Expertly researched, American Journeys: From Ireland to the Pacific Northwest (1847 – 1900), Volumes One and Two, details the family's struggles during the Great Irish Famine, emigration from Ireland to Boston, the journey across the United States, the Oregon Trail, and the Panama Canal. A Female Doctor in the Civil War follows Dr. Abby Kaplan, trying to become a surgeon during the Civil War. She was first introduced as a little girl in Volume One of American Journeys. Being a lifelong learner, Richard loves pursuing the research for his historical fiction. It is frequently accomplished while RV traveling with his wife, Carolynn, to libraries, museums, and historical sites around the country. Having a career that is portable permits traveling to many spectacular areas of the United States. It also provides opportunities to visit our adult children, grandchildren, other relatives, and friends.

Read more at https://villagedrummerfiction.com.